THE LADY IN WHITE

A TALE SET IN ROCHESTER, NEW YORK

THE LADY IN WHITE

A TALE SET IN ROCHESTER, NEW YORK

Zachary Finn

PRESS

Published by Vulpine Press in the United Kingdom in 2023

ISBN: 978-1-83919-487-0

www.vulpine-press.com

To Rochester. You run deep in my veins, old friend.

And to Bruce and Natalie: my strange best friend who knows the scents and smells of Rochester better than I, and my other strange best friend, who keeps me exploring.

Thanks for all those walks to the Castle, you two.

Dear reader,

I tried not to get bogged down in history or let facts get in the way of a good story, or maybe I did…I suppose you'll be the jury, judge, and executioner as it is. Either way, the tale of the Lady of Lake Ontario, The White Lady, or the Lady in White, whichever you prefer, is one that, like all good stories, is malleable in the telling.

Here's my take. I hope you enjoy it.

-zjf

"I stood here, and saw before me the unutterable, the unthinkable gulf that yawns profound between two worlds, the world of matter and the world of spirit; I saw the great empty deep stretch dim before me, and in that instant a bridge of light leapt to the unknown shore, and the abyss was spanned."
-Arthur Machen, *The Great God Pan*

Part 1
Mirages

Chapter 1

I found Professor Dawdson at the decrepit Hotel Celeste in the Fall of 2015. He'd been all but missing for the better part of twenty years, his research rarely cited and his papers collecting dust in the school's library. As far as I knew, he hadn't stepped foot in a classroom during that time. None of his work had been transcribed or added online, and there were no books or articles during his absence to speak of, either. Dr. Dawdson appeared to have become a footnote himself (Chicago style, I should add).

If the rest of the world was forgetting Dr. Dawdson, that was all the more reason for me to talk to him. I had convinced myself early into my own research that an interview with him might prove beneficial, and truth-be-told, there was a bit of curiosity prodding me to hunt him down. Dawdson had a touch of legend to him; not enough to push anyone besides myself to action, but enough to add the spice of adventure to the whole ordeal.

An interview with a secluded scholar of yonder past? What secrets might he know?

Some days I wish I'd never met him, but most times I'm glad I did. I suppose the purpose of writing this is an attempt on my part to understand what I saw, to make sense of it all or something along those lines. Or perhaps it's just because a story like this *must* be told, because it's how I truly got to know the city I'd called home and studied for all of my life, one I *thought* I knew.

Take your pick.

I'd tracked Dr. Dawdson to the Hotel Celeste thanks to a history professor who had both worked with him and stayed in tenuous touch, and who shall remain unnamed. The hotel was my best chance at locating him, she told me, when I cornered her at a university function the spring before.

"He's not well, you should know. I doubt he'll be willing to talk. Times have been…tough for him," she added before being whisked away to talk to another professor.

I'd tried to call to schedule the meeting, but each time the receptionist had only laughed and hung up after telling me there wasn't any Doctor at the Hotel Celeste. Not a great sign, I know, but success belongs to the persistent or some other platitude like that. If scheduling a meeting was not an option, well, perhaps an impromptu trip to his residence might do the trick. As such, I made my way to the hotel on a sunny October afternoon hoping to make an introduction.

The hotel itself spoke to the high hopes Rochester once possessed. If it hadn't been left to rot, the building might have remained a centerpiece of Rochester. But the bones were still there, and even if the hotel had seen better days, and the structure maintained an air of prominence and opulence that demanded respect. Sort of like a mausoleum, I suppose.

There was this beautiful art-deco sign that jutted out from the building over an aluminum plated overhang. **HOTEL CELESTE** written in sans serif, so nice you *had* to stop and admire. The smooth-faced stones running beside the entrance were dark, and at one point in time they surely glistened. Sandwiched between the two black columns was more smooth stone, though this stuff was white. Just in case you didn't get it the first time, Hotel Celeste was written once more above in black lettering.

It was like looking at a mirage of the thirties: you could practically see the specters of past visitors hovering through the glass doors ahead of you, wearing floral silk dresses and pinstripe suits as they entered the old building. You could smell the cigar smoke, and hear the faint beat of swing music playing beneath, chatter of decades past still reverberating off the surrounding walls as if they were just spoken.

The place was still stuck in another time...but only if you squinted.

When I first laid eyes on the Hotel Celeste the years had, as I've mentioned, taken their toll on the place. Though it appeared timeless, times had not been good to say the least. I'd stood on the slow corner in a busy city both trying to see through the grime smeared windows and trash strewn walkway that lay before me while stealing my resolve. Even the cab driver, who dropped me off, mentioned I should look for another place to stay; keep in mind this was after spending a twenty-minute car ride together with him only grunting at my attempts at pleasantries. I thanked him for his concern, but as he pulled away there was a small voice that told me to chase the car down and head to somewhere, anywhere else.

But I didn't.

Instead, I stayed on the corner for a minute and peered through the fog of time and decay, back to when the hotel would have attracted bohemians and business folks alike. Eventually, the cold October wind forced the mirage I'd carefully constructed to evaporate, leaving behind a derelict structure. I would have to go inside it, if I was ever going to have the conversation with Dawdson that had drawn me there in the first place. I took a deep breath and made my way to the entrance.

Before I go on, I should probably introduce myself. My name is Jason Green: Rochester native and, during the time this story takes place, doctoral candidate in History as an Americanist with a focus on religious movements and folklore.

Now it's Dr. Green.

I'm also an animal lover, horror movie fanatic and brown belt in Brazilian Jiu Jitsu (though I've been focusing on no Gi lately) in case you were wondering. Sometimes it's tough to maintain that personal identity as you are subjected to the miseries of academia. I like to think I did. And besides, I figured I ought to include the "get to know your professor as an actual human-being" with the fun facts I tend to tell my students during their first class, to remind you, dear readers, I *am* an actual person and not simply a character dropped into this strange story I'm about to tell you.

Back to my research.

Given my interests as a scholar, my hometown of Rochester was ripe with possibilities. With its location on "Clinton's Ditch", or rather, the Erie Canal, Rochester has been described by historians as one of the first inland boomtowns of the United States. As Paul Johnson described in *A Shopkeeper's Millennium,* this led to tensions when workers, whose life expectancy rate was—how shall I put this—*not great,* would arrive and partake in behavior that would make a frat boy blush. So, you've got discontent workers, a culture awash in booze, a growing, transient population and...voila, a sudden burst of religious development meant to quell these societal ills.

You've got Charles Finney, Smith finding the golden tablets down the road, and of course the Fox sisters, who I'll get to shortly. Religious sentiments gave way to social and political reform: from abolition to the women's rights movement, it's no coincidence that both Frederick Douglass and Susan B. Anthony are buried in Mount Hope Cemetery. The canal brings new arrivals, new economic opportunities, and new modes of thinking—all of which converge in Rochester, which was not only rapidly growing but smack dab on the canal, and near Lake Ontario.

I just tried to describe a history that enough books have been written about to fill a library, but I'm trying to keep this thing going. In short: Rochester is rife with history, religious development, and in contrast, a rich counterculture of folklore that emerged in the flower/flour city.

All of which made me lick my historical chops.

So, although I'd left briefly for my undergraduate studies, I was set on continuing my studies in the city I called home. The city I loved. After receiving my Bachelor's in History, which cost me half of a house, I spent a few years patching together jobs as a teacher's assistant in middle schools with volunteer work at local historical sites. Money was tight during this time, but I was determined. I was admitted to a school that shall remain nameless (Note: for the sake of anonymity all names, businesses, etc…save for my own have been changed in this manuscript), and in 2015 I found myself hard at work trying to complete the dreaded dissertation paper that would decide my future before funding expired.

The working title at that time?

Facts and Fanaticism: The Scientific Debate within the Spiritualism Movement, 1848–1900.

This is why I was seeking out Dr. Dadwson, who, though unheralded, had written a monograph in the late 1970s looking at E.W. Capron's career, life and writings. Capron would serve as the Fox sisters' manager and was active in suffrage circles, having acquaintances such as Susan B. Anthony, Frederick Douglass and Lucretia Mott. In fact, he carried out a detailed conversation with Anthony about the concept of conversations with the dead. Plus, he published his own book, "Modern Spiritualism: Its Facts and Fanaticisms, Its Consistencies and Contradictions" from which the quote in *my* title was derived...all of which is to say, I wanted to talk to the man who knew Capron best.

***

Even before I opened the door, I knew I was walking into a mess. The glass was smeared with God knows what. The mystery substance left behind sooty streaks across the paneling, and it looked like some ghostly apparition was attempting to claw its way free from behind. It was sunny out behind me, sure, but through the dirty glass door the lobby was a dark, cavernous place with only a flickering bulb providing any light. I could make out a few silhouettes of either people or furniture inside, but little else. I opened the door slowly and stepped inside.

I was greeted by the noxious smell of some discount lemon scented air freshener sprayed liberally about. The cleaner was doing a poor job of masking the smell of piss, cigarette smoke, and a rot I couldn't quite place, that filled the greeting area and lingered beneath the chemical mask. The place looked as bad as it smelled too. The tile floor was splattered with intermittent blobs of organic colors ranging between red and brown; I shuddered thinking about what had left those particular stains behind. Dead flies were littered across the floor, and in each visible corner were giant plastic rat traps, which gave me a hint as to what that rotting smell might be. Beyond that, a thick layer of dust coated nearly every surface in sight.

There wasn't much in the way of decorations either. Two couches took up the bulk of the space, both of which looked to be victims of an especially persistent machete attack, judging from the number of rips and tears they had suffered. Stuffing ruptured from the gashes like smoke from a volcano, and between the sofas was a small wooden coffee table, that was nearly blue with ink due to the sheer amount of graffiti decorating it.

Beneath the flickering fluorescent light sat a check-in counter, behind which sat a man who I guessed to be in his sixties. He was balding and the top of his head glistened beneath the overhead light, and though it was tough to tell with him seated, I ventured he had to be at least six foot six. He looked like the stereotypical enforcer in a mob-movie, and he seemed too preoccupied with the book he was reading to even notice my existence. A calendar still open to April 1993 sat on the top of the counter facing me; I presumed it commemorated the date of the last time anyone cared enough to clean the lobby.

"Dobs…someone's here," a raspy voice said from behind me. I turned and realized there was a woman standing in a doorway that I assumed led to an upper floor. A cigarette hung loosely from her lips as the smoke trailed up above her. She was standing directly beneath a smoke detector that, given its faded yellow color and the fact there was no blinking light, *probably* had a battery change around the last time someone cleaned. She stared at the man behind the counter with tired eyes, then scooped the cigarette from her mouth and looked towards me.

"He doesn't hear all that good. Got clocked in the side of the head real hard and lost his hearing when he was breaking up a fight in the lobby. I was there that night, they got him good." She looked back at him and stomped her foot.

"DOBS!"

That got his attention. Dobs's head snapped up and he stared about the lobby confused as if he'd forgotten where he was, before finally noticing me. He blinked rapidly and leaned forward slightly. As he did, I noticed there was a scar running down his face that started at his temple and disappeared beneath the faded polo shirt. I assumed his job was part bouncer too.

"Lookin' for a place to stay? We have a room or two. It's not the Ritz, mind you. Also, mind you, we won't put up with any…trouble. No trouble while you're staying here, you got it? Now who dropped you off?"

The question caught me off guard.

Why the hell was the hotel clerk giving me the third degree?

I looked back to see if the woman was still there, but she'd disappeared leaving behind only a wisp of smoke.

"I don't see how—"

He turned his head, so his left ear was facing me.

"Police? Parole Officer? Some protection agency?" He paused and then his voice softened. "Don't mean nothin' by it, I just need to know who to bill."

"Isn't this a hotel?"

He let out a dry chuckle then coughed. It sounded like Velcro being pulled apart and it filled the whole room.

"I suppose, though I can't remember the last time we had anyone stay here *without* getting put up. This is more of a…what's it called? A halfway house, or a place to stay when there's nowhere else. If you're looking for a hotel there's one down the road 'bout a half mile."

"It's not that, and I wasn't dropped off either. I'm looking for someone. John Dawdson. Dr. Dawdson. I heard he might be staying here." I held up the copy of his book I'd bought from a used book website and pointed to the name.

Dobs leaned over the counter and scrunched his face together as he read from the cover page. As his face relaxed the scar became a crawling caterpillar making its way up his face. With each twitch of expression, the caterpillar would extend or contract on its never-ending journey. I tried not to stare, honest. Eventually he sat back in his chair which groaned loudly.

"Sounds familiar. I think I know 'em—old timer?"

"He would be about sixty or seventy," I guessed.

"Yea…Yea I think I know him. He's on the top floor. Don't speak much. Been here as long as I have. Didn't know he had any family."

"I'm not—" I let the words die in my mouth. No use getting into specifics.

"I haven't seen him leave today. He normally goes out for dinner, but like I said, I think he's still up there. You can go up there and knock, room 501. He's the only one on the top floor, can't miss it."

"Thanks," I said as I turned towards the stairway before turning back. "Say, if I did want a room for the night, what would it run me?"

"Say again."

"If I wanted a room, what would it cost me?" I repeated as loudly as I could without shouting.

"Fifty a night, plus tax and fees. Like I said, there's a hotel down the street." He leaned back in his chair again and shrugged. "You seem like a nice enough kid. You'll see. This isn't like most hotels you've ever been to. Top floor, can't miss it."

With that he returned to his book, and I began my climb.

***

The stairwell was not all that different from the lobby, and as such, it seemed like something from a horror movie: flickering lights, puffs of cobwebs like cotton candy in the corner, and an echo that bounced around the space with each step I took. The whole nine yards. I kept waiting for a masked figure to appear and begin the ol' game of cat and mouse. Even though a horror movie antagonist (or protagonist, depending on how you watch them) never appeared, I hurried up the first flight as quickly as I could, bounding two or three steps at a time. However, when I arrived at the first-floor landing curiosity took over. Rather than turning and making my way up to the next floor, I stopped and paused for a moment, thinking back to standing outside the hotel and seeing that faint hint at what the hotel *had* been once in all its past glory. Within seconds I wanted, no needed, to see what the place looked like inside before I ascended to Dr. Dawdson's floor and started my scholarly business. I decided to peek my head in and look about the first-floor hallway for a moment. Then, I told myself, my curiosity would be quenched, and I could continue my mission. Simple enough.

The door on the landing was painted the worst shade of brown I'd ever seen, and the small glass panel situated above the knob had been smashed out. Fairly recently too, judging by the twinkle of glass shards on the ground beneath it. Not that I thought anyone would run a broom through the stairwell mind you, but surely the busy rush of feet up and down the staircase would have dispersed the broken fragments about. Perhaps this should have been a deterrent, but it didn't. Curiosity had its ugly hooks in me. I carefully stepped around the larger pieces and turned the handle, then stepped into the hallway on the other side closing the door behind me.

A blood red carpet with gold trim lined the way. I'll admit, I was initially taken aback by how nice this section appeared given the state of the lobby and stairwell. The wallpaper, though old no doubt, was in remarkable shape and continued the art deco style I'd noticed out front with a dark blue backdrop and neatly arranged outlines of golden palm trees that reflected the light from above. Fantastic chandeliers that ran the length of the way for as far as I could see. I could see at least ten doors running down both sides, each painted the same deep red as the rug with gold calligraphy labeling the respective room number. It was like I had stepped foot into a completely different hotel.

The soft, sorrowful song of a woman singing echoed from somewhere within, her voice calling out like a siren. I couldn't tell if it was a recording or someone from within one of the rooms, and I stood awestruck for a moment.

This was exactly how I imagined the hotel would look before I stepped inside and allowed reality to shatter the illusion.

I was about to step further into the hallway when I was abruptly yanked back into the stairwell. I hadn't noticed the door open behind me, and it happened so quickly I had no time to brace myself before I tumbled back into the landing with glass crunching loudly beneath my feet. The chandeliers gave way to fluorescent light bulbs, and the warm glow of the hall dissipated into the cold glare of the stairwell.

"You're not supposed to go in that one. That's one of the off-limits halls."

It was the woman from the lobby. The cigarette was still clamped in her lips, and she stared at me with wide, unblinking eyes. "That's off limits. Don't go in there."

She squeezed my arm tight, but there was something comforting in her grip. I assumed she was unwell but even if some idiosyncrasy made her scared of the hall, at least she cared enough about my well-being to protect me.

"Off limits. Got it," I said, and the woman relaxed her hold on my arm. "Thanks for helping me get Dobs earlier, by the way."

She grinned in response and brushed her grey bangs from her face. I guessed her to be in her sixties or seventies, though when she smiled there was a glimmer in her eye that made her twenty again for a passing second: even then, the similarity to looking at the hotel from the outside did not escape me.

"He's nice enough…can't hear well though, like I told you. Got whacked real good a few years back. Sorry I grabbed you like that—just can't be going to off limit space. *That,* that can get you in trouble." The smile left her face as her eyes widened in concern.

"Got it. I won't go in there, promise."

She nodded, relaxed, and her face softened into a smile once more, then she placed the burning cigarette out on the wall until the thin trail of smoke disappeared and dropped it on the stairwell. With the cigarette out of her hand she immediately turned to the sleeve of her sweater and started pulling at a loose thread as she stood there, clearly not trusting me enough to leave me on my own.

"Say, I haven't ever seen you before. Are you new here?"

Realizing I had a chance to do some recon, I decided to take my time talking to my new acquaintance.

"Sort of, just visiting I suppose. I'm Jason. I'm looking for—"

"I'm Deborah, though folks around here call me Deb or Debbie. Been here nearly all my life, so I know them all. Well, most of them. There are some new folks I might not have met, and some people only stay a night…"

Her voice trailed off as she looked up the stairwell as if she heard something, though I was standing right next to her, and no noise caught my attention. I followed her gaze and looked up the ascending flight of stairs, which seemed much taller than five stories. In fact, peering up the stairwell it seemed impossible that I was in the same building I'd admired outside as the stairs kept climbing past where I would have guessed the roof to have been. For the second time in those few minutes, I felt as if I'd stepped out of the Hotel Celeste. I was so lost in my thoughts it took a few seconds before I realized Deb had started talking again.

"…father moved us in sometime around the 1960s when he got the job at Kodak. He passed away not long after, mom too, in a car accident. I stayed here taking care of my siblings and never left. They did though; got a brother in Seattle, a sister in Cortland, another sister who stayed here…"

I nodded politely and added the occasional, "oh wow" as she listed the whereabouts of her siblings, then immediate family, then distant relatives for the next several minutes. She was so proud of all of them I couldn't bring myself to pull away, though I'd occasionally steal a glance away to stare at the seemingly endless tower of stairs that lay above. At one point Deb must have noticed as she changed the subject of her cousin, Emily, who was now working at Disney and how she was planning on visiting her there that spring, on a dime.

"Who did you say you were visiting again?"

"I might have forgotten to mention it. Dr. Dawdson –John Dawdson. He was a professor and—"

Deb's face dropped so instantly I didn't bother finishing the sentence. It was night and day: from a radiant smile proud of her family to looking like I'd just told her said family had been abducted.

"The man at the top of the hotel," Deb managed to say, after regaining some bn. composure. Though the words meant nothing to me, she said it with such purpose that clearly there was some deeper meaning I was oblivious too.

"The clerk, er, Dobs, told me he was on the top floor. He said he was the only one up there too."

"Do you know him?" She whispered as she looked up.

"Not personally, no. I'm studying at the school he taught at for a few years and have been reading some of his old research and, well, I was hoping to meet him to talk about what he discovered."

Deb opened her mouth as if she was about to say something, then shook her head. She then rolled up the sleeve she'd been picking at to reveal a watch, and, in the most obvious display of being done with conversation I'd ever seen, tapped her watch and said, "oh, it's 3:20! I must call my sister. It was nice meeting you Jason."

With that, Deb turned and walked up the stairs without giving me another glance. Her footsteps echoed throughout the corridor, and eventually the heavy slam of a door let me know I was once again alone. I took a moment to process the strange encounter, and I'll admit, I was once again tempted to turn back around and make my way back home. You see, although Dr. Dawdson's research was important to my own, as I mentioned earlier, he was also a bit of a department legend. Not for a good reason, mind you.

The story, or stories since there's so many different tellings, goes that when Rochester was in its historical heyday, meaning the mid to late-seventies when you had Genovese and Lasch at the University of Rochester, and the previously mentioned Johnson's, "A Shopkeeper's Millennium" was hitting bookshelves (while these names might be unfamiliar to most, they were/are *big* names in the field…in short, Rochester both had name historians and was being written about by historians) Dawdson was hired by another college in the area to chair the department. He was a Harvard graduate whose dissertation was well received, and he appeared to have all the makings of a bona fide superstar in the field.

Well, relative superstar I suppose, it's a niche audience after all.

The first year started great: somehow, despite a full course load Dawdson managed to still turn out published paper after paper. Even if his work was since forgotten in the school's library there was a *monstrous* amount of it he left behind, especially considering it was all done in a career that essentially lasted only three years. I counted five peer reviewed articles, one book, and a good number of published reviews, all of which accumulated to a workload most professors would be proud to accomplish in twenty years, let alone three.

But that gets me to reviews.

Given the busy course load and the sheer amount of research he completed it was clear Dawdson was passionate—though more likely the better way to describe his drive is as obsessive. How he managed to do everything that first year is absolutely mind blowing, and clearly something had to give. If the legend was true, that something was his mental well-being; supposedly it was a bad review that set him off. The review was highly critical of the book I'd brought with me that afternoon. Though the reviewer was of modest reputation and the same age as Dr. Dawdson, meaning young and just starting out, and their criticism would most likely have been swept away in the otherwise overwhelming praise of his debut monograph, Dawdson couldn't ignore it.

The story goes that after the review was published in some academic journal that, realistically, probably had less than one hundred subscribers, Dawdson lost it. He authored a scathing essay about every academic paper the reviewer had themself authored, going as far back as locating their master's thesis and claiming plagiarism for a wrongly cited quotation. Petty, but certainly not damning; however, it didn't end there.

He went on to contact the chair of the department the reviewer worked for and demand their resignation, threatened the journal that the review was published in with a lawsuit, and generally unraveled in a manner that burned every bridge he'd worked so hard to build. Supposedly there was even a specific time of day (most telling of this story claim from 4pm-5pm, though I've heard later as well), that Dawdson would slip off to make calls to everyone and anyone to bitch about the review. The whole office would clear out during this time since his shouting, even from behind a closed office door, made it impossible to get any work done. So Dawdson would sit alone in the history department's offices bellowing as some poor sap who was likely so taken off guard they could only sit there and listen.

Every. Damn. Day. As dedicated as he was to his publications, he was equally as dedicated in this one-man war he waged.

Even though the college's administrators tried their best to look the other way—keep in mind he'd been brought in to make their history department competitive with the other local universities and was the prized professor at that time—eventually it got so bad they had to address the issue. They tried to have him focus on research and dropped his course load; when that didn't help, they switched and did the opposite.

Nothing worked. Though his classes were still decent and well attended, and he was still publishing at an impressive rate, Dawdson refused to drop the campaign against the reviewer. They had other professors talk to him, they reached out to the reviewer to offer an olive branch, they did everything they could to smooth over what was quickly becoming a PR nightmare in a small world where everybody knows everything. *Nothing worked*, Dawdson kept trying to get his revenge. It was getting so bad that the college was getting ready to cut ties with their golden boy and who could blame them? It was also so public there was no way they could shovel it underneath the rug like the other professorial indiscretions so common during this time. The writing was on the wall when they removed Dawdson as the chair. Everyone batted down the hatches expecting the worst as the calls became longer (he even began sleeping in his office) and for the first time, his class quality began to decrease to the point of registration reducing to half of what was expected. The downward slide continued.

That is, until he started on a major next project. It was so sudden, everyone who knew him was left wondering whether they'd imagined the past year. One day the calls stopped and instead of shouts, only the machine gun paced rappings of his typewriter could be heard. When classes resumed, all accounts from students were glowing praise. He'd grab a drink with the department when invited, and- get this-he even began making *jokes* about the negative review. It was a complete about face. Dawdson returned to his old self as far as those involved were concerned, and I'm sure all involved let out a long sigh of relief the fall of his third year when he seemed to forget about the review that he'd spent the last year raving about.

Although he would never reveal what the project was, when asked, Dawdson would simply smile and note that he believed it would be his *Magnum Opus.* The fact he was in his twenties and was claiming this probably led to some eye rolling from the older faculty members, but he was clearly determined and I'm sure everyone was happy to have Dawdson return to form.

So, the first semester went well, holiday break commenced, and before leaving Dawdson told his colleagues he would be spending it at some archives out of state. Nothing too strange there. A month passed, December turned to January, and the staff had a faculty meeting the day before students returned. As such, all of them arrived at the history department offices around the same time.

Well, *almost* all of them.

One of the professors, and I assume you've pieced together who, had apparently been spending a good amount of time there during the break. Like, living-there amount of time. The scene was complete chaos. There was a pistol on his desk along with several empty bottles of whiskey, and upon finding out he was no longer alone Dawdson started yelling about "the never-ending chaos," and "the multiple selves of the damned" and "the shadows now seen" all things that, as you can imagine, did not bode well for his mental state. His research had consumed him, and regurgitated a broken man. The police were called when he continued to grow increasingly more agitated, grabbing professors and screaming about the voices and what they knew and how close he was to solving it all. Eventually Dawdson was taken away by officers, most likely to a psychiatric facility to provide the help and support he needed, and subsequently let go from his position. From there, he essentially disappears from the academic record.

One more thing: his office was in complete disarray. Used markers and pens were all over, and papers and open books scattered across every square inch, which all things considered, isn't *all* that strange, however, on those open pages only certain words would be highlighted. Not sentences, just single words. There were so many books spread about it was impossible to walk though his office without stepping on a few. He'd also taken a marker and drawn a giant circle on one of the painted brick walls, which he then filled in completely until it looked like a giant black pit. In front of this faux-cavern sat his office chair, facing it directly. Supposedly it took the cleaning crew weeks to get it cleaned for future use.

A strange scene, no doubt, and a tragic end to a promising career, which gave my visit to the hotel a gothic flare that did not escape me as I reflected on the stories I'd heard from multiple fellow students by that point, each with their own flavor of emphasis. How much of the story was hyperbole or exaggeration? Well, before visiting I would have guessed most of the story. Now, well…you'll see.

Chapter 2

I continued up, only stopping to take a quick peek at each floor as I passed it. Each was different, though I quickly realized they fell into two categories: dated yet well-kept or completely left to decay. It wasn't every other floor or anything like that. There was no discernable pattern I could locate. And, to that point, I realized the numbering system the clerk in the lobby had mentioned must have only related to one type of these hallways, as I climbed well past five floors on my way up.

The nicer floors ran the decorative span of decades, ranging from the art deco glamor of the twenties to the floral chaos of the seventies. These hallways were clean and well kept, even if some of the wallpaper and design elements showed the faded hint of age. Though with each of these nicer levels I noticed a layer of what appeared to be smoke lingering above the floor, which was easily explained away when thinking back to my introduction to Deb. Just someone enjoying an evening toke, I figured. The other hallways? Let me tell you, those looked to have been ripped from a horror movie asylum and dropped in the Hotel Celeste.

Graffiti covered walls as stained as the lobby floor. The markings ranged from the standard phallic outlines and sophomoric obscenities, to the more disturbing "Welcome to Hell", or "We are Damned in this Hell" tags that were pretty bone chilling given their location. No decorations lined these halls; no tables or paintings to offset the ramshackle backdrop. Occasionally a barred window could be seen at the very end, but that was it. Trash littered the hallways, leaving behind a fetid smell of decay that greeted me whenever I opened the door and peered into one. They were more of a dark, sinister alley than they were a hotel or apartment or whatever the Hotel Celeste was.

I should add a personal note here: I was completely enamored with this weird fucking place. I mean, absolutely spellbound. I could not wrap my mind around it, and I was loving every second of exploration on my way up to see the troubled professor I've thus described.

Floor after floor, landing after landing I climbed, peeking my head in to see what each hallway looked like before I continued my journey. I have no idea how many halls there were in total, though my best guess is at least twelve, but eventually I arrived as far as the stairs would take me. In front was the first wooden door I'd seen at the Hotel Celeste.

Up to this point the only evidence of human occupancy had been the clerk and Debbie; however, as I stood there, the clatter of footsteps reverberated below me. It sounded like a stampede, too. Occasionally a voice would break through the clamor with a "hey!" or a displeased groan. I looked down at my watch; it was 4:15pm. A bus had likely just dropped off the bulk of the hotel's occupants, and if I needed to ditch Dawdson I had a built-in excuse of needing dinner. Truth be told, I'd grown a little nervous at the thought of being alone with Dawdson, but with the new arrivals someone would hear me if I called out for help.

With that, I entered the "fifth" floor which seemed a carbon copy of the first floor I entered and knocked on the only door contained throughout, 501. I heard some movement from within. Dawdson was home.

It took a few minutes, more stirring, and another knock before the door swung open and I was greeted by a short, distinguished man. I don't know what I was expecting him to look like, and I think the...dualistic, shall we say, nature of the hotel had only further thrown me for a loop, but the man who greeted me could not have been the same one from the stories. Hell, he looked like he had just made his way back from the lecture hall: tweed suit, glasses barely situated on the tip of his nose, an armful of books and I kid you not, a pipe protruding from his jacket pocket. His hair was grey and neatly parted to the side, and a carefully manicured mustache rested above his lip. He stared at me like I was a freshman who had just arrived during the last five minutes of office hours asking what a thesis was.

"Dr. Dawdson? Dr. John Dawdson?"

He tilted his head to the side and furrowed his brow. He opened his mouth to respond, then closed it and stared. It took him a moment to finally find the words, and I realized it was seeing his book tucked beneath my arm that stopped him in his tracks.

Finally, he answered. "Yes..." His voice was hesitant, unsure. Then he took a deep breath and regained his professorial composure. "Dr. John Dawdson, though I don't often hear the title these days," he stuck out his hand. "Now, might I ask who you are?"

I shook the extended hand, and introduced myself. He nodded along politely as I discussed my research and my discovery of his publications in the school's library. Naturally, I left out that I was most familiar with him from the tale of the professor that was used to scare graduate students about the dangers of academic obsession. As I spoke, it seemed impossible that the man in front of me could have been the boogeyman described; that being said, the fact that

24

I'd found him in the Hotel Celeste lent itself to those stories. I shrugged my concerns off as I spoke at length about my proposed dissertation. The whole time he simply nodded and smiled, staring at me with eyes that seemed both distant and curious.

When I was done with my spiel I held up his book. "I was hoping to talk to you about your research, if you wouldn't mind. I'd be happy to come back wh—"

Dr. Dawdson turned his back to me abruptly, and walked into his room. There was a second where I was certain he was about to shut the door in my face behind him, but he kept walking, leaving it open behind him. I was at a loss, not knowing whether he wanted me to stay in the hallway or follow him. I'll admit, the thought of following a stranger, much less a storied stranger— docile though he might seem— into their room screamed in the face of common sense. It also went against everything I'd learned from watching countless B horror movies and slashers growing up.

But when he didn't return, I did what any person whose head was clouded with the smog of academic aspirations and a gut feeling that their project was missing *something* would in my situation. I followed Dr. Dawdson inside.

***

There was a long walkway leading into Dr. Dawdson's apartment, making it difficult to see anything beyond the small, doorway sized opening before me. As I made my way, I reassured myself that, surely, if I was to yell someone below would hear me. Besides, my roommates back home knew where I was going, so it wasn't as if no one was aware of my whereabouts. *I'm safe,* I told myself over and over as I walked, which is something that rarely needs to be reiterated unless you are, in fact, unsafe.

I stepped out from that walkway and my jaw dropped. There in front of me was one of the best vistas of Rochester I'd ever seen. A long window wrapped around a nearly 180-degree view, unfurling the city in front of me. I could see Kodak towering high in the distance and the Redwings stadium just beneath. Cars, which looked to be no larger than ants from the vantage point, sped and wove through roads beneath. The city seemed so close and so distant; so small yet so large. I knew I was sitting there in the middle of it, but for a brief moment I had the strangest feeling that it might all disappear in an instant. That feeling I first felt outside, that I was staring at a mirage when I first saw the Hotel Celeste, was becoming stronger, more convincing. Somehow the whole urban landscape beneath was part of the phantasmagoria I found myself in, starting from standing outside the hotel to my strange adventure within. Everything here was not what it seemed, and all it would take was the smallest puncture to release the floodgates containing whatever lay behind.

It wasn't just the hotel. There, from Dr. Dawdson's perch I was convinced that whatever was happening had seeped into the city of Rochester itself. *A ripple, a slight flutter of the curtain? Or maybe that's not Rochester beneath us.* I blinked my eyes as if to clear the disillusion and told myself I was letting the strange nature of the day impact my mental clarity. It took a few seconds to silence those voices, but eventually I returned to admiring the view, and soon I was so engrossed in hunting familiar landmarks that I started forgetting why I was there in the first place.

"It's quite the view, isn't it?" Dr. Dawdson asked. I turned, my hypnosis broken and looked around the space not realizing until

26

that moment that I'd drifted through the room and was now standing directly in front of the window. It took a moment to find him, but eventually I saw him standing in the far corner of the giant loft, fingers tracing across a row of books in evident pursuit of a particular title.

The apartment was massive. A bed, king sized I guessed, was neatly made and tucked away in the corner of the cavernous room opposite Dr. Dawdson. Bookcases lined the wall, floor to ceiling, stuffed with ancient looking leather-bound books and various curios I ventured were from his studies. A recliner and sofa sat in the center of the main area, between which was a small wooden table covered with more books, these ones opened to certain pages. A yellow legal pad was also open, the facing page half covered with scribbled notes. Naturally, I might add, a giant map of the central and western portion of New York spanned one of the few splotches of painted white brick not hidden by shelves. Two globes sat beneath, and I felt myself pulled into their orbit. Upon closer inspection I realized they were a pair, one celestial and one terrestrial, both yellowed and peeling from age.

The smell of leather, tobacco, and that general hint of spices which old books so often have filled the apartment. It was a rather pleasant living situation, one which I could easily see myself sliding into upon retiring.

As I admired the space, Dr. Dawdson made his way to a bar cart and busied himself pouring two drinks. I watched from the corner of my eyes making sure there was no sleight of hand additions to the glasses, but all he did was pour from a large bottle with a distinguished looking label. He took a sip of the drink I presumed was his, then joined me by the globes and handed me the other glass filled with an amber colored liquid. As he did the two ice cubes collided about inside, clanking loudly.

"It's whiskey. I should have asked, but if you're working on your dissertation, I assumed you could use a drink."

"Thank you."

Not wanting to be rude, and having seen him prepare the drink, I accepted and took a quick sip, and I was surprised it burned less than the cheap whiskey I was used to. I took another, slightly longer pull, and found myself relaxed. The apprehension I'd felt earlier drifted away. *This is exactly what any old timer's place would look like, perhaps the stories were exaggerated.* The echo of the words I'd heard from the professor emeritus rang once more, *"he's not well,"* I quickly shuffled it away, assuming she must be talking about his health.

"So, you wanted to talk about Capron, was it?"

"Capron and the spiritualist movement in general. Just trying to get a good grounding in the original research before I make my argument. Your book, your biography on Capron, has already proven so helpful."

"Mhmmm…" he gestured over to the center of the room and took a seat on the sofa, then nodded towards the leather recliner. I took a seat, and pulled out the notepad I'd tucked beneath Dr. Dawdson's book, ready to jot. The glass of whiskey was still in one hand, while the other held my pen above the teetering notebook that had found its final resting place on my knee. As I readied myself to take notes, Dr. Dawdson busied himself with preparing his pipe. Removing the pipe and a small cloth bag from his jacket pocket he looked in my direction.

"I apologize, it's been some time since I've had visitors. Do you mind?"

"Of course not. And thank you for inviting me in."

He grunted and nodded to say both thank you and you're welcome, and soon the pipe was packed, lit, and the smell of tobacco wafted through the room. He leaned back into his chair and crossed his legs, the whole time staring at me with a look that seemed to imply curiosity, or at least mild interest.

His voice was muffled when he finally spoke from around the stem of the pipe, a puff of smoke enveloped his face.

"Mr. Green, I'll be up front with you. My studies…my *research* has taken me on a divergent path from the book you carry with you. Sure, there is overlap, much in fact, but I fear an honest conversation between the two of us may prove useless to your own thesis."

He sat back further and sunk into the sofa, and though he tried to speak in an even, emotionless voice, a tremor of frustration rumbled through.

And why's that?

I couldn't say it aloud of course; sitting in a chair, notebook in lap, I already felt enough like a therapist or reporter. No, that wouldn't have done. I had a premonition of the eye roll and subsequent, "get the fuck out," or, "look at the time," which would have been sure to follow such a ridiculous prod. The cryptic answer about his research was too much. I thought about the stories, that final project that seemed to fix things until holiday break when it all unraveled. How could I not try to find out more? That same surge of curiosity that sent me exploring the hotel like some 19th century archeologist defiling some ancient cultural site had the crossbar and strings, and I was just a marionette pulled by forces bigger than I. In this case, the bitch goddess curiosity and potential discovery was the puppeteer. I took another sip of the whiskey and figured what the hell? I was here against all odds, might as well shoot straight.

"Is that why you left [redacted school]? Your research didn't align with the department."

"Not quite, though it would have led to that, I'm sure. Oh, I'm sure there are stories about how I left; maybe some are closer to the truth than I'd like to think, but the research I'm talking about was never explained in full to my colleagues. No, no, it could never. *They* could never."

He turned his head and stared in my direction, a look of pure despair sweeping across his face. The corners of his mouth were drawn downwards, and his eyes softened, and for a moment I was worried he was going to break down sobbing, a scenario which I was woefully inadequate with knowing how to handle.

Luckily it never came to that. He regained his composure with a deep, raspy breath and sat up stiff as a board. "Now Capron—"

It's rude to interrupt, but I felt a monologue coming on and wanted to get it out before the moment passed. I'd like to think I said, but more likely I blurted: "I'd be interested in hearing about this research, if you'd like." And I did. I really, *really* did. I didn't care how off the rails it was, or how meandering and pointless it might prove. I *had* to know.

He raised his eyebrow and pursed his lips.

"Okay then. Let's see how serious you are. Truth be told, it would be nice to talk about it to someone, and even if you think me a raving fool, what's the harm in that? That's the story they tell about down at [redacted college] anyways. My research, as you'll see, may have broader implications for historical understanding than even I realize. Before I go on, whether you think I've lost it completely halfway in, promise you'll see it through? That's important to me."

He looked at me, a sudden shadow of concern cast across his face. *He's lonely up here,* I realized. Even if I wasn't interested— which I certainly was—I would have stuck around to listen. I nodded. "To the end."

"What if I told you, it was about the White Lady?"

"The kid's ghost story about the Durand Eastman Beach?"

"See," he threw his arms in the air in frustration.

"No, no, go on. I'm sorry, just— not what I expected," which was the God honest truth. I don't know *what* I expected, but a local legend about a ghost woman who haunts the shores of Lake Ontario accompanied by her two dogs searching for her missing daughter was certainly not it. I was familiar with the story though. Like everyone I knew who grew up in the area, I'd first heard about the White Lady of Durand Eastman as a kid in fourth grade from one of my friends' older brothers who was looking to scare the shit out of us little kids. Given my interest in folklore, I'd done some digging into the legend later on and always came up empty; it seemed as if the story was just the standard "lady of the lake" narrative that was so popular in the old world, and repurposed for Lake Ontario *à la* Washington Irving-style.

Similar to the stories about Dr. Dawdson, there were several different iterations, but they all boiled down to the White Lady or Lady in White haunting this old stone pavilion overlooking Lake Ontario and seeking revenge for her daughter, and like I mentioned, accompanied by her two dogs who she purchased in life to help locate her missing child. After dying and returning as a ghost she continued her mission of revenge. If she found you in her territory and didn't like you, or you were a bad person (typically

31

this part of the legend only included males, as the backstory often included a guy either killing or kidnapping her daughter) she'd haul off and throw you off the edge of her "castle", which again is a rather unassuming stone pavilion dug into a hill overlooking the lake. A forty, maybe sixty-foot drop, max.

So, in short: I was familiar with, and surprised to hear that researching an old ghost story is how Dr. Dawdson had been enjoying his forced retirement, but to be honest, there was no way in hell I wasn't sticking around to hear whatever he had to say. I figured at worst I'd hear a good ghost story, which was more than okay with me given the fact I didn't have much time to watch horror movies and was missing them dearly, and at best, maybe he'd located something I could include in my research. Either way, a win-win for me.

"So, you'll listen? The whole thing." Dawdson's face lowered as he stared at me, his brow furrowed in unwavering concentration. Any hesitation, any wrong answer, and this interview was over.

"Yes, yes, please. I'd truly love to hear about it."

The Faustian verbal agreement, so began my hellish fall.

"Okay then. Well, here it is…"

***

I didn't move from that seat for the next three hours. Looking back, it's a good thing my roommates were prone to forgetting, as otherwise I have no doubt Rochester PD would have had a missing persons report after finding out where I was. As for Dawdson, the fact that his lectures were well attended even as things went south soon made perfect sense. Historian, storyteller, omen of terror…he did it all. He described feelings, thoughts, and places in a way that put me there in the story. At the time I assumed this omnipresent, third person way of telling history was simply creative liberty taken by a bored old man, but…well, again, you'll see. I'll do my best to capture it in the way Dr. Dawdson saw fit to describe it.

This is the tale he told me.

Part 2:
Behind the Veil

Chapter 3

In 1849 Rochester was growing, as it had been since 1825. The Erie Canal had brought wealth and new settlers to the region that once belonged to the Haudenosaunee, and just as importantly, it sent goods back East. The Geologic Survey, which had been completed between 1836-1842, proved there were untapped natural resources, ripe and waiting to be plucked like a plump empire apple that the region would become famous for. The transient and often violent decades of the canal construction still lingered in the minds of many, but the wounds had scabbed, and the rose-tinted lens of the past led to tavern talk of the old times when the world seemed more wild, where a person could set out and stake their claim with a bit of luck, wit, and guts.

Of course, these nostalgic and oftentimes slurred conversations were had by the survivors: not the child Irish workers whose bodies were never discovered following a gunpowder induced cave in, the immigrant ditch digger who ended up on the wrong side of a pistol after an argument, or the missing women from the brothels whose fates would never be discovered. No, their stories went untold. There were the small subsistence farmers whose properties were swallowed by larger and richer growers as the money flowed along the canal and, similar to how the political party his death inspired had fizzled out, William Morgan's death was a thing of the distant past and no longer on the tip of wagging tongues primed by libations.

Rochester was not only growing in population, but had also changed from a frontier space to a youthful metropolis with all the merchants and craftspeople needed to supply the demand for expensive wares and an emerging upper class. Stores with imported china and fineries lined the main streets, as did bookstores and expensive taverns and hotels and giant churches and places of worship that spoke to the city's ambitions.

...but it didn't take a long walk to step outside the bustling streets or the covered Reynolds Arcade where vendors hawked their goods to an increasingly wealthy clientele. A few streets in one direction, a short carriage ride perhaps, and a person could find themselves back in those places that hadn't changed all that much. Where the *new* hadn't yet set claim; where the stories not told in the bars of expensive taverns and hotels still took root, and were more than stories.

Such was the case with the Fox sisters, who first heard the rappings of a murdered man thirty miles west of Rochester in their family's farmhouse. The injured spirit, as fourteen year old Margeret Fox called it, responded to their requests for knocking, and did so in a fashion that scared the Fox's parents enough to abandon their house and send the sisters to Rochester where Margeret and Kate joined their older sister Leah.

(I should add, at this point Dr. Dawdson made note that he felt the Fox sisters were faking; but enough historical debate exists for you to draw your own conclusion, dear reader.)

The Fox sisters' claims were a match that fell into a bed of dry kindling in Rochester. Religious fervor was so ardent that the area was referred to as the "burned-over district" because it was ablaze with the fires of zeal, but just as importantly, they found a world that had seen recent technical developments such as the morse code. If a person could now communicate with someone miles away, if geography was no longer an adequate barrier to stop conversations, why should death?

So, when the Fox sisters appeared at the Corinthian Hall in Rochester on November 14 to demonstrate, an audience gathered to bear witness to a new phenomenon, one sure to change the world.

And the world was sure to change, especially for one woman in attendance that evening.

***

It was November and outside a cold wind blew, rattling wooden signs and making all those who strolled the streets pull their jackets and shawls up a little higher, but inside the packed Corinthian Hall four hundred spectators huddled together warming the space with their collective body heat. The occasional low whistle of a steam radiator located within the building would indicate another blast of heat, and soon, many of those in attendance were fanning themselves with pamphlets as beads of sweat formed on their foreheads and their clothes began to stick. There was a dull murmur of conversation as the crowd waited, with strangers whispering to their neighbors about what they might witness. Most seemed to think a public humiliation awaited; that the so-called spiritualists would soon be caught in the act. If not hostile, the crowd was certainly incredulous. Some even glanced about the giant hall trying to find some hidden device or tool that might be used in the trickery. The smell of booze emanated like a noxious gas from many of those in attendance and cigar smoke hung like storm clouds above the gathering.

Those looking for early signs of tampering found themselves disappointed. No evidence of recent modifications could be located in the pristine structure. The Corinthian Hall was the most recent addition to the growing center of Rochester, the building less than a year old, and everything from the floors to the walls to the benches had a luster about them that spoke to that newness. Despite the hushed, damp nature of the crowd, the air in the cavernous Corinthian Hall was charged with excitement. A public shaming awaited, most likely, but there was an off chance they might see something spectacular. Something they could brag about witnessing.

Mary was lucky enough to find herself a seat along the aisles of benches that sat on either side of the building. She sat above the galley below, giving her a view of the whole building. Looking down at the amassed crowd she felt her pulse quicken. Mary had never seen so many people in one place, and all at once she felt the surge of humanity pressing down on her, gripping at her neck tightly and weighing down on her chest like a nightmare where she couldn't move. She took a deep breath and the feeling passed. Mary removed the shawl that she'd draped around her neck to the bench beside her, then she busied herself examining the crowd: women in dome shaped skirts with high and tight bodices intermingled with men wearing tailored suits or frock coats and vests beneath, which clung as tightly as the bodices in many cases.

Mary's mind wandered as she looked at the sea of mutton chops, beards and barley curls below. She thought about what the lecture might mean for her: one, final conversation with her mother. A thing robbed of her all those years back. Closure? Contentment? An understanding of her mother as a person, as a woman and not just a parent? Perhaps all of those things, or maybe just the chance to say goodbye. Mary felt her pulse quicken again, but this time in joyous excitement. A smile grew across the young woman's face as she surveyed the wavering crowd beneath.

She was so distracted she didn't notice the row of men and women who were entering the building from some hidden backway as they took their seats on the platform in the front, facing the audience. It wasn't until a blanket of absolute silence fell over the audience that Mary realized the presentation was about to start. The stillness was interrupted by some taunting and subsequent snickering.

"Where are the damn ghosts?!" a man cried out and the audience interrupted in laughter.

"Charletons," another man cried out.

"Hell awaits those who lie and spread false beliefs." This was met by a round of cheers from the audience, who continued to toss out insults and barbs.

This went on for several minutes, until the audience eventually quieted when they realized they weren't getting a rise from those at the front who had taken their seats and stared out at the crowd. She'd never been to one, but the calm faces of resignation that peered out towards the crowd made Mary think of an execution. Though it was mostly quiet, a few giggles could still be heard from various pockets.

"I believe it is seven and time to start," someone from the front table said, though Mary couldn't make out who spoke. She strained to see, and even though she had one of the better seats in the house, it was still tough to make out a few of the faces furthest from her. If the goading was meant to have an effect on the speakers it certainly failed, she decided. Whoever called the start of the meeting spoke with enough confidence to halt any further jabs for the moment, and the faces she could see were confident and unshaken, save for an older couple sitting on the edge who fidgeted nervously and looked away from the crowd.

"I want to thank you good people for joining us this evening," said the man at the center of the table, now standing.

All eyes were on him. His voice was loud and clear, and it filled the giant Corinthian Hall like the retort of a cannon. Like most of the men in the crowd, he had mutton chops and was wearing a frock coat. He leaned forward, hands clasping the table behind which the panel of speakers sat and stared out into the crowd, face scrunched in a scowl.

"There had been much said of the Fox sisters here, sitting beside me," he gestured to two women to his right, "and our aim today is to correct much of the misinformation that has spread so quickly. We are joined not only by two of three sisters, but also Mr. and Mrs. Post, dear friends of the Fox family who though, originally skeptical, soon saw the truth to these claims."

The man then gestured to the man and woman sitting at the furthest end of the table from where he stood and closest to Mary. The Post's seemed the least comfortable out of everyone at the head of the hall. Both looked down at the table in front of them, barely casting their eyes up to the crowd when introduced. She felt bad for them, clearly, they didn't want to be there. Mary hoped the audience had gotten most of their vitriol out and would settle down, though that quickly proved not the case.

After the man paused following the introductions the audience rediscovered its voice. A few of those in the crowd hissed and someone in the back shouted "Frauds!" so that it filled the hallway.

"Show us the spirits," grew from a single voice in the back to a cheer that included most of the audience.

42

For a moment it seemed as if the whole gathering might break out into chaos, but the man raised his hand and bellowed, "Order! Order! To any doubters among us I simply ask you to wait 'till the end." The audience lulled to silence once more following another fit of laughter and a few eye rolls below. All of those in attendance paid admission, and they wanted to see their money well spent, one way or another. The crowd calmed and waited.

Mary looked back at the stage and was surprised to see how young the famous sisters were. Sure, all the newspaper reports included their respective ages in the reports, but it was another thing to see them in person. One was a teenager and the older one, (*Leah Fish, the sister they've been staying with since fleeing Hudesville,* Mary knew from one of those articles), looked to be only a few years older than Mary herself, who had just counted her twenty third birthday. She guessed Kate was somewhere else, too young to attend such a meeting. The newspapers claimed Leah was contacted by the spirits to prove their claims publicly after spending a month in the parlors of local residences. Admission was twenty-five cents. Mary jumped at the chance.

The man started talking once more, a notable change to his voice. "Our AIM," he said again, louder, his voice dripping with indignant rage like a preacher at a Sunday pulpit chastising his flock, "is not to subject you to *interpretations* or *thoughts* or *guesses,* but rather," he slapped the table and paused.

The loud clap forced many, Mary included, to sit upright in their seats as if a teacher had caught them daydreaming and slapped their desk with a ruler.

"To present you merely the well proven FACTS and allow *you,* the good people in attendance, to draw *your* conclusions. As you will hear; no, as you will *experience,* the sisters beside me, here in front of you tonight, have presented us with the evidence and proof that something exists beyond. Through science, through religion, and through the FACTS, we might hope to understand what this means."

Mary remained still as a statue, worried that if she moved the spell would be broken and the spirits might not appear. Surely, whatever was to happen required her undivided, unmoving attention. She felt like a child again, sitting in a church sermon and knowing any fidgeting would bring rebuke or worse. There was no information in the article about *how* the spirits would appear, simply that they would. Might they come swirling in from the ceiling above? Or calling out from somewhere unknown? She soon realized she was holding her breath and let out a long quiet exhale as she waited.

The man shuffled some papers in front of him, the quiet rustling filled the Corinthian Hall that remained frozen in silence, still hanging on his last words. His hooks were in. Rowdy as they were before, his speech worked like magic. Just like Mary, they were bracing for whatever was next. When he resumed his voice was softer, quieter, and it seemed the whole crowd leaned in to hear better.

"We at the table will tell you the events that have led to the gathering this evening, beginning with the manifestation of Mr. Splitfoot as he soon revealed himself as in Hydesville, the communications since, and then the spirits have promised to make themselves known today to you, here in the hall."

He gestured around, arms wide as he peered up towards the balcony. His words continued on in an echo that reverberated about the space. As they died off, the man thrust his fist against the table and leaned his face forward. Again, his voice lowered as his face grew solemn.

"Of course, while this may convince many of you in attendance this evening, skeptics may claim these manifestations as works of forgery or of fraudulent means, we will then appoint a committee for further investigations. The revelations are too valuable to have any room for doubt. Have we any objections?"

No response.

Mary expected someone to stand up to make a point or an inquiry, but no one moved. Someone down the row from her shifted on the bench, and the loud creak that followed roared throughout Corinthian Hall like a crash of thunder. All eyes fell upon the unlucky fellow who nervously glanced around, concerned his indiscretion might get him thrown out. After a second all eyes returned to the front as the man at the head table let out a soft chuckle.

"Yes, yes, thank you for demonstrating sir that the acoustics in this hall should do quite nicely for our spirits."

There were a few giggles from the crowd below and several smirking faces, and the air of tension that had permeated the room seemed to break. It was as if a silent, collective sigh of relief was had by all those in attendance, and for the first time Mary allowed herself to squirm slightly in the bench to find a more comfortable position. The corner of her lip even curled up into a slight smile.

"Shall we begin with the first night, when Catherine and Margaretta first heard the noises that would soon lead us all here today? The farmhouse in Hydesville the family occupied has a reputation as being haunted, and soon…"

The man, who eventually introduced himself as Eliab Wilkinson Capron, continued for another twenty minutes telling the story all those in attendance already knew. About the rappings that, dropping their formal names almost immediately, Kate and Maggie reportedly heard, which continued for several nights following the initial appearance of the sound. How the neighbors were brought in to witness the phenomena after a code of communication was established with the presumed spirit, who eventually introduced itself as Mr. Splitfoot. Lastly, how the entity explained it was the spirit of a man murdered in the house, a peddler by the name of Charles Rosna, and the Fox family's subsequent abandonment of the farm. A few prodding questions were occasionally shouted out from one of the drunker or bolder members of the audience, to which Capron would only reply, "questions at the end," and continue. The break between questions grew longer after each one until eventually Mary was certain the audience had taken Capron's instructions to wait till the end.

The man knew how to hold court.

The background information was told in an exhaustive manner and Capron spared no detail, small though it may seem. Although Mary knew the story well, she leaned forward as Capron spoke, captivated by his way of relaying the history of the strange occurrences. He spoke with such confidence, such vigor, that anyone in the audience who doubted the validity of the story *must* be forced to reconsider. His adherence to the "facts", a word he seemed to use at least every other sentence, reminded Mary of a scientist. *There was no way this man could be tricked into believing a prank*, Mary thought, thinking of all the articles that had been published claiming to debunk the Fox sisters and all of their followers.

"Which brings us to today. As advertised, Leah, their older sister, and Maggie will make contact for you good folks as they have for private audiences over the past several weeks, here in the lion of the west, this great city of Rochester. And, also as advertised, a committee shall be established to experience the phenomena on a more intimate scale. I will turn the floor over to Leah and Maggie to commence their work. Before I do, however, I need to remind those in the audience absolute silence is not only necessary, but *critical* to the success of this venture. The spirits can be meek at first, but as has been established earlier," he smiled a big showman's grin, "noise travels well in this hall, and they have promised to visit this evening. Complete silence of the audience will allow *all* to hear. We will take a minute for anyone who might want to leave."

He paused to look across the sea of faces. No one moved and Mary sat back in her seat, resuming her statue-like posture. She took a preemptive deep breath.

"Alright then. Maggie, Leah: the floor is yours."

The two sisters rose from their seats. There was no doubt they were related: both had soft, oval faces with dark walnut brown hair and similarly dark, piercing eyes. Again, Mary was taken aback at how young they were, but she was also surprised at how confident they were before a crowd of four hundred spectators. No wavering, no eyes glancing nervously about; no, both Maggie and Leah seemed completely at ease in front of a crowd that no doubt included several doubters. Again, Mary felt her confidence in them soar. *Surely these girls are telling the truth.*

Both sisters closed their eyes, while Mary's grew wider. She didn't want to miss a thing.

A minute passed. Nothing.

A seed of doubt was planted. A wave of worry washed across Mary's face; her eyes grew wider in concern.

What if it was only in Hydesville? What if I can never talk to her again. What if-

A soft *thump* sounded to her right. For a moment she thought the man had shifted on the bench again, but a hushed gasp across the crowd proved otherwise.

"Quiet," Capron said, his voice harsh despite the smirk.

The younger of the two girls spoke now. "Spirit, are you here? Please let these people know your presence," she peered around the room, starting at the wall opposite where the noise was heard. Slowly her gaze moved to the back wall, then to the wall behind Mary, and finally, after what seemed an eternity, to the spot where the first noise had been heard.

thump *thump*

Looking out to the crowd, the older of the two sisters spoke next.

"They are here."

Another gasp, another call for silence from Capron.

"Are there more than one of you?"

Another doubled response. This time Mary noted the noise was less of a thud, and it sounded more like the sound of someone snapping their fingers together. Still, it came from the initial spot of the first response. The older sister spoke again.

"Thank you for joining us this evening. There are those who doubted your ability to communicate with the living in attendance, and your presence tonight should change that."

A series of snaps and rappings followed. Mary had trouble telling where each one came from. It sounded to her like the noises came from all over, like there was something alive and crawling within the surrounding walls.

"There are many here this evening willing to communicate, it seems. Is Mr. Splitfoot in attendance."

snap *snap*

"Then you have followed us here to Rochester?" the younger Fox sister asked.

snap *snap*

Mary's heart fluttered. Capron's instructions took hold at last, and the audience managed to hold its collective gasp this time. Still, everywhere she looked Mary saw eyes opened wide in a mix of surprise and horror. A few of the men below were dabbing at their perspiring faces with handkerchiefs while others tried to puff out their chests in feigned confidence, though it was evident from the way their eyes darted about that their bravado was merely for show. However, most of the men and women below simply looked around in bewilderment.

The Mr. Splitfoot, the murdered peddler who had first broken through to communicate with the Fox sisters was in attendance; here, in the Corinthian Hall in Rochester New York. For the first time that night Mary felt herself bristle with fear.

Mr. Splitfoot is what we called the devil. She thought back to the games and teases from childhood: *Mr. Splitfoot will get you…here comes Mr. Splitfoot…better hide from Mr. Splitfoot.*

A wave of fear washed through her as the surrounding audience and space became blurry as if grew distant. Mary wanted to get up and run out of the giant hall out to safety. Her heart beat faster, her breath quickened, her head felt lighter, a surge of adrenaline coursed through her body— but then a thought broke through.

One last conversation.

It was like wading into the still chilled waters of Lake Ontario on a spring morning, suddenly Mary felt herself at attention once more as the panic was shocked back to interest. The hall regained its focus and though below the audience remained in a state of shock, the sisters were now moving about from behind the table, pointing to various spots on the walls. Meanwhile, the row of men and women at the front table joined in gesturing towards various directions.

"Mr. Split foot, are there more than ten spirits with you?" One of the sisters asked, though Mary couldn't tell which one with them moving about.

snap *snap*

"Twenty?"

snap *snap*

"Thirty?"

snap

"More than twenty spirits of the deceased here with us this evening," it was now Capron who spoke as he stood up from his seat. A final flurry of rappings rattled throughout the Corinthian Hall, which seemed to even have an impact on Capron whose confidence was betrayed for the slightest moment as his eyebrows shot up in startled surprise at the commotion. The two sisters exchanged glances from the corner of their eyes, then returned to their respective seats.

Capron regained his composure almost immediately with a sudden upward tilt of his chin and a puff of his chest that reminded Mary of sketches she'd seen of the knights of King Arthur's round table. He then opened his arms wide as if embracing those gathered in a familiar embrace.

"And now you good folks have seen the validity of these reports. That these are not abstract claims or falsehoods or the curious and mistaken minds of the young women sitting next to me. No good people gathered before me, what we are dealing with, are *facts*."

***

Capron took questions from the audience for the next twenty minutes, always serving as the mediary between the crowd and the sisters. A few in the crowd continued to hiss or boo on occasion, though they would quickly be silenced by those surrounding them. Most of the questions were about particular persons who had passed on, and there was half a second where Mary considered asking about her mother, but Capron worked away from specific answers and only promised that further connections surely loomed in the near future.

The hall was still warm, and the stale smell of sweat hung heavy in the air. All around spectators fidgeted about their seats, uncomfortable but unwilling to miss a second of the presentation. Another whistle from the steam radiator made everyone flinch in surprise, then the following burst of warm air cascaded on those around it, including Mary, adding to the stuffiness of the lecture hall. Mary's dress clung tightly to her neck seemingly intent on strangling her.

Eventually, somebody opened one of the windows near the front entrance of the hall, and a cool gust of wind blew in from outside. Someone next to Mary let out a long exhale and muttered, "about damn time." He was immediately shushed by someone near him.

"We have time for one, final question before we must move on to the business at hand; of forming the investigative committee that is. Now…yes, yes. You, there!" Capron pointed to a man sitting in the second row who then stood from his seat. Knowing all eyes were on him the man paused for a second, reveling in the attention, and ran his hand through his bushy facial hair. He then turned his head both ways to look at the surrounding audience and cleared his throat.

"*Ahem* now, might other persons, other people, serve as conduits as the Sisters? Or is this a unique ability impossible to replicate?" He nodded at Capron and the head table and took his seat.

"An excellent, excellent question sir. One I was hoping might be asked, in fact."

There was a boyish excitement in Capron's voice now, the pitch rising higher than it had at any point during the past hour. Again, Mary was struck by the man's sincerity. *Surely this was no con.*

"Already it appears those with the ability to communicate with the spirits have increased, including Leah Fish here, older sister to both Maggie and Kate, who has joined her sisters in communicating with those who had passed. And *rumors,* a thing that I hate to report but that I have a feeling contains some validity, of others have been reported to myself and my associates here. It is not all that unfeasible…"

Capron shuffled the stack of paper in front of him until he discovered the note sheet he was looking for, then continued.

"No, no, take for example the ancient histories of this world that account for similar interactions. Stories and traditions even older than the holy book of course, but take for example the story of King Belshezzar, son of Nabonidus, and his palace. How, might I ask a sceptic, is the hand of the spirit that appears to write on the wall any different than what we have seen here tonight? I might go further to ask, how is the translation done by Daniel any different than those of the Fox sister? Would you deny the validity of the book of Daniel?"

Capron went back to looking at his notes, then realized he had not finished answering the question. His head shot up and the words flooded out of his mouth as if to make up for lost time.

"That is to say that there is precedent for these communications, and that, to your point good sir, it appears as if the lines of communication between the spirits and our world will continue to grow, with more eyes and ears willing to receive their messages. That there are more conduits, perhaps even a few in this room, who might develop the abilities to communicate with the deceased, I have almost no doubt. The Fox sisters may prove to be the forefigures of a soon mighty movement, one sure to change the world as we know it."

Some in the audience jeered in response, others returned to hissing out or calling out names, and some cheered—but perhaps none clapped louder than Mary.

***

It was a long walk home that evening.

As the presentation came to a close a committee was appointed, all men, to attend a smaller "seance" as Capron had called it. It was promised that their findings would be published in the newspapers to either confirm or deny the credibility of the sisters, then the crowd was dismissed. After sitting in the Corinthian Hall and hearing the rappings, Mary had no doubt that those involved could only make one conclusion: that the sisters were telling the truth. That it *was* possible to talk to the deceased. Even more fantastic? Spirits were not only in the little farm in Hydesville, they were everywhere. The Otherside was near at all times. She felt the company of the dead in that packed hall that evening.

As the crowd poured into the outside world it seemed everyone was in a state of shock. Occasionally a couple or group might whisper amongst themselves as they passed Mary, one of the last people to leave their seat, but for the most part it seemed as if everyone was busy trying to make sense of what they'd witnessed. It took some time for Mary to make her way outside as the entrance was bottlenecked, with the crowd only slowly dispersing outside. Perhaps it was the cold November air that made them hesitant to leave, or maybe it was out of concern that they might miss one final act of the evening. Whatever the case, the crowd moved slowly.

As she stood waiting to leave, Mary looked about the wall closest to her: there was no evidence of being tampered with, no recently disturbed plaster or signs that there might be some foul play. As far as Mary could tell, the wall was as it had first been built. Though everything in her wanted to believe, and she told herself she was convinced beyond a doubt, some small, cynical voice kept prodding.

It could have been faked. Someone could have been outside the walls, or perhaps it was just a parlor trick you fell for.

She scanned the wall once more and after still finding it undisturbed, she found it easier to ignore those thoughts.

Finally, the floodgates broke, and the crowd surged forward, bringing Mary with it into the cold November night. She passed through the row of Greek Corinthian columns that lined the front of the building. A few stragglers still milled about in front of the

Corinthian Hall; most, however, had disappeared into the night, either boarding carriages or beginning their walk home, just as Mary would that evening. She crossed a bridge over the Genesee River, its waters green and rushing beneath her, and listened to the roar of the Genesee High Falls that had claimed the famous daredevil Sam Patch's life all those years ago. Like the Genesee River, her walk would take her in the direction of Lake Ontario that evening. After crossing the bridge, she stayed on Main St. for a few hundred feet, then turned left.

The streets were dark, only occasionally lit by the soft glow of a gas lantern overhead or a candle shining in the window of the shops and houses she passed as she walked through the city. For the most part the night was quiet as people settled in and prepared for the next day; there were, of course, some exceptions. Mary quickened her pace as she walked past a tavern, whose clientele she could hear hollering and yelling two blocks away. The smell of smoke filled the air as she approached, both tobacco and burning wood. It was an enjoyable change to the sour-stench of the packed lecture hall. Still, pleasant as the smell and thought of a roaring fire might be, Mary was keenly aware of the dangers that her being alone posed, and she didn't dare consider taking a detour. She kept walking as fast as her feet would carry her.

The building was dark, and though she only cast a quick glance into the window as she hurried past, through the grime smeared window she could make out the orange glow of a fireplace which cast the silhouettes of at least thirty people packed into the tiny establishment. It was nearly eight at night and Mary guessed many were already in the cups. As she passed, the roar of drunken conversations reached a crescendo, the sound of which followed her another three blocks past. Her pace didn't slow even as the shouts gave way to a distant murmur, and eventually to silence.

The cluttered wall of buildings that lined the cobbled streets soon gave way as well and the backdrop of the city was replaced by woods and farmland. Even the road pittered out to a dirt path, which Mary knew she'd be on for another four miles or so before arriving home for the evening. After leaving the city Mary let out a deep breath that she hadn't been aware she was holding. Though she was alone on the country road, Mary felt significantly safer than she had as she walked past that packed tavern. Her calves burned from the pace and trying to keep flat footing on the uneven walkway, and for the first time since leaving the lecture she allowed her pace to slow slightly.

The effects of overheating during the crowded presentation was soon a distant memory. The night air nipped at her exposed neck and face, and her ears stung from the cold. Mary pulled the shawl she'd brought with her for the walk around her shoulders, then buried her hands in the warm material and brought it higher until it covered most of her face. Her mother had made her the shawl two years before her death, and though the color had since faded to a muted red and the ends had frayed, the shawl still kept her warm. Mary wrapped the shawl around her face so that she could still see the way in front of her. The road lay ahead in a nearly straight line before disappearing entirely into the dark expanse, and although she didn't have a light with her, the full moon above cast enough light so she could make her way. Mary stared at the stars above and the endless expanse of cosmos that swirled about the clear night sky. The beauty of the heavens only added to that gut feeling she'd felt in the lecture hall. *Surely, with all that is unknown what the Fox sisters claim is not only possible, but probable.* She thought back to the intact walls of the hall that clearly had not been tampered with, the responsive nature of the rappings, and how Capron had made his point like a scientist or priest convinced in their convictions. All of that pointed to one conclusion for Mary: *One last conversation.*

Another voice echoed from the back of her psyche. It was one that only occasionally broke through, but when it did it whispered and rattled like wind through reeds, and forced her attention.

And the dreams...

Yes, the dreams. At times Mary convinced herself she'd grown accustomed to them, though she knew it was a lie. They started around the same time she'd read about the Fox sisters and first entertained the thought of talking to her mother. The dreams were always different, but the voices and the fog were always there, and sometimes when she woke Mary had the strange feeling that she'd been told something she was supposed to remember. That the voices were *trying* to communicate with her. Most of the time, however, she simply woke drenched in sweat trying to untangle the darkened room from the strange dreamscape she'd been wandering.

The dreams slowly dissipated in her thoughtstream as her mind returned to the Corinthian Hall. *The last question...* the one about *others* being able to communicate with the dead. For a second, she allowed herself to believe that the dreams were exactly that; that she was privy to the same hidden knowledge as the Fox sisters. The idea passed quickly though: the dreams were simply her active imagination taking hold of her growing interests, she told herself. Mary resumed trying to remember everything she could from that evening while shielding herself from the cold.

After another minute, Mary stopped walking to figure out how far she had left. The fields running alongside the road had been harvested bare, the tall rows of wheat that typically surrounded the farm had been cut down, leaving behind rows of stumps that reminded Mary of a porcupine's back. Without the wheat to obstruct her view, Mary could make out the glowing windows and the silhouette of the Smith's farmhouse about a quarter mile away from where she stood, which marked the halfway point, and less than a hundred yards past their house began the forest that contained hers. At night and from a distance the woods looked like a dark impenetrable fortress, though Mary knew the road continued through it.

Her legs were no longer sore and wanting to get home sooner rather than later, she returned to the quickened pace she'd managed when leaving Rochester and made her way to Irondequoit. Somewhere from the distant forest that loomed ahead an owl hooted, as if spurring Mary onward.

***

It took another half hour for her to arrive home.

Just as her breath was beginning to fog in the cold night air and the warmth of the shawl seemed to die away, dropping constantly from her face so that eventually Mary gave up and just held it to her stinging ears, the clearing of her property began. It was subtle at first; in fact, most people would have never noticed and simply walked right by continuing on the dirt road that would take them all the way through Irondequoit to the shore of Lake Ontario, but Mary knew the trail like the back of her hand. A wide split in the brush and foliage that ran along the way, marked by two thick elm trees whose leaves had long since dropped. Though the forest was filled with other elms, poplars, and maple trees, even the passerby who failed to note the entranceway they formed would note these two particular trees due to their sheer size and mangled trunks, which resembled a large coil of snakes, each attempting to reach the top of the tree first.

Mary walked through the elms and reached both arms out as far out as she could to trace her frozen fingers over the thick bark at the same time. This was something she had attempted to do every day as a child, and since that fateful day when her wingspan was finally wide enough to touch both she'd continued to perform this little ritual every time she returned home. Even when her fingers were so cold, she could barely feel the rough texture of the bark as they passed over.

From there, it was another twenty feet or so before the forest gave way to a large clearing that included the house her father, then mother, had left to her after she passed. It had been built by her grandfather in 1822 and though the subsequent owners had done their best to upkeep the place, time and weather had worn the wooden siding down to an ashy grey that gave the old house an almost translucent glow in the dark. The forest around her rustled as a breeze blew through and the smell of dying and moldering leaves filled her nostrils. Above her, a few trees managed to hang on to their orange and red plumage that rattled against the wind, though most of the trees she passed were barren, and their leaves formed a slick layer on the walkway Mary traversed. With each step she could feel herself sinking in before she made contact with the packed dirt of the trail beneath.

She was almost there. A single lantern she'd left burning before making her way to Rochester was still lit next to the doorway. The promise of warmth was within distance, Mary lurched forward and braced herself against the wind as she again quickened her pace. A branch cracked beneath her feet as she continued towards the front door, and immediately the night was filled with the sound of harsh barks and the pounding of paws.

"It's just me," Mary said as loudly as she could through chattering teeth as two bulking forms appeared in front of the house. The flickering lantern behind them cast long shadows in her direction and the illusion seemed to triple their respective size. Their nails tapped against the wooden porch that groaned beneath their weight as they stood guard.

"It's me," Mary said a little louder.

When they realized who it was, the two large bulldogs, Neppy and Morta, stopped barking and sprinted in her direction, crashing into her legs in a whirlwind of wagging tails and excited pants. Warmth radiated from their bodies and Mary leaned into them, wrapping her arms around each of the two dogs. Their fur smelled like smoke and musk and the woods, and Mary knew she was home in the way that only seeing one's dogs can signify.

"You've been sitting by the fire, haven't you?"

Both looked up at her with eyes and jaws wide open, rapidly panting in excitement at her return. They followed her the short distance to the doorway then into the warmth of the house. The fire in the stone mantel was still going, though the logs she placed in before leaving had burned down to nothing more than blackened chips, beneath which red embers smoldered amidst the grey and white ash. Not wanting to lose the flame Mary shut the door behind her and hurried to the fireplace, grabbing a piece of wood on her way over. She set the log in as gently as she could; still, a burst of sparks, crackles, and smoke exploded as the piece of dry wood settled.

The fire roared to life and Mary pulled a seat closer to the hearth. As she settled into her chair and wrapped herself in a blanket that had been draped across the back of it, both Neppy and Morta selected a spot on either side of Mary, spun about twice, then curled up on the carpet as close to the fire as they could get. Mary guessed it to be nine at least, and though the excitement of the day was still fresh in her mind the effects of a ten mile roundabout trip in the cold took their hold. The fire grew distant, disappearing at the end of a tunnel, and soon Mary was asleep

***

"Mary...Mary..." a voice whispered in the darkness. She couldn't tell who the voice belonged to, either. It was unfamiliar and seemed so...distant. Everything seemed distant, for that matter.

Around her the world was dark, nothing but a black canvas, and there in the center of all that nothing was Mary. She couldn't remember how she'd gotten to wherever she was; it was as if she'd just appeared or germinated into existence. The voice continued to call out her name, but each time it grew fainter and farther away.

Mary took a step towards where she thought the origin of the voice was, and all at once the black backdrop gave way, and once again she was sitting in the Corinthian Hall. Her memory was hazy, but Mary could recall being there recently, even sitting on the same bench before, but it all seemed so...so...

Distant.

The Corinthian Hall was packed with people. Mary tried to concentrate on the crowd to perhaps pick out a familiar face or some clue as to what she was doing there, but each time she did the hall seemed to ripple and lose definition. She next tried to move. Lifting her arms to wave to someone proved impossible, however; it was as if her

61

whole body was stuck in quicksand. And although she could hear the rumble of conversation around her, it all seemed to blur together into a maddening hum of nonsense. Above it all rose the whisper.

"Mary…Mary…"

In an instant the hall was empty, and Mary alone sat glued to the bench. She still couldn't move her arms or legs, but now she could move her head about freely to look around. Mary looked each way, down the long benches and towards the front table, and tried to call out for help. Though she tried her hardest, the best she could manage was a soft whimper that died in her chest. The room was hot, *she remembered, not exactly sure where the memory came from. Now, the room was freezing, and she longed for a blanket, or a*

shawl!

The word exploded into her thoughtstream like the retort of a gunshot. She strained her neck to see if a shawl might be draped across her shoulders or on the back of the bench. Both were uncovered.

"Mary…Mary…"

Another blast of cold air that chilled her to the bone and made Mary's skin crawl. She tried to move, she tried to shout, but she remained stuck in the empty Corinthian Hall. Something bad is here, *the same internal voice that told her to look for the shawl said once more. A feeling of dread rose from the pit of her stomach and flooded Mary's senses.*

Something bad is here. Something bad is going to happen.

The voice chanting her name grew louder, and in between intervals a new assault of noises began: a mix of rappings, knocks and thuds on the wall behind her. It sounded as if someone was trying to burrow through the wall. If they did, given her current state, Mary had little hope of defending herself. She writhed and tried to pull herself around, but her body was at once too heavy and too light to move.

Doomed, doomed!

The internal voice cried out in conviction like a preacher grasping the pulpit. The inferno of chantings and rappings went on for an eternity, it continued as time lost meaning to the stuck Mary who could only listen and watch the empty hall in front of her fail to provide any answers.

At some point, the giant hall went dark. In the pitch black the noises reached a crescendo: the whispers louder, the rappings and thuds reverberated on the bench behind her; it was drawing nearer. They *were close now. Whatever engulfed her was their space, she realized. Whatever was making the noise controlled the expansive bedlam.*

The darkness and cacophony lasted for another moment, then the oil lanterns were re-lit by an invisible force, and the room was illuminated. As the light returned, Mary heard a noise that sounded almost like a gasp behind her, then silence. For a second a sense of relief washed over her. It didn't last. Mary felt her skin tingle; there was something wicked in the silence. It was when Mary realized she wasn't alone in the hall any longer that the tingle of apprehension increased to full-fledged, skin-crawling terror.

Two long shadows draped across the room on either side of Mary. Neither moved at first, but based on the way the shadows were cast Mary knew they were standing right beside her, staring down in her direction. Their frigid gaze burrowed into the back of her skull and all she wanted to do was run from that horrible place, far, far away from whatever surrounded her, though she knew her body wouldn't allow it. Even when she tried to swivel her head as she had managed to do before, once more Mary found herself completely unable to move. She felt a wave of fear rise from her stomach to her chest to her throat, but just as it had before, the scream of horror died before it could leave her mouth, fizzling out to a soft whimper. A howling gust of wind filled the hall,

whipping about in a frenzy that scattered anything not bolted to the
floor: pamphlets flew about the air like white doves escaping captivity,
and Mary's hair blew across her face and mouth adding to the scene of
confusion. The wind screeched, bombarding her senses, and all Mary
wanted to do was cover her ears and bury her head in her arms.

They won't allow it…they want you to see, Mary.

All around her the Corinthian Hall danced in a tumultuous
disarray, the shadows moved and leapt about, their origins a mystery
refusing to step into her line of sight.

Though she couldn't see who was behind her casting the shadows, it
was evident the silhouettes cast across the floor of the hall were clearly
human in form. Two shadows turned into three. Then four. And soon,
there was a whole army standing behind her staring down; more than
should ever have ever fit into the building, giant as it were. They
wriggled and wreathed and intermingled and jumped forth in a melee
of chaos. The two closest to her leaned in close and whispered, their
breath chilled like a gust from a mausoleum.

"Mary…Mary…we're all here. It swallows everyone, every bit.
Look beyond the veil, Mary. We're waiting for you."

***

Mary woke, gasping for air. The fire in front of her was still
burning, though the light it cast had dimmed since she first threw
the log on, and outside of the area directly in front of the flames,
the house was engulfed by darkness. Her mind was busy at work
separating the dream from the immediate reality, and the threat of
danger still loomed and called for action. Mary swung around so
that she was kneeling on the chair she'd fallen asleep on and
searched the room, half expecting to see a collection of shadows
preparing their attack; but though dimly lit, Mary could see that

the house was empty save for Neppy and Morta, who stood growling at a spot next to the door. The guttural noise rumbled through the room and made Mary's hair stand on end. After a few seconds the growling stopped, and not long after Neppy and Morta rejoined her side.

Mary took a minute to look about the first floor to be sure they were alone: she could see the darkened outline of the small dinner table she ate at, the collection of pots and pans she cooked with strewn across the counters, and the washbin she cleaned with was all she found though. Beside her, Morta was standing and whimpering, eyes wide with concern while Neppy remained glancing about. Her throat was sore; it took her a moment to realize she'd been screaming in her sleep. After convincing herself it was just a dream Mary turned around and settled back into the chair facing the fireplace.

"I'm alright, I'm alright. Everything's okay. Just a strange dream." The words came out fast,more for her sake than the dogs, still, she cast a glance towards the two of them. Both remained on edge.

For a moment Mary thought about the dream, and the fear she'd felt when she was stuck in it reared in her gut. But it passed. It was easy enough to explain the nightmare away, as she *always* did: the lecture, the walk home, the new, strange possibilities that now presented themselves; surely the dream was just her brain attempting to process things. Once that was settled in her mind the blanket she was cocooned in, and the fire worked their magic. Mary's eyes began to close, her thoughts became more abstract, and soon, she was back asleep.

Neppy and Morta did not fall back asleep, however. The two dogs would spend the rest of the night watching Mary closely, only occasionally standing to circle around the chair or the perimeter of the house, never relaxing as they hunted for the source of the rappings that had first woken them before Mary's screams.

They were guard dogs, after all.

Chapter 4

The next morning Mary woke feeling refreshed. The dream was a distant memory, made all the more forgettable by the rays of sunlight that poured through the kitchen window and filled the whole first floor. Rather than thinking about the shadow that filled Corinthian Hall in her nightmare, Mary focused on the sister's presentation from the night before.

All morning as she prepared breakfast, went about completing chores around the house, and saw to the garden outside, she thought about the presentation. Still, at times when the sun cast long shadows as it draped across the surrounding forest Mary found herself looking about nervously.

It was an abnormally warm November day for western New York, and Mary rolled up her sleeves as she worked the plant and herb garden next to the house. Most of the vegetables had already been harvested and pickled for the winter, though a few of the more robust varieties needed to be pulled. Though it was nice now, the weather could turn on a dime and Mary wanted to get as much done today as possible. As she picked the last carrots and cabbages of the season, her mind strained to think of another comparable revelation that could so significantly alter a way of thinking.

The signing of the Declaration of Independence.

It was monumental, no doubt, but as she dug into the soft dirt with her shovel, angling it back to lift a clump of dirt that contained a carrot, she realized a more fitting comparison was the discovery of the Americas or writing; those moments in the past where the world grew seemingly overnight as a new way of thinking emerged.

She grabbed the carrot at the stem and shook, the dirt that had stubbornly stuck to it cascaded to the ground below. Mary then tossed the dirt smeared vegetable in the basket beside her and went back to digging out more.

***

The farm had seen better days, certainly, but Mary had done her best to manage the upkeep in the years after her mother's death. Her father and grandfather, the former she could barely remember and the latter she never met, had passed away in quick succession. Though hundreds of miles away, in one of those bizarre and cruel twists of fate, both father and son had passed away of typhoid fever within a year of each other. Her grandfather's inheritance would have been substantial enough on its own with his wealth amassed as a land speculator. Her father further added to the family coffers, too, as a country lawyer and farmer in a then prospering region. He had left behind enough money to take care of Mary and her mother. As Mary's mother told her, it was during his last month while his health deteriorated that her father labored to craft a will that would include proper allotment of money to see them supported in the years to come.

And his efforts had proven fruitful. In his last acts he carved up the vast amount of acreage he'd purchased when Rochester was still finding its footing as a boomtown and land was still cheap. He saved the house and surrounding few acres for his loved ones, of course, and rather than selling the remaining farmland as most would, he rented them out for low prices, even at that time, for fifteen-year contracts, knowing that though the value of the property would grow the passive income would support his family after he passed. He selected local farmers he knew he could trust— thanks to his time as a lawyer he understood the local landscape of characters better than most—and the money from the rented acreage continued to support Mary. In fact, knowing the actual value of the property they'd rented, many of those farmers who had already owed her father for settling tricky land disputes would deliver a small percentage of their crop to Mary every season in remembrance. Her mother had instructed her to sell those plots after the contracts concluded, two years in the future, which would provide another windfall of money.

This information had been passed down from mother to daughter as Mary grew up in a series of conversations that seemed random at the time, but planned carefully by her mother in hindsight. When Mary's mother talked about her father to her, her eyes would grow distant and a small smile, one that only appeared during these conversations, would cross her face. It seemed strange, but perhaps because her father passed away before she could capture him in her memories, or maybe because these conversations with her mother highlighted his efforts to retain the property, in Mary's mind her father *was* the house and acreage left behind. The farm was her connection to him.

It was his legacy.

***

The gardens lay bare when she was done that morning. Mary took a moment to even out the dark freshly turned dirt before bringing her haul to the creek that ran behind the house to wash them off.

The basket was heavy with large heads of cabbage and giant carrots, and it required both hands to carry it. As she walked past the front of the house Mary had the sudden urge to talk to somebody. She set the woven basket down in front of the porch and called out to Nappy and Morta, who she expected to come bounding out from behind the house after using the dog door located on the back entrance. She called out again, and when neither appeared she walked to the front door and opened it.

Both dogs were lying on the floor and Mary watched their heads and ears shoot up as she peered in. When they saw who it was, however, the dogs rested their large heads back down on the rug.

"You two act like you didn't sleep all night and most of the morning, c'mon. Up!" The command was followed by a shrill whistle. Neppy and Morta rose to their feet and shook, which seemed to stir them from their drowsiness as immediately after the little rising ritual was completed both bound towards Mary ready to take on the day.

"There we are," Mary said as she kneeled down to pet both dogs. "I need some help cleaning the vegetables, my fierce guardians."

She stood and made her way outside, closing the door behind her as the dogs trotted beside her, one on either side. Neppy and Morta were her mother's idea but even as puppies, little more than wriggling balls of wrinkles when they first got them, the two dogs gravitated towards Mary following her whenever they could. It never ceased. After her mother's death they had refused to leave her side as Mary wept, crawling into bed with her during those sad days following the accident, even occasionally whimpering themselves.

She loved them and they loved her. Though she knew some of the farmers in the area described her as being "alone" in the house her father built, she wasn't. Mary knew that.

As she hoisted the basket of vegetables up in her arms, Mary started her spiel. "They packed that Corinthian Hall; you wouldn't believe how many people were in there."

They stepped off the porch and onto the grass. "It wasn't cheap to get in, either," she continued "Let me tell you. I was lucky Johnson paid for two months in advance."

Morta looked up at Mary while Neppy seemed content to simply trot beside, and the three of them walked around the house towards the creek.

It was hotter than the day before, and the sun warmed the three of them as they made their way. The smell of fall was all around, and Mary took a deep inhale to capture all the earthy, musky and sweet scents that filled the air.

"It was a fair price though. Even if it was only the lecture it would have been worth it. The man who spoke, Capron his name is, well he was convincing enough in his own right."

The clearing ended quickly, and they stepped into the line of trees that marked the start of the woods. The path was well traveled but narrow. The dogs moved from her side with Neppy taking the front and Morta the back. Mary looked over the heaping pile of vegetables down at Neppy as he led the way, his tail wisping back and forth. The motion of his tail seemed so carefree, so lackadaisical, Mary couldn't help but smile.

"I wonder what the spirits would say to dogs?" She paused. "You probably already see them, don't you, you perceptive little devils?"

The trail wove through forest and foliage that during the spring and summer months were thick and full; however, this late in the fall the curtain of bushes and leaves had been drawn to reveal deeper into the woods than could typically be seen. The naked trees stood in their skeletal state, their leaves that had been so vibrant only a month before now dead and crunching beneath the trio's feet as they made their way.

"It's coming up," Mary said to the dogs as the thoughts of spirits and rappings momentarily vanished, drowned out by more pressing matters. She felt a sudden wave of guilt that she hadn't grabbed a flower or two from the garden as the pioneer cemetery emerged amidst the trunks of trees running along her right. During the summer the cemetery would remain hidden until you stepped into it; however, during fall months you could see it as far away as from the trail. She placed the basket on the main trail and took the even narrower path that led towards the small outcrop of faded tombstones and markers about thirty feet away.

The dogs followed, and perhaps it was only in Mary's mind, but the sound of their paws seemed to grow lighter with less of the excited pitter-patter that had previously marked their trip. It was as if they were walking in reverence. It was at that moment that Mary decided that, should spirits communicate with the living, and she was confident they did, they would certainly do so with human's four-legged friends as well.

They stopped at the edge of the plot. A shambled stone wall ran around the outskirts; most of the rocks had fallen over, victim to the battering snow and wind-storms that rolled off Lake Ontario only a few miles to the north. A simple, faded wooden sign rested against the moss-covered pile of stones beside the opening that served as an entrance, despite the fact the "wall" was less than a foot high and could easily be stepped over: "Pioneer Cemetery Est. 1799".

Her father had made the sign shortly after discovering the plot the first fall they'd lived there, so Mary's mother had told her during one of their visits to pay respects to both him and other long forgotten occupants of the old cemetery. The year had been selected based on the earliest tombstone contained within. Sensing a moment to rest, the two dogs plopped down in a sun-covered patch of grass just outside the cemetery and watched Mary with tongues hanging from their open muzzles.

She stepped through the opening and made her way past tombstones that were barely distinguishable from the stones used to make the wall. Some simply had a year and last name carved in, while others, slightly more elaborate, would include a full name and simple epitaph. Mary passed "M. Saunders, died 1803," who was "to god", and "S.S. Lackskey, died 1799" who was "called to the shepherd." There were thirty-three markers in total (Mary had often counted them as a child), and most were between the years of 1799 and 1804 and represented the first, unlucky wave of settlers who had made their way to the western portion of the state following the "Treaty of Hartford" between New York and Massachusetts. The land belonged to the Haudenosaunee before, and many of the foot trails Mary grew up walking were old trade routes and hunting paths used by the Seneca.

All of this had been told to her by her mother through a series of visits.

She wove through toppled markers swallowed by high grass towards the back corner where the two most recent additions to the cemetery lay; the only added since 1804 for that matter. "Here Lies William H. Browncroft: Loving Husband and Father. Friend to All. May 1806 to September 1831. Age 25" read one. Besides it: "Here Lies Cornelia S. Browncroft: Devoted Wife and Mother. December 1809 to June 1846. Age 37."

While she cleared the whole plot twice a year—once in spring and again in August—Mary checked her parents' markers every time she headed to the creek, making sure no weeds or high grass ever found their way near the patch above where they were buried. She had visited only two days before to clear the leaves, and resting at the foot of each respective tombstone was a dried goldenrod she'd found during one of her walks. Besides the flowers, their plots remained unblemished.

Mary closed her eyes and felt the sun on her face. The wind blew across her and the smell of fall, those pleasing traces of spices and natural decay, once again filled each slow breath she took. The wind whistled as it passed empty branches and flurried dried maple leaves about. For a moment Mary could hear the sound of her mother's voice carried on the breeze, softly singing as she used to during their walks. The memory was as sweet as the smells, but soon the winds died, and the forest was still again, save for the occasional chirping of birds in the branches above.

She let out a deep sigh.

"We'll talk soon." Mary turned, then stopped in her tracks. Her head went light, and at once the surrounding forest seemed to recede until it disappeared, leaving her alone in the cemetery. There was a flash of darkness, quick as a blink, and when the light returned Mary found herself surrounded by figures milling about the cemetery. They were blurry, too spectral to discern for certain who or what they were, and there were so many it was difficult to focus on one form. She opened her mouth to scream…

Another blink and she was alone.

Mary hurried out of the cemetery trailed by Neppy and Morta who stayed close to her side.

***

After washing the vegetables in the creek and returning to the farmhouse, Mary decided to take a trip to Ford's General Store and Mercantile to buy food for the week and to see if any reports from the lecture had been published in the newspaper. Though the small shop was less likely to include the array of papers a shop in Rochester might have, the walk towards the shop that sat towards Irondequoit Bay was much quicker and Mary decided to take her chances. She grabbed a carrying basket and made her way out the door, still shaken from the vision in the cemetery.

She passed fields of harvested wheat rented out by her father's will, the farms of families she knew since childhood, the school she'd attended growing up, taverns she'd had meals at and the Irondequoit post office where she received her mail before arriving. Each was alive with activity as farmers hustled to prepare their farms for the harsh months ahead, students rushed around the outside enjoying the brief reprieve of recess before returning to their studies, and folks grabbed a midday meal or busily read their mail on the front porch of the post office. Most of those Mary passed she'd known all her life, and they would wave and exchange pleasantries with a smile.

There was something about seeing the surrounding hustle and bustle that put her at ease. The dreams, the cemetery...all those things slowly subsided to the back of her thoughts, again explained away as symptoms of her imagination. Her mother always said she should be a writer, after all.

The bay soon unfurled itself in front of her and from the ridge above Mary could see the mercantile swarmed by wagons carrying sacks of goods from ships docked at the harbor. From where she stood, they looked like ants funneling around an ant hill. She hurried down, excited to see what news might be carried along with the items for trade.

When she arrived, a few men were busy unloading giant sacks of grain from an open wagon onto the front deck of the shop. Sweat droplets beaded their foreheads, and they nodded and tipped their hats as she walked by before resuming their business. Four horses were tied to the fence that ran along the porch, their bodies twitching and swaying as they were bombarded by flies, zigzagging about. Past it all, water lapped at the shore of the bay as ships bobbed like apples in the water.

Mary walked through the swinging doors of Ford's and, to her surprise, found the store nearly empty, save for Ford himself who was busy cleaning off the counter. Even hunched over trying to scrub away a particularly stubborn spot, his giant form dwarfed the glass jars filled with spices and stacked precariously on top of each other beside him. A bell jingled as the doors swung close behind her and Ford stood upright and looked up from his work. When he saw who it was, he grinned.

"Morning, Miss Mary; how are you on this fine November day?" he asked, throwing the rag over his shoulder.

Ford's shirt was dirty, stained with what looked like either mud or coffee, and his beard and hair were both wild and unkempt with grey streaks running through both. A scar ran from his eyebrow down to his chin, and when once she'd asked about it as her mother was busy looking for something in the store Ford had simply smiled, leaned in and whispered, "your mother would have my hide if I told you the story. Someday, perhaps." Then he'd given her a peppermint stick and sent her off. The lingering curiosity about the scar stuck around. Someday Mary hoped to hear the story, though she felt childish whenever she tried to work up the nerve to ask again.

Ford had been one of her father's closest friends before his death, though her mother would always point out their *stark* differences whenever the two of them had left the store. Each time Mary would simply giggle and roll her eyes; even as a child knowing what her mother was saying—Ford was a little too rough around the edges for her taste. After listing the differences in temperaments, Ford's love of whiskey, the many, many hours he spent hunting and fishing the marshes to the north, she would always add, however; "don't take it all to heart though. Ford's a kind man and that's what matters."

Mary never forgot that, and Ford never proved otherwise.

"Hi Ford, just buying some supplies for the week."

"Of course, of course. I was wondering when you'd be in this week. Well, you know where everything is, but you need help just holler. I'm gonna go check on those boys upfront. Got a big ol' shipment of potatoes coming too."

He stepped out from behind the counter and made his way out the swinging doors, leaving Mary alone in the store. A counter ran about the main space, and throughout the center was an island of rough wood shelves, topped with every variety of food and spices one could think of. Barrels and containers of fruit and vegetables that were stored in the cellar beneath were intermittently placed throughout, and glass bottles of milk and wine from the local vineyards were scattered about. To a first-time visitor the shop might be chaos, but to Mary it all made sense.

She found the barrel of apples in the back corner and plucked half a dozen that looked the best. Mary then gathered the rest of the items she needed: tea, milk, cheese, eggs, salted pork and potatoes, filling her basket as she went. It took her less than fifteen minutes to complete her order. She then brought the items to the front counter and laid them out so her bill could be added.

Ford's gruff voice sounded from outside the door as he spoke to one of the shiphands. Though she couldn't hear what they were saying, his voice was animated in a way that let her know the conversation had his interest. Mary decided to take a look at the papers to see if any from that morning had arrived.

She drifted over to a small wooden stand that housed the newspapers and began leafing through them. There was the Monroe Democrat, The North Star, The Rochester Courier, The Rochester Evening News, there were even a few slightly older papers from New York City and Albany…it went on and on. None from that morning, however.

The bell jingled and Ford returned, muttering to himself as he made his way to the counter. Mary met him with her empty basket in her folded arms.

"Is everything ok, Mr. Ford?" she asked when she noticed the solemn look across his usually jovial face. There was a haunted expression that appeared for a moment, which was quite unnerving. He looked up at her as if for a moment he'd forgotten she was there.

"It's a crazy world we're livin' in, Miss Mary. I'll tell you. You remember that peddler boy who went missing last winter, Richards I think his name was?"

"Yes…yes! The boy from Rochester who came out this way to sell some goods or another. He went missing in February if I recall. There was some speculation that he ran off with the shop owner's money. I remember reading about it in a newspaper about that time."

"That's what they thought, him runnin' off and all. But the Thomas boy loading right now says he heard from one of the other boys at the dock that they just found his body. They think he was murdered now."

"That's awful!" At once the thought of the murdered peddler communicating with the Fox sisters crossed her mind, as did those long walks home she so often took herself. She knew everyone though, a traveling peddler wouldn't know which houses and farms to avoid. *Dangerous line of work.*

"I tell you, it's like those years after the canal was built. People were going missing left and right, no one thought to report it though since it was so...so..."

"Frequent?"

"That's it, frequent. I tell you, I reckon those marshes I'm so fond of huntin' have more lost souls than you'd care to imagine." Ford paused and looked down at the counter, his brow furrowed in concentration as if he was about to continue. All at once his face relaxed, however.

"Now this ain't proper talk with a young pretty lady such as yourself, is it."

He started moving each item Mary had laid out on the counter as he mentally calculated the tab. "Fifty-two cents," he said when everything had been added.

"Mr. Ford..." Mary turned her head and mustered the best schoolteacher glare she could manage.

"And not a cent more, I won't take it you hear."

"You're too kind to me." Mary counted out the change and handed it to Ford, who took the coins and looked down at them in a state of shock.

"How did you get here, might I ask?"

"I walked," Mary responded.

"With money on you? No, no…not after what happened to that peddler boy. From now on I'll track your tab like I do with most of the farmers 'round here and collect when I'm by your farm."

"Mr. Ford, that's very kind of you but you already do so much, and I don't mean to be an inc—"

He waved his dirt covered hand, cutting her off.

"You could never. It's best, I think. Most people forget or purposefully ignore them, but," he tapped his head, "I ain't smart as you but I got a good memory. A lot of those folks from the old days are still around, and the way I see it, some of those bad apples ain't change all that much." He picked up one of the apples Mary selected and hoisted it up in the air so that the light caught it.

"I don't mean to sound fatherly, and I know you can and do take care of yourself," he added quickly. "It would help an old man sleep better at night, if that's alright with you. I know you got them nasty, mean guard dogs at the place to take care of you. Who sold you those good-for-nothing mutts anyways?" He smiled big revealing a half-broken front tooth.

"An old friend of my father," Mary said, returning the grin. "Of course, if it would make you feel better, we can plan payment that way. However," again she tried to look as stern as possible, "I will be paying."

"Of course. Might start chargin' you double even. Seems fair."

Mary shook her head in feigned disbelief and loaded her basket with the groceries.

"C'mon now. I'm takin' the wagon into the city to buy some traps. I'll drop you off on the way back."

"Well, actually, if you're heading to Rochester…"

It was as if everyone in Rochester and the surrounding townships was looking to take advantage of what was sure to be one of the last warm days, and as such, decided to converge into the city at that exact moment. Ford deftly maneuvered the wagon around other riders who seemed oblivious to the fact they weren't the only ones occupying the road. Occasionally, when a wagon or rider on a horse did something especially egregious, he'd shout out a string of curses then sheepishly look to Mary and apologize to her while she fought valiantly to contain her laughter.

Dust filled the air like a cloud, making Mary's nose twitch as they made their way.

The wagon bumped over the rough roads leading through the city, eventually slowing to a crawl as they became smoother yet more congested. Walkways were packed with throngs of people hurriedly moving about, and all around a charge of excitement hung in the air. It was as if any moment a festival or celebration might break out. Mary had never seen the city so alive.

At every corner a newspaper boy stood, satchels stuffed full of the latest prints, hollering at all those who passed by about the strange happenings at Corinthian Hall. Mary felt a flutter of pride at having been there to witness it all.

"I ain't never seen the city like this in all my life," Ford said as they crossed the same bridge Mary had the night before on her way to and from the lecture. They lulled to a stop as something blocked the road beyond their sight. Mary took the pause to look around. To her right the giant hall stood; in the daylight it looked like some magnificent temple or political arena from ancient Greece, still fresh and glimmering in the sun in all its splendor.

Ford was looking towards a building on the opposite side of the road.

"See that building there, Miss Mary?" he bumped her shoulder with his and then gestured to a large structure that sat on a corner. The building had glass windows running across the first floor. Above, it was a very orderly brick structure with rectangular windows evenly placed across five floors. Between each floor were various signs of businesses that occupied the space: hardware, tobacco, and a leather shop all included.

"What about it?"

"That's where one of my most best-selling papers is produced. *The North Star,* have you seen it? It's published by Frederick Douglass, I reckon you know that name."

"Oh yes! I read his book a year back."

"Well, that's where the office for the newspaper is. I sell at least ten everyday…maybe more. A few of the local farmers buy it regularly, then there's always one or two of the workers from the ships who'll buy it when they're passing through. I don't ask since it's not my business, but I think a few of the shiphands I see from the Canadian ports used to be slaves themselves who escaped."

"Just dreadful, the whole thing."

"I read it myself, on occasion. Hurts my heart, if I'm being truthful." He stared at the building then turned back to Mary.

"And it sells."

Mary was about to ask why Douglass selected Rochester as the base for the newspaper, but before she could do so the wagon was moving again, and Ford was looking over his shoulder for a place to tie the wagon.

"There we are," he said after a minute, quickly pulling up on the reins and directing the horses to a tying post on the right side of the road. Once they were beside it, Ford hopped down from the driver's seat and began hitching the wagon. As he worked to secure the horses Mary inspected the building they were in front of. Like the building Ford pointed out containing *The North Star,* this one was a tiered collection of shops ranging from a book publisher to a brewery on the first floor. Through a window on the first floor Mary saw a giant wooden vat she assumed was used for brewing the beer.

"There, should be all set," Ford approached her side of the carriage then reached his hand up toward Mary.

"Thank you." Taking his hand as she stepped down onto the road. "That was much quicker than walking."

"I can't believe you walked all alone from here to your home last night," Ford said, shaking his head in disbelief. "How late was it again?"

"Around seven. The sun was just setting." No harm smudging the truth, she figured.

"Well not today. We meet back here at say, five?" Ford pulled a battered pocket watch from his trouser pocket and opened it. "That's about an hour and a half away, is that enough time for your running around?"

"Plenty of time, thank you dearly Mr. Ford."

"Five it is, I'll see you then."

Mary watched as Ford made his way towards the gunsmith and hunting supply store a few blocks down. Though the crowd on the walkway quickly surrounded him, he stood head shoulders above most so she could see him nearly the whole way. Eventually she turned, not knowing exactly where she was headed. She started walking and soon, whether through the ebb and flow of the crowd or some strange pull she didn't realize, Mary found herself headed in the direction of the Corinthian Hall.

Of course, any newspaper boy worth a damn would be hawking their papers at the site.

She smirked after realizing the wagon ride with Ford had left an imprint on her internal vernacular.

The streets in the daylight were dirtier than she remembered them. Large clumps of horse manure lined the side of the road, adding to the fetid stench of the filled street gutter. The smell of rot emanated from piles of waste and muck too large to be sucked down into the drains beneath, and as this sludge cooked beneath the sun above, the smell became so unbearable that Mary had to cover her breath when she walked past. Even the smell of fresh bread from the bakery she strolled past couldn't cancel out the horrific one that drifted up from beside the walkway.

Cutting across the oncoming traffic Mary headed down State Street. She could see a crowd gathered in front of the Corinthian Hall: those gathered were a mix of all races, all genders, and all ages standing beneath the doorway leading to the entrance where their attentive gaze lay. Mary guessed there had to be at least two hundred in total.

Though the mass of those gathered was quiet, even from a distance Mary could hear a single, bellowing voice addressing them and she quickened her pace. She arrived and stood on the very edge of the gathering, and though it was impossible to see over the wall of folks in front of her, the voice carried.

"...the disbelievers at the Rochester Democrat, for example. Through sources of good repute, it has been reported that, after the selection of the esteemed committee done at the hand of yesterday's gathering of nearly 400 of this city's most upstanding individuals, that the *newspaper*—and I bristle to call it that—had a story set to print. Would you like to know what this story was to say?"

The call received an uproarious cheer from those around Mary. Someone near the center called out, "Go on! Go on!".

"Alright then…I should note everything mentioned henceforth will be expanded on at length at tonight's gathering here at the Corinthian Hall." Mary felt herself leaning in with the crowd as the man paused. Although she couldn't see the speaker it felt as if he was about to whisper a secret. She held her breath, worried that any sound might deter him from going on. There was silence, but only for a second.

"The story set to be printed," his voice started low but grew in volume with each word, "was, in essence, a defamation of this new *movement* started by those young sisters. Though the article set in type was eventually scurried, which you'll hear why in a moment, the general gist, if you will, was the discovery of fraud of the sisters. Rather than WAIT, the paper prepared to deal a scandalous death blow to this blossoming idea. But why now would the newspaper not run the story, you might ask? Why was the story, written and set to print for immediate distribution, left to die?"

Another pause.

"Why, the committee report was made. Those selected to investigate the validity of the sisters had gathered together and codified their account. Not one, not two, not three, but five witnesses of high moral standing, chosen by public decree, investigated and made their report. Remember, we deal in FACTS, not assumptions as certain *newspapers* might." With that last statement the identity of the speaker was revealed to Mary, who now knew it to be Capron. He continued.

"With the report fully commenced the *Rochester Democrat*, who had been fully convinced that further rappings were no longer likely to the degree of preemptively writing an article stating such, was forced to abandon *its* report. Now, good people, I shall relay the findings of the initial report, which will be fully corroborated with newspapers both reputable and some…less so."

The audience cheered and in the brief burst of excitement enough bodies moved around so that Mary could see Capron standing on the steps. He was alone and wearing a top hat, but other than that he looked the exact same as he did the night before. Same jacket, same air of being both distinguished and on the defensive. A country lawyer before a jury.

"The initial site chosen was the hall of the sons of Temperance, as a few members of the committee had a familiarity with the structure, which again, would prevent any tricks or sleight of hand as I know have been accused. It goes without saying that neither Maggie nor Leah had ever stepped foot within the structure. The rappings were heard throughout the floors and walls, and a number of questions posed by the committee answered. Still, wanting to make sure due diligence was seen the committee had decided an additional sitting was yet necessary, this second gathering at a private estate commenced earlier this afternoon, not…" he produced a pocket watch from his jacket and flicked the cover open, "not but two hours ago. I might invite each of the members to join me on those stairs here to announce what they saw. A formal report will be presented this evening, of course, make no doubt."

He took a step down from the stairwell and pointed towards the front of the crowd, a man similarly dressed as Capron stepped forward. He then climbed the stairs and turned to address the audience.

"The manifestations presented themselves as such…"

***

An hour passed as Mary stood listening to each man who told their story, faces flashed with excitement and words flying out a mile a minute, and who was then subsequently replaced by another member of the committee that continued in a similar manner. None of the accounts were all that different: all mentioned the tapping, rappings, and questions posed in the hall belonging to the sons of temperance, then continued on to the private house where things became even more lively.

Here, the men reported sounds coming from outside the door upon entering and being seated, as well as knocks from various closets about the room. The men admitted taking precautions to make sure they were not being tricked: one mentioned placing his hands on the sister's feet to make sure the noises they heard were not from something as simple as their footsteps. The man swore to the crowd that as he did so the rumbling of footsteps could yet be heard behind him. Each committee member added in their own way that both Maggie and Leah were fully cooperative throughout the demonstration, and tried in earnest though they had, no explanation for the sounds could be deduced.

The ending was a whirlwind: Capron had emerged from the crowd to detail the sisters' agreement to a "thorough personal examination by a committee of ladies, if so desired" and appointed another committee to investigate, including a congressman from Leroy. It was decided that their report would be made the next evening to an audience in the Corinthian Hall. As the crowd dispersed, Mary had already made up her mind she would *certainly* be in attendance.

***

That night Mary found herself staring into the cemetery with her heart racing and toes sinking into the cold moss beneath. She couldn't remember how she got there. The night air bit at her skin and made her shiver, and the forest surrounding her rippled in the wind.

Why was she here?

The evening had started out normal: she found Ford in his wagon promptly at five, the cart packed with various hunting traps and necessary supplies, and the drive back to her farm was rather uneventful with him talking about what the city *used* to be like. When she got home Mary prepared a quick meal, ate, and then she sat outside on the porch with Neppy and Morta until it was too dark to do so. She had even gone to sleep as normal, unlike the night before, climbing up to the loft where her feather mattress lay and reading by the candlelight as she typically did.

As the candle burned and the light flickered, a wave of drowsiness washed over her. That was the last thing she could remember, *being deeply, deeply, tired...*

...And then coming to, awaking in the pioneer cemetery. In front of her she held the same candle that was used to provide light in bed, though its glow did little in the engulfing darkness. The wind picked up as did her shaking; her only protection against the elements was a thin nightgown, which did little. Beside her were both Morta and Neppy, which provided a little comfort. The dogs

88

had followed their owner out on the strange midnight trip, curious as to the strange break in ritual but refusing to leave her side.

The suddenness of finding herself there was startling enough, but the woods surrounding them took on an especially haunting nature during the night. The moon was high, nearly full and directly above them, and in contrast the blanket of surrounding forest seemed especially dark and foreboding. The pallid face peered down and cast a grey light across the nightscape.

An owl hooted from the tree line above, the noise echoed throughout the forest like the screech of a banshee. Mary wanted to turn and run, but something kept her from moving. It wasn't the same paralysis from the dream before; no, this was something different, a voice or a premonition from inside. *You're supposed to be here. You're supposed to experience something, Mary,* it said with a voice as fleeting as the wind that blew about the cemetery. Fog began to rise slowly from the ground, swallowing tomb markers already difficult to see in the darkness. It happened fast, and in one of those strange realizations that only happens in moments of stress or fear, Mary realized she'd never seen fog form before. *Did it typically form so quickly?*

Soon it was up to her waist. Only their ears, fully perked upright now, could be seen of the two dogs. She was standing just outside the stone wall.

Go in. You have to go in.

Mary moved forward. Her feet were bare, and the ground was both cold and slicked with condensation, so she was careful with each step. She kept walking until she was in the center of the cemetery. Again, something within told her to stop.

Mary looked around: the cemetery layered in fog, the jaundiced moon above, the dark woods all around. She should have been petrified, and in the way of knowing she *should* be scared, that perhaps danger lurked all around her, she was apprehensive, but...there was something else; a curiosity that overpowered the fear.

What was she doing here?

The dream from the night before had come back to her in bits and pieces throughout the day, which only added to that feeling that she was on the verge of learning something new. She peered over the brink, and what lay below might be life changing, either for better or worse, but she couldn't pull herself away. She had to know.

The wind blew louder, beneath its wail Mary could hear something else. A rustle of leaves? The snapping of a twig? A...a whisper. It was so faint she could barely untangle it from the wind, but she was certain.

"Who are you?" Mary said. Her voice trembled slightly. She repeated the question, this time her voice was steady. "Who are you? What do you want?"

"Mary...Mary..." It was the voice from the dream. The one that had called out in the Corinthian Hall. Now it was here, in the cemetery, beckoning once more. "Mary...Mary..."

The dogs were beside her now, their growls gruff and menacing.

"We're waiting for you. All of us. See what awaits all, Mary."

The fog around her flurried in an instant, and from the chaos forms took shape. Human shapes grew from the grey mist, their bodies like spires of smoke climbing into the night sky. A cacophony of voices filled the cemetery, raspy whispers calling out to names of people Mary had never heard before, pleading and begging. Mary heard questions about loved ones and calls for forgiveness as well as simple sentiments called out from the mass of wriggling forms taking shape around her. So many voices called for attention it was difficult to untangle, but through the discord Mary noticed a strange thing: some sounded the same, as if there were multiples of the same spirit calling for attention. Not that it mattered, in seconds the madness reached a crescendo and all the voices joined together in a deafening wail that forced her to cover her ears. Eyes wide, she watched the forms pulsate as the mist around her transformed into a grey curtain. Her curiosity outweighed her fear, and Mary stood spellbound as she witnessed the strange show.

A sudden gust of wind carried it all away in an instant, however, and Mary and the dogs were standing alone in the cemetery with not a patch of fog remaining. One last voice was carried away in that wind.

"Mary…Mary…there is no escaping. Chaos awaits all. We've chosen you, Mary."

***

"You have to be careful when you're cutting!" The warning was followed by a lighthearted laugh that filled Mary's stomach with warmth. How old was she in this memory? Seven or eight, she was almost certain. The paper in her hand was cream-colored, the black ink still wet so she was careful not to touch it.

"Remember what we're doing. You have to cut carefully, or they'll all fall apart." Her mother smiled, placing her hand on Mary's shoulder. Safety…happiness…warmth…they were the feelings that interlaced with the memory. The sewing scissors worked through the paper like a sharp knife through butter, its blade working around the outline her mother had sketched out.

"You did perfectly Mary. Go get a donut."

"With—"

"With cinnamon!"

Feet pattering across the wooden floor, the smell of cinnamon and spices wafting through the kitchen, it was like being there once more. She took the warm pastry in her hand and turned; there was her mother, a fluttering line of humans running between her hands. Mary smiled; she'd cut it right! She walked closer, the donut an afterthought as she traced her fingers along the cutout.

"That's why we folded the paper, and asked Mr. Ford to find us a long sheet. That way we only had to cut one out and we got…" she folded them together like an accordion and then extended them again.

"There's so many of them!" Mary marveled, finally biting into the donut. It practically melted, though the cinnamon stuck to her lips in crumbles. The happiness was as warming and filling as the treat.

"There all the same though, all from that first shape you cut. Kind of like a person, wouldn't you say?"

Mary raised her eyebrow and tilted her head.

"Each person has so many different parts, wouldn't you say?"

She brought them together so there was just one, once more.

"One person…"

She stretched it back out so the figure extended, the same shape seven times, as if holding hands with itself.

"…but different versions."

Mary's head remained tilted, and she let out a questioning grunt.

"Someday you'll get it…careful now, you're getting cinnamon everywhere dear!"

***

A jarring bump from a man who'd had too many drinks brought her back.

He spun, nearly toppling over after colliding into Mary, but managed to get his feet beneath him as he continued his oblivious weave through the crowd. The Corinthian Hall was even more full than the first night. Mary guessed there to be over five hundred men, women, and even some children in attendance, all of whom chatted excitedly with their neighbors. The hall was so packed the entrance doors remained open to allow the audience to spill outside. It looked as if everyone in Rochester had turned out to hear the third report.

She looked towards the bench where she sat the first night and wished she was sitting there once more. Still, she was just happy she'd found a space to watch the lecture and wasn't forced to stand outside. The crowd pressed in around her until it was nearly suffocating. Trying to distract herself, she looked about the space and noticed a podium had been brought out and placed beside the table. It was a new addition, and one fitting of the conversation ahead she had no doubt.

Though she tried to distract herself, it proved impossible. All around excited conversations stirred about what the report might entail, and Mary was soon drawn in:

"…heard they caught em' in the act! An apple tied to a—"

"The fraudsters are set to be expo—"

"Possessed! Possessed! One of the committee members began speaking in tou—"

"I heard the sister were able to—"

The atmosphere was tense, like the first presentation. But unlike that first presentation, those in attendance were clearly there for reasons other than amusement: these folks had strong feelings, one way or another. The carnival had morphed into a trial. Their voices were loud, and many looked like they had something to say. Mary tried to hear each conversation, but there were too many to follow along. It seemed everyone around her was privileged to a different rumor, and though she could catch little tidbits of each, another conversation would soon start derailing her earlier eavesdropping.

You have to find your truth, dear... Her mother's advice, from some reading or writing lesson years back, echoed in her mind. She'd always told Mary she was meant to be a writer, and that being honest was the cornerstone of the best authors. Here, listening to a million different opinions rumbling through the giant hall, that advice made perfect sense.

Along with the conversations, all around her the smell of tobacco and alcohol wafted from the crowd, and a puff of cigar smoke floated in the air above from someone in front of her. The grey cloud of smoke sent shivers down Mary's spine. Her mind went back to the cemetery and the fog, which looked so similar to the billow of smoke that hung overhead. *What if it reached out? What if it took a human form and cried out like the fog?* The smoke dissipated into the space above and was soon replaced by another puff.

The fear gave way and was replaced by something else—pride.

Whatever happened last night, it had chosen Mary. It was *her* name called out in both the dream and the moonscaped forest; it was *her* who had seen the forms emerge from the fog and the shadows cast in the hall; it was *her* who heard the whispers amongst the tombstones. How was she any different than the Fox sisters?

"You see that one," a man beside Mary interrupted her thoughts and pointed to the row of people filing along the front. "There! The one with the cane. He's a senator…wonder what he has to say about all this. Oh look, there's the two sisters, not the youngest one though.'" Leah and Maggie followed closely behind the senator.

"That's the older sister, Leah, I believe," Mary added, nodding towards the woman behind them.

"They all look so stern. Think something bad happened?" The man asked as his face dropped with concern. Though he was wearing jacket and trousers, Mary noted multiple worn patches throughout. The shoulders in particular had nearly given way, the once black color weathered to a sickly grey.

"Wonder if it was something bad that made em' so somber. Like a funeral up there. I paid good money to be here. I wanted to hear n' see it." The man's eyes were wide and for a moment Mary worried he might burst into tears.

"I'm sure they're just tired. This is at least the third of these talks, plus the demonstrations," Mary said, which seemed to do the trick.

"Yes, yes, that's right. Oh, quiet now I think."

The audience hushed in unison.

Mary squinted, trying to get a better view of the committee in the front of the hall. She noticed that, as her neighbor mentioned, each seemed more serious and less animated than the committee before them who'd spoken on the steps of the Hall. Whereas the first committee seemed like excited schoolboys stealing away to a circus to visit the freak show, this one seemed like a row of sour professors about to tear into a disappointing pupil. Though Capron was there seated beside the rest of them, a man Mary had come to associate as the ringleader of the operation, another man stood and walked towards the podium with a stack of papers in hand. He was tall and wiry, and the man moved as Mary imagined a scarecrow might if brought to life. When he arrived behind the podium, he paused for a moment, waved his hand to the crowd, then, after bringing his glasses to the very tip of his nose, he began.

"I have been chosen to speak on behalf of the committee, which consisted of," he cleared his throat and looked down at the notes, "Dr. H. H. Langworthy, the honorable Frederick Whittlesey, D. C. McCollum, William Fisher, and the honorable A. P. Hascall, who have all agreed to the report I am about to read. It goes without saying that these men, selected because of their station and reputation, are of the *highest* regard."

He stopped and tilted his head upwards so he might see better through his glasses, then peered around the hall as if expecting someone to challenge him. He reminded Mary of a schoolteacher looking for a giggling pupil. He was met by silence.

"I, Arthur Haddleton, was appointed to record the happenings as they were, instructed to only record the factual happenings. The investigation commenced at the office of Chancellor Whittlesey. Along with myself and the esteemed committee, we were joined by the three Fox sisters who need no introduction, and their associate, Mr. E. W. Capron who I'm sure many of you are familiar with."

Every head in front of her bobbed up and down in recognition.

"As expected. Now, on to the report."

Haddleton continued talking, but his voice was suddenly distant. Mary strained to hear, then looked around at the rest of the audience to see if anyone else was having difficulty making out his voice. Nodding heads and smiles seemed to indicate it was only her.

A low hum rattled through her conscience. It sounded like the buzzing of a bee surrounding her, and Haddleton's voice continued to seem farther and farther away. He was talking from the far end of a tunnel, growing farther and farther away with each passing second.

"Mary…Mary…"

She looked around again. No faces chalked with surprise. No one looked around to see where the voice was coming from. It was only Mary who could hear the whisper filling the hall.

"Mary…Mary…"

The whisper died out, as did the humming in her ear, and Haddleton's voice returned. A bead of sweat dripped down Mary's temple. Her armpits grew damp, and a sudden chill washed over her.

Haddleton's voice cut through.

"Even when moving the girls about and standing in between, the committee stated in its entirety the rappings could still be heard. Throughout this the good Doctor Langworthy, using a stethoscope to ascertain any…" his voice fumbled, and he looked down at his notes. "Any…any…ah! Yes. Any *movement* of the lungs. Doctor Langsworthy reported no fluctuation could be dedicated when the noises were heard. In short: no machine or mechanical device was used, nor was there evidence of any sort of ventriloquism. It is in the mind of *this* committee that no fraudulent means produced the rappings. Thank you."

Haddleton gathered his papers and the audience responded in a mixed manner. Some clapped excitedly, while others jeered or looked about in frustration. Mary, still reeling from hearing the whispers, could only look about in shock as the audience grew more animated. There was, for the first time, a notable rift in the crowd between those excited no fraud was detected and those disappointed. The more vocal on both sides began to shout out, channeling their anger or excitement at the head table and each other. For a moment it seemed a riot might erupt.

"Tricked by mere children!" A heavyset man with the bushiest mutton chops Mary had ever seen pointed at the table, his voice rising above the clamor of the audience. He stood near the front just a few standing rows in front of her to the right.

"A committee of grown men *tricked* by a child and their handler. I thought I'd seen it all."

The arguments that had broken out in the crowd dimmed. Realizing the moment to seize the floor, the man with the mutton chops lifted a cane he'd been balancing on and tapped it on the wooden slabs beneath. The clatter silenced anyone still talking as all eyes fell on him.

"Sir." Haddleton half-stood behind the podium clutching his notes to his chest, face wide in surprise. At first looking like a bank robber caught in the act of fleeing, he quickly realized he was still responsible for leading the report and returned fully behind the podium.

"Sir, as you were saying? Please lead with your title and name for the audience so your comments can be *recorded*."

If the prospect of having his words printed was meant to scare the man, it had little effect. He puffed out his chest and launched into his spiel.

"My name is W. L. Burtis. That's Mr. W. L. Burtis." He gripped the lapels of his jacket and poked out his chin, then slowly turned to face the audience. "What we have here is an easily deducible case of fraud. Plain and simple. I wager ONE HUNDRED dollars that these sisters won't dare to have me serve on the next committee. While their gimmicks might fool the untrained eyes," he turned and gestured towards the front table, "I have both experience and the abilities to detect tricks used to convince *lesser* men. I repeat, I wager one hundred dollars they won't have me on the next one."

The crowd roared in approval.

Capron leaned in and whispered something to Leah, then stood and replaced Haddleton, who bounded to his seat as a look of relief crossed his face.

"Mr. Burtis not only will we have you on the committee, we *welcome* you to it. What better evidence to the legitimacy of our claims than to turn such a hardened skeptic as yourself. Also, we won't make you pay this hundred-dollar fee you've seemed to offer."

The man beside Mary who had spent the better part of the lecture muttering quietly to himself started fidgeting with excitement. Finally, after a few seconds of silence he called out, "What if he doesn't find nothing? What does he wager then?"

"A new beaver hat," Burtis responded.

"Those in favor?" The crowd cheered in support, while Mary whispered to the man beside her.

"From a hundred dollars to a beaver hat? Seems someone had a change of heart." Her neighbor chuckled a raspy chortle in reply.

"Burtis, you shall serve on the next committee. Any—"

"My name is Leo Kenyan, and I will jump from Genesee falls like that drunkard Sam Patch if I can't locate the trick."

More cheers commenced from the crowd.

"Mr. Burtis will be joined by Mr. Kenyan, so it seems," Capron added. More names were hollered, and once more a committee was established. At one point, Burtis called out again, "to see that some

99

device is not being used, we demand that a committee of women be formed to inspect them prior to *our* inspection." The crowd jeered and Burtis reveled in the attention. Sweat poured down his temples and he busily dabbed his forehead with a handkerchief. The light reflected off his glistening face as he held his head high, extending his chin out at an unnatural angle. Though she couldn't see, Mary was certain he was standing on his tiptoes. All around her the audience grew more agitated as people snickered and called out further taunts towards the front table.

A loud **ahem** silenced them. It wasn't Capron or Burtis whose call for attention hushed the rowdy crowd. Leah Fish, formerly Fox, stood to address the crowd, staring down from her elevator stoop behind the table. She peered directly at Burtis, whose confidence seemed to waver for a moment. The cane which he'd used for the past discussion to wave about wildly or slam on the floor to call attention back in his direction slowly lowered to the ground for its intended purpose. Even his posture grew less certain. From her position Mary could just make out that he averted his eyes from Leah's downward glance.

"Of course, Mr. Burtis. We have offered this to each committee, I should note. A search will be permitted, before *and* after, if you'd like. Is that suitable to you…Mr. Burtis? And when all is completed a wager of a…*new* beaver hat shall be exchanged. Is that right and agreeable."

Her voice was neither angry nor indifferent; a current of *something* bubbled through, however. Was it rage? Bitterness? Both would be justified given the crowd's treatment, Mary supposed. *No, no, it wasn't that.* She struggled to find the word. Then it hit her: *She's confident; mocking even. She knows Burtis is trying to make a name for himself, and she plans on showing him up.*

This is her stage. This is their stage.

"I see and agree to the terms." Burtis replied. That was the last he spoke to the crowd that evening.

A few final odds and ends were haggled out. Where they would be, how the report would be authored, and the committee of women who would inspect Maggie and Leah were all established in mere minutes. The lecture adjourned and the animated crowd began to file out of the Corinthian Hall.

Once again Mary found herself towards the back of the bottlenecked gathering trying to exit out the front door. A few of those in front of her swayed back and forth on sea legs from a night of drinking, and Mary tried to take a step back to prevent them from crashing into her, but found there wasn't much space for her to move as the crowd pressed in, all wanting to make their way outside. Conversation roared around her, though with each passing second, they grew further away, more distant until it was silent.

The room went dark.

***

The lights flashed on, and Mary was back in the Corinthian Hall. It was almost the same as she remembered, however now it was empty. A quiet still hung in the air. Mary was still standing within view of the two wooden doors, both were closed, and the windows beside were pitch black.

I must have fallen asleep or fainted…and no one noticed?

The thought was absurd, but it was the only thing that made any sense. Maybe those in the crowd thought she'd drank too much and simply left her behind to sleep it off. Or maybe they were all so focused on getting out they really didn't see her collapse.

It must be late and whoever closed the venue though it better to leave me in here than bring me outside.

An act of kindness, no doubt.

Her head was swimming and the light from above made her squint. She'd only been drunk once, a simple misunderstanding of the potency of roman punch served during a fall festival, but as best as she could recall this was how she'd felt that evening as she stumbled home: simultaneously feeling both as light and as heavy as she ever before. Everything seemed less defined than normal as if a slight fog had filled the room. Mary blinked her eyes hurriedly, hoping to return things to how they should be. It didn't work; the room remained hazy.

She walked towards the door, not knowing if she planned on walking home or remaining in the hall for the rest of the night.

I'll see how dark and cold it is. If they left me in here, surely, they wouldn't mind me staying until morning.

The thought made her skin crawl. She couldn't point her finger on *why*, but something about the giant lecture hall at night made her uneasy. Mary made up her mind that, unless it was freezing, she would try for home. She arrived at the set of doors and pushed…

…and nothing. Neither budged. She tried again. And again. The door stayed shut. They neither swayed nor opened slightly.

The lock must have been set from the outside, and it wasn't a chain or anything like that.

Mary remembered that it was a new building someone was undoubtedly keen on protecting, and surely, they had invested in a heavy-duty lock.

Strange they left me in here then.

She felt a tickle of fear in her stomach. All the sudden it seemed like the walls were pressing down on her and she had nowhere to hide. The crashing sense of claustrophobia quickened her pulse and breath. Mary backed away from the door towards the center of the hall hoping the feeling might pass. She stepped over lecture pamphlets that were distributed outside the event and now littered the floor. The paper crumpled beneath her feet, adding to the sound of her raspy breath that now filled the space. Her eyes darted around looking for another exit, one that someone may have forgotten to seal off where she could possibly escape into the night. It was a big building, surely there had to be another way out.

Her eyes fell on the wall to her left behind where she'd sat during the first presentation. It was then Mary realized she wasn't alone. There, in the same seat of the same pew where she'd first watched Leah and Maggie speak to the dead, sat a form. The haze intensified around it, and no matter how hard she strained her eyes, it made little difference. The pew's occupant had a vaguely human form, though it was tough to tell where it ended and the space around it began. It was like staring into the beam of a lighthouse. A strange pulsating energy seemed to radiate from the figure that appeared to emit no color while simultaneously glowing. The figure stood up.

"Mary…Mary…"

The voice rushed around the hall like a whirlwind, bombarding her from every direction. In an instant the pew filled with more of them, as did the pews behind and in front. Then the gathering space in front of her, and soon, the whole hall, save for a five-foot clearing directly around her, was filled with human forms. The call of her name was replaced with the call for a hundred other things. Voices beckoned her from every direction,

"Tell my sister—"

"I didn't mean to. You have to tell them I didn't mean—"

"It was Patrick Smith. Patrick Smith killed me on Dece—"

Some of the voices wailed while others simply spoke, even keeled with no hint of emotion. The voices drowned out her own as she tried to call out to ask what they were and what they wanted with her.

"Tell her that beneath the porch there's—"

"He's an innocent man they locked up for my death. He ain't have no—"

"Love you Mary, we—"

It cut though the wailing cacophony like a knife and finally Mary found her voice.

"Mother, where are you? Where are you?"

She looked across the sea of indistinguishable faces and the fear subsided for a moment. They still called out, each asking for a request of some sort but Mary ignored them as she hunted for her mother. Even if she could make out their faces, there were too many. They engulfed the hall, multiplying with each passing second until it seemed the structure itself might burst at the seams and a flood of ghostly occupants would pour into the surrounding streets.

Mary didn't care, she darted around followed wherever she went by a small circle of space they seemed to avoid no matter how fast she moved.

"Where are you? Where are you?" she cried out over and over to no answer to her question save for the outpouring of requests.

"Tell Jaxon I loved h—"

"I died a hero. Please, tell my mother I saved my comm—"

Frustrated Mary screamed. "Quiet! Quiet! I have to find her, then I'll help you! Just leave me alone!"

The room emptied out in an instant; all forms vanished save for one.

"My name is William Richards. I was murdered on February 18th as I walked towards this cursed city. A band of four brothers fell upon me, the oldest took a long knife and—" the fog lifted, and Mary stared at a rotted corpse with ashen grey skin and a slick sheen of blood that still gurgled from the open wound across its neck. "And slit my neck from ear to ear, laughing like the devil himself as I pissed and shat myself while the life left me."

The wound erupted in a fountain of blood that poured down the front of the shirt and trousers that were as decayed as the body they covered. Behind him the Corinthian Hall disappeared; they were left floating aimlessly against a black backdrop.

"I had nothing of value on me, save for some handkerchiefs and tin cups I was selling at the time, couldn't have cost more than twenty five cents total. They dragged my body to the swamps along the lake and threw me in an outlet that hadn't frozen yet." His eyes grew distant and welled with tears. Mary's voice was no longer in her control; if it were, she would have screamed at the first sight of the body. She could only watch.

"I remember sinking into the water…it was so cold. The coldest thing I'd ever felt in my life, Mary, you have to understand how frightened I was. Mary, it was so cold…" The corpse sobbed. Tears rolled down a face missing much of its tissue. The sinews of tendons and muscles that controlled the jaw were exposed, working hard as the face that was more skeleton than skin and flesh continued talking.

He's just a boy. He's just a boy.

105

"I remember sinking into the mud. It clinging to me like a thousand slugs or leeches attaching to my body as the cold water filled my lungs and mouth. I was dead but my mind kept going and Mary it was so dark and cold, and I was so afraid, and they didn't have to kill me why did they kill me I just—"

The words poured as violently as the blood leaking down the front of the young man's body. With a gasp the rapid-fire stream ceased. The young man coughed then leaned back his head as an inky black bile spewed from his mouth, bubbling and gurgling like the blood from his slit neck.

After a moment, he wiped his mouth and stared dead-eyed at Mary, the terror passed.

"There is nothing that makes it matter, Mary. Any of it. The chaos of this world continues to the next. It took me into its depth like the bottom of those damned marshes. I wish to see those bastards join me. The Brixley brothers, all four of em', are responsible for my death. I will wrap my rotting hands around their throats and—"

"Why me?" Mary's voice broke free for a second. Finally, she was able to blurt out the question that had haunted her since the cemetery. "Why me?"

The murdered peddler looked at her with eyes sunken into an all too exposed skull, and for a moment the rage softened to a look of pity. Though no physical change took place, the look of sadness in his eye made him appear as a child again.

Sixteen and killed for twenty-five cents.

"I'm sorry. I truly am. Some things are just unfair like that. Trust me, I know," another pump of blood cascaded down his body. "You were just the only one to listen, I suppose. I'm sorry."

In an instant, the body of William Richards was in front of her, less than an inch from her face. She could smell the stagnant pond water and piss and shit and rot as it leached from his body, the scent assaulting her senses. She felt herself sinking into the murky depths, the water filling her lungs and mouth and a searing pain across her throat.

"The Brixley brothers killed me, William Richards aged sixteen, by way of a knife, stole my copper rings and handkerchiefs, then threw my body into a pond. I demand my revenge. I am here. The Brixley brothers—"

***

Mary came to—again in the Corinthian Hall, and again, not alone—with a gasp. Staring down at her seemed to be a hundred concerned faces, all of which were also pale with fear.

"She's done talking. Miss, you must breathe," someone said.

"Is that water coming from her mouth? Why is it…oh god, it's green!" One of the men surrounding her exclaimed, his voice cracking at the final exclamation.

"Just stay there, don't move, miss," another man told her. Then he turned to the crowd gathered about Mary and added: "and someone will want to get the sheriff. He'll want to hear this."

Part 3
The White Lady

Chapter 5

The next year was a blur for Mary.

From the interviews and questions from the sheriff to the fact that the news about what happened to Mary in the aftermath of the third lecture spread like wildfire through the Rochester community, everything remained in a constant state of change while Mary became a local celebrity. A few of the local newspapers picked up the story, though news of the Fox sisters seemed to overshadow Mary's experience on the regional circuit. She was fine with that, truth be told, as even the status as a local celebrity proved difficult to manage.

***

The ground was covered with a fresh dusting of snow. As Mary walked through the two giant trees that marked the entrance to her property, she noticed fresh prints leading both to and from her house. Mary had a feeling she knew exactly what she'd find. She shook the droplets of melted snow from her hair and shoulders as she got closer. Smoke billowed from the chimney, promising warmth.

As expected, an ivory-colored envelope rested on the porch. Written across in elegant, looping letters was one word: "Invitation." Similar invitations were a daily find: some were left at Ford's shop, others, like this one, would appear somewhere along the path to the front of her house after being thrown hastily down as some poor servant or delivery man, sent on behalf of a wealthy family, was chased off by the dogs. While the invitations were frequent enough, finding one all the way on the front porch was a rarity.

Mary bent down and scooped up the envelope. She muttered to herself, "whoever dropped this off must have been fast," then threw the envelope on top of the basket she carried. She was greeted by both Neppy and Morta who swarmed her, working around her body as their tails wagged in excitement.

"I'm surprised you let them get all the way to the porch. You guys are losing your touch" Mary scratched behind both dog's ears, then she set down the basket containing goods from Ford's store on the table. She held the envelope in front of her, turning it every which way in the light. "Another parlor demonstration, I'm sure. If I never see another parlor again it will be more than alright with me."

She set the envelope down and returned her attention to the basket, stripping off her cloak and jacket as she peeled back the piece of cloth she'd laid over top. Some snow fell onto the table as she did so. Instantly the white powder melted, leaving behind a few droplets of water Mary wiped onto the floor.

"There it is." Mary reached into a basket and grabbed the newspaper that was rolled up into a tight bundle. She let out a long sigh and looked down at the dogs who had joined her by the table. Both Neppy and Morta tilted their heads out of curiosity.

"We knew this was coming. Still…"

She opened the newspaper to the second page and laid it out on the table. On top the newspaper was dated November 2, 1850. It was a few days old, but it had the article she'd been looking for.

Scanning the wall of text, it took her a moment to find the heading she was hunting:

TRIAL OF ALFRED BRIXLEY AND BROTHERS CONTINUES: BROTHERS CLAIM ALFRED ACTED ALONE

The article ran two long columns beneath. Mary read it carefully, occasionally reiterating a sentence or sections aloud.

"Called to testify, the youngest of the brothers, Thomas, claimed eldest acted alone in the gruesome deed…Rings and other wares were found in possession of Alfred…the suspicion fell when local spiritualist claimed to be contacted by the murdered peddler whose body was discovered after…" She went back and read the article a second and third time before closing the newspaper.

"They could have used my name at least." She made her way towards the fireplace. As always, the dogs followed. Mary grabbed the poker beside and jabbed it into the flames, kicking up a flurry of red sparks as the flame rekindled.

"On second thought though, it's probably best they didn't." Mary thought back to the conversation at the store. Ford had warned her that, though known to be trouble, the Brixley's were well connected enough to make her life difficult. According to an earlier report, even before her vision the four brothers were suspects due to the youngest's affinity for drink and talk. His wagging tongue wasn't enough to garner anything other than a few questions, that same report announced, but when interest was rekindled thanks to *her* a whole host of evidence was discovered. All four had been arrested, but if the most recent article was to be trusted, only the oldest would be convicted. The other three had turned on him pretty quickly, it seemed. Mary felt a twinge of guilt knowing a man would be executed, but it quickly subsided. The memory of the poor peddler, decaying and bleeding, was fresh enough in her memory to remove any guilt. If the papers were right, Alfred had what was coming to him; and it's not like she had any say in the matter, it had just…happened.

Looking down at the paper another thought crossed her mind. *What if they want revenge?*

Like the guilt, this thought too quickly disappeared.

"You two would scare anyone off, besides." she said with a smile as she looked down at Neppy and Morta.

***

The sun set and the window in the kitchen filled with a golden glow that cascaded across the first floor, basking everything in its warm light. The fire crackled while Morta and Neppy rolled on their backs so it might warm their bellies. A book lay open on Mary's lap, a cup of tea so recently poured that wisps of steam rose from it and sat on the small table beside her. If there was a winter chill outside, inside the house was as cozy and inviting as anyone could hope for.

Mary's gaze rose from the book she was reading and moved to the window. The same layer of snow that coated the ground on her way from Ford's store still iced the branches of barren trees and blanketed the occasional outcrop of white pines that lay intermingled in the facing forest.

The thought of leaving the house and making her way into the cold made Mary shiver in anticipation, but she was ready. She *had* to. By this point it was a nightly ritual and all she needed was for the sun to disappear completely. She went back to reading.

With each passing minute the shade of orange cast by the disappearing sun grew darker, and Mary had to focus harder on the words she was reading as the light became insufficient. When the words were on the verge of disappearing, she went and threw another log on the fire, which provided a touch more light—certainly not enough to read by, however—and a plume of smoke. Still wanting to spend some more time with her book, she made her way to the kitchen to grab a candle and a holder. The smell of the pork she'd fried for dinner still hung heavy in the air and grew stronger as she approached the iron pan used to cook it, which hung beside the window. The candle lay beneath, but Mary was drawn to the view of the setting sun outside. She stopped and stared through the glass pane at the outside world.

A blood red line striped the horizon.

Give it half an hour, she told herself as she continued staring out the window. Then it would be completely dark.

The dusk sky, a kaleidoscope of colors made richer as the end approached, like the orange and yellow of leaves soon to crumple and die, stopped Mary where she stood. The splashes of color across the night sky were so beautiful, yet so chaotic. Lost in the expanse before her she could practically hear those voices from the void of her dreams; those voices that whispered long lost secrets and begged to be heard. That told her how to listen and find them in those nights after she'd seen the peddler.

Chaos and madness...

Mary was so close to understanding it all. The letter upstairs proved testament to that, they'd shown her how to open the entryway and now she was just exploring *terra incognita.* Soon she would know her way around, and then she could find her; then she could cut through all the voices and strangers who she'd found so far.

Then she could find her.

Mary scooped up the candle and returned to her chair, stopping only briefly by the fireplace to carefully light the wick using the now roaring flame. With enough light to now read, Mary returned to her book as the two dogs snored with deep, rasping breaths.

Mary flipped back to the title page:

AUTHENTIC ACCOUNT OF THE APPEARANCE OF A GHOST IN QUEEN-ANN'S COUNTY, MARYLAND PROVED IN SAID COUNTY COURT IN THE REMARKABLE TRIAL OF JAMES THOMAS HARRIS VERSUS MARY HARRIS: FROM ATTESTED NOTES, TAKEN IN COURT AT THE TIME BY ONE OF THE COUNCIL. 1807.

She'd searched all over to find it. Finally, after frequenting every bookstore within the city and asking each bookseller where she might find either a copy or someone who might have purchased the obscure account, she'd been put in touch with a lawyer who'd bought it sometime back. He'd been willing to part ways with the book for her services. The seance was easy enough—they always were—and he'd happily given her his copy when completed.

Scribbled throughout were the man's notes. Best Mary could tell, the lawyer had been scouring the trial account for a court case of his own, occasionally jotting down a note or circling an idea or argument he might borrow. Or perhaps it was just mere curiosity in the strange tale; after all, he had been keen to participate in a seance in exchange for the book.

Whatever the reason the man saw fit to trade, Mary was grateful. The book was, besides being marked and difficult to find, weathered and printed on cheap material and who knows whether she'd ever be able to find another copy. At forty years old the spine barely held the pages, a few of which would slide out if not handled in the same manner one might hold a baby. Mary treated it with care.

Slowly flipping from the cover page, she returned to where she'd left off, reading about the ghostly apparition that appeared to a man in a cemetery to see his inheritance left to the four illegitimate heirs he left behind.

Dusk settled, Mary read, and as the minutes passed it grew darker outside. She eventually closed the book saying aloud to the dogs as she did, "I think it's time we started our business." Mary laid the book down on the side table, then thought better and set it on a pillow, which she then placed on the table once more. Sensing the call to activity Neppy and Morta started to stir from their resting spots by the fire.

"I heard musical instruments are being used now too by some other spiritualists. Too bad we don't have any with us here. Oh well, we might try that in the future." She made her way towards the ladder then climbed to the loft carefully, candle still in hand, where her bed was located. The dogs stood at the foot of the ladder staring up, watching as Mary disappeared over the ledge above.

Next to the mattress left behind by her parents was a small dresser, which too once belonged to her mother. Mary made her way towards it and slid open the bottom drawer. Contained within were all her mother's worldly belongings, save the furnishings still spread throughout the house. Mary scanned the array of items, which included her mother's wedding ring, a locket on a silver chain that had been gifted to her by Mary's grandfather, and a small graphite and ink drawing of her father completed the year before his death. There was a single white and blue plate, blue willow china her mother had often bragged, resting on a piece of cloth Mary had placed beneath it to safeguard one of her mother's prized possessions.

There was also Mary's sole addition to the collection: the letter, penned by her, detailing how to break through to the Otherside. One of the spirits told her to write it down, just in case, and she'd listened, and so she'd recorded the instructions to contact the dead. She traced her finger over the envelope, knowing how valuable the contents were and what people might do to have them…

Finally, she found the silk wrapped parcel she was looking for: contained within was a silver-plated daguerreotype of her mother. Like the print of her father, it was completed shortly before her death.

Mary set the candle on the wood planked floor beneath her and removed the daguerreotype from the drawer. She peeled back the silk wrap, revealing the leather, rectangular box beneath. The protective box was beginning to streak from her constant handling. In the spots where the brown coloring of the leather had rubbed away, a stained copper tint was left behind. Mary thumbed the hook-latch and opened the case: on one side there was a purple felt backing; the other, a silver image of her mother. She tilted it back and forth in the light of the candle, watching as the image seemingly changed color depending on the angle.

The memory of cutting the paper doll chain flashed through Mary's mind. Why, she didn't know, but something about the dualistic nature of the daguerreotype and how it worked to capture her mother seemed strangely familiar to their conversation that evening. Mary sighed and the memory drifted away as she inspected the image.

Her mother would have been thirty-seven in the moment her likeness was captured for the daguerreotype. Even without the pine-green coloring of her eyes, which seemed to glisten with excitement when she spoke, seemingly drained and replaced with a lifeless metal tint, the kindness from her gaze still emanated from the still. Though her mother was told not to smile, Mary, and perhaps only she would notice, always noted how the corner of her lip was pulled up slightly, bordering on a smirk. It made Mary happy—thinking of her mother battling not to grin as the image was taken— with a childish short of glee she rarely felt anymore.

Though she'd looked at it daily for the past two years, Mary still took time to inspect it each evening. Her mother's head was tilted slightly, and her hair, though neatly parted in front, spilled out in a plume of curls behind her. It was silver in the depiction, of course, but she saw the chestnut brown with just a hint of copper that it had been back then. She was wearing a plain dress, Mary knew it to be dark blue, with a white split collar, between which the locket from the drawer hung about her neck; it was a simple image, but it still amazed Mary to hold it. Her mother, dead for over two years, seemingly stared back from beyond the grave at her. *She looks so young.* Yet thirty-seven, which is what she was when the still was completed, seemed so old to Mary, so many years away, yet…

Is that what I'll look like?

A tear trickled from the corner of her eye. All the missed conversations, all the moments of joy and happiness robbed of her mother. She'd lost her husband and been forced to run a farm and raise a daughter on her own.

Was she happy? Did she have a chance to do any of the things she wanted to in life before death and disease changed her life and then her own life was cut short?

119

It was so unfair. The tears streamed down her face as Mary looked at her mother and she thought about her death, as random and as senseless as anything could be: trampled by a horse whose owner lost control of it after it was frightened by a gunshot from a tavern. She'd been in the city visiting a friend when it happened. As she stepped onto the walkway to make her way back home the horse careened into her, killing her on impact. To make it worse, the rider managed to get control of his horse shortly after and simply rode off, never to be found.

How could that be allowed to happen? Why did her mother have to die? Why could the rider go off to live whatever life they wanted to while her mother lay on the street, dead with a broken spine for the simple crime of visiting a friend?

Kneeling beside the mattress Mary stared at the daguerreotype for another minute before closing it, re-latching the hook lock, and enclosing it back in the silk wrap silk. She had a chance to find out, to answer those questions. More importantly, she had a chance to let her mother know what she meant. Mary wiped the tears from her eyes then carefully carried it down the ladder with her as she returned to the first floor. She then bundled herself in as many layers of coats and overcoats and wrappings as she could manage.

"Morta, Neppy, come." The three of them made their way out the back door and into the night.

The tops of the grave markers and tombstones were powdered with snow, and her breath fogged in front of her as she stared into the pioneer cemetery. Closer and closer to breaking through, she could feel it in the pit of her gut. She stepped past the crumbling wall, and as always Morta and Neppy stood on the other side watching Mary as she made her way to the center.

Into the chaos, Mary, she thought, concentrating with everything she had as her body and mind sunk into the abyss as that poor peddler's body had.

The nothing, the darkness, the churning ichor, the…

***

Chaos

Darkness surrounded her, but it was different from the darkness of the night sky or what one sees when they close their eyes. It was complete. No light or reflection or color broke through. All-engulfing, though when Mary looked down, she could see herself without problem, as if some unseen light cast down on her with exact precision. She was nearly translucent in the glow. She looked from her arm and saw there was a shimmer of something beneath, something swimming (above or beyond or through, she couldn't tell), trying to break through the void around her. Mary held her breath. She was a lone actress on an empty stage, but there was someone, or something in the audience. There was a ripple in the murky depths. What would emerge?

And in an instant the show curtains were pulled back, the scene set: Mary was back in the cemetery, though it was different than before. No snow covering the ground or icicles hanging like fangs from branches above. Instead, the ground was barren with only the dried husk of vegetation left behind. It was mushy beneath her feet, and the tombstones that had been little more than knee high now towered above her, extending upwards like strange megaliths into the sky above. A shroud of fog covered the landscape swirling about though no wind blew.

Though she should've been used to it by now, fear coursed through her body as she stood surveying the strange scene. *You shouldn't be here. You should leave.* She turned around and neither Neppy nor Morta were in sight; instead, standing where the entrance should have been, was the silhouette of a gaunt man. A loud wail filled the cemetery as the shadow slowly transformed into something of slightly more substance: a grey mist that blended with the fog beneath, yet maintained its vaguely human form.

"I'm suffering you bitch, why did you drag me out to talk? I'm suffering so," it groaned then dissipated into the blanket of fog.

"Where did you go?" Mary cried out. No response. She sprinted towards where she had last seen the spirit, only to hear the sound of its moans begin behind her.

"You BITCH!" its voice rose then caved-in as a pathetic string of whimpers and snivels replaced the shout. Mary turned and saw the spirit had reemerged beside a particularly large tombstone. The misty form became slightly more substantial as it leaned against the weathered stone that was nearly triple its height: long grey fingers gripped the marker as the spirit braced itself to keep from falling. Stringy hair fell from a partially caved in skull down to shoulders that sloped downwards at an unnatural angle. Again, Mary felt fear bubble in her gut despite the fact she should have been used to seeing apparitions in similar states. The afterlife, the realm she'd found, rather, was not always kind to the dead. His tall, skinny frame seemed nearly broken in half, his hunched over body like a tree snapped in a windstorm. His skin was the same color as the blanket of fog that extended up to his knees, a sickly grey that was both unnatural and grotesque. Shirt and trousers that looked like they were made of burlap clothed his skeletal frame, though much of the material was worn through and revealed the mangled body beneath.

"Are you…are you able to talk?" Her voice sounded distant, almost as if it was coming from behind one of the surrounding tombstones. She barely spoke above a whisper and yet it seemed to carry from all around. The fog swirled in front of her as if the words had caused some disturbance.

A dry cough slowly transformed to a cackle. "I don't suppose I have any choice. You dragged me here. Why the h—"

"I'm looking for someone." Mary produced the daguerreotype of her mother from the folds of her dress, unwrapping it as she kept her eye on the spirit in front of her. Without thinking or looking she unhooked the lock, opened it and waved it in the air towards the gaunt man. "Her, this woman. I would like to talk to her. Have you seen her? She's…she's buried here too. After you, most likely."

Another coughing fit that gave way to a wicked laugh filled the cemetery.

"That's not how this works. You don't get to make your way here and start demanding what you see. No, no—" he stopped for a moment, and when he resumed the tone of his voice softened. "A wagon. I know what you're thinking, "how didn't ol' Deacon see a wagon coming?" I gotta be honest, I'd had a bit too much of that hard cider and was pretty in the cups." He tapped the tombstone. "I guess I hung around a bit after, don't remember much of it, then they buried me here." Risley's spirit stared up the height of the marker. "This is all that's left. I'm…nothing. I'm," his voice rose higher, "forgotten! It was for nothing. My existence meant *fucking* nothing. OH god it hurts, it hurts so bad. Why did you drag me here." His form began to lose shape as his ashen skin started to steam.

A flash of…*lightning*? That was the closest Mary could come to placing it. As her eyes adjusted to the sudden flash, she saw the man was still there, though…different. Younger, maybe thirty or so, and still thin but now sinewy and packed with muscle. The decay was gone though still an unnatural pallid shade of grey. Even with the hint of death still set in, the man was now pleasant to look at. Handsome even. A smile passed across his face, and when he spoke his voice was full.

"Oh, I don't mean none of that. I got my little boy n' girl out there in the big wide world. I'm sure he's a lawyer now, just like he always wanted. Her? I'm sure she's out there doing great things. She was a hellfire growin' up, that's for sure."

Another flash, and life began to drain from him once more. With each second, he grew worse.

Please answer, she waved the image of her mother at the rapidly dissolving shape.

"It won't make sense because you want it to, Mary" a voice that wasn't her internal dialogue cut across her thoughts. The intrusion was familiar from past dreams and escapades into the…well she still didn't know what to call it. Though she was used to it, the voice made her shudder. It was the one that first reached out to her and still always made a point of turning up towards the end of her visions.

"Have you seen her?" Mary asked, the desperation rising in her voice as she waved the open daguerreotype in the withering man's direction. If he had, he gave no indication. Rather than responding he began screeching out in an incomprehensible jumble of noises. His form continued to deteriorate until there was only a tendril of smoke left where the gaunt man had once stood, staring up at his tombstone.

124

She was alone in the cemetery. The giant tombstones began to change, becoming newer as years of decay and weathering were stripped away.

Mary stepped forward but before she could move any farther the fog began rising higher, climbing up Mary's body until she had to stand on her tiptoes to see above it. She called out again, but no one answered. The mist engulfed her, and Mary was lost in a sea of swirling haze that wrapped around her like a blanket that grew darker and darker and...

***

The sound of Morta and Neppy barking brought her back.

Mary opened her eyes to the snow-covered cemetery with appropriately sized tombstones and no fog to be seen. The moon and stars shone from above; no ripple moved through the vast expanse. She turned and looked at the dogs who silenced immediately. The cemetery settled into serenity as Mary stood, rage boiling in her chest.

She let out a scream of frustration that shattered the still night. Mary was tempted to make her way to the gravestone marked Risley and kick it over, it wouldn't take much but she stopped herself.

It's not his fault, they've all been like that.

Each form, man or woman or child, had been similarly dispositioned. Some rambled on about their deaths, others simply cried or sobbed, while others spoke nonsensically, seemingly unaware that they were dead. They would have conversations with her, though never about her mother or how she might find her. Throughout their conversations they would change; she would see different versions, shifting between their younger and older selves, with emotions that changed just as frequently. Each night Mary found herself unable to get any information, but she felt close. And by her count she'd spoken to almost everyone with a tombstone.

Her mother might be next.

The thought was not as comforting as it once was, especially given the state of some of the other spirits she'd seen. They were all so disoriented and…strange. Besides that, the state of their—not bodies, though spirit didn't seem the right word either—*apparitions,* she finally decided on, were quite jarring. Though if she took a shovel and dug into the ground Mary was quite certain she would find little more than bones or skeletons beneath (save for her mother who was recent enough to have not withered away completely, a concept she tried to push past without dwelling on), the *apparitions* were all so full, though in various states of decomposition. It was rather grisly to see.

After the bellow of frustration followed a chain of echoes that seemed to go on longer than it should, the cemetery was once again placid. The snow glistened beneath the moon and stars overhead, and Mary let out a deep breath that turned to fog in the frigid winter air. Behind her Neppy and Morta whimpered, and an owl hooted somewhere in the distance, disturbed by Mary's scream.

"Let's go back." She turned and walked through the opening in the cemetery, the disappointment evident in her tone. The dogs seemed all too happy to oblige. They turned and trotted beside her as they made their way back to the house—though as they left both kept a sideways eye on the tombstone of A. Deacon, watching carefully as a wisp of fog rose from its base.

A knock on the door was swallowed by the sound of Neppy and Morta barking furiously as the dogs sprinted towards the back door. Mary moved quickly, sliding a chair between them and the dog door before they could make their way outside.

"They're picking me up. I have a talk."

Her assurance did little to convince either of the dogs, who, prevented from rushing out the back, busied themselves circling around the first floor growling as ferociously as they could while their nails pitter-pattered against the wooden floor. Over a year of similar interruptions and the dogs were still not used to it, too hard-wired were their instincts as guard dogs. Another knock sent them into an increased flurry.

"I'll meet you by the road," Mary called through the door above the din. She couldn't make out the muffled response, but she assumed it was the driver agreeing. The sound of heavy footsteps pounding on the front porch grew more distant, finally giving way completely as the driver met the path. The dogs' ears remained perked, though their frantic rush ended, and both sat down at various posts throughout the first floor. A minute passed before either relaxed completely.

During that time Mary rushed about the house, finally finding the shawl she was looking for draped across the back of her chair opposite the fire. She threw it over her shoulders and stopped for a moment. *Grab the daguerreotype,* something inside her said. Mary had never thought about it before, bringing the image of her mother to a gathering, but the idea made sense this evening. Perhaps it was the lack of luck she'd encountered at the cemetery, or perhaps it was the sudden appearance of the thought; whatever it was, it spurred her to action. Mary climbed the stairs, carefully tucked the silk wrapped image in her dress, and made her way back to the first floor.

As she sprinted towards the door, she turned to Neppy and Morta: "You two be good, I'll be back later."

Both dogs began to stand, and Mary quickly cut across the room and stepped out into the night. She could hear soft whimpers from behind the door.

"I won't be long," she whispered, then turned to walk down the path towards the main road.

It was January and Mary was thankful she didn't need to walk to the city like she used to before the invitations. Even during a mild winter such as the season had been, the walk to the main road was bitter. The snow from the previous week had melted, leaving behind only barren frozen earth. A mile would have been unbearable.

Two pinpoints of light shone through the naked branches of bushes and trees before her; it took Mary a moment to realize they were lanterns hanging from the carriage. As she emerged through the two gnarled trees, she found the finest carriage she'd ever seen pulled by two of the largest horses she'd ever seen. They neighed at her approach and steam filled the night around their muzzles. The light of the lanterns reflected off their dark brown coat, giving them an almost brindle appearance. Growing impatient, the pair tapped their front hooves on the packed dirt road beneath. The carriage behind them shuttered at their slight movement. It was much smaller than the wagons she was familiar with, and the boxy design of the carriage bed was completely enclosed. It wasn't until she was close enough to touch it that she saw it was painted dark blue, and the hood of the carriage leather.

"This way ma'am." A tall man with a thin, sharp face accentuated by his wispy facial hair that did little to conceal his pointed chin opened the carriage door. "Miss Mary," he said with a slight dip of his head. He held his hand to her, and Mary used it as she stepped up into the bed of the carriage. Once inside, Mary sat on a cushioned bench facing the driver's seat. The pillow beneath her was a dark red and looked as expensive as anything she had in her house. Mary's stunned face asked a question words couldn't.

"It's fine, isn't it? Your hosts imported it from England, or so I'm told. They've had some modifications made to it. Wanted it more robust, or so I'm told. It's supposed to be a city carriage, but your hosts have need to visit the countryside often." He pointed to the horses then the lamps. "I added those, and a second hitch. Helps with the country roads. There are even springs beneath." The pride of his modifications seeped through his voice.

"It's fantastic," Mary said, completely awestruck.

The driver closed the door behind her and took position in the driver's seat.

"The roads are bumpy for the first few miles, ma'am. Not even the springs can help with that. Once we're closer to the city they smooth out nicely, 'm just glad there's no snow or ice on the way" he called from over his shoulder.

With a loud "*Hyah!*" the driver started the reins, and the horses were off. Though the carriage was enclosed the winter air seeped through openings Mary couldn't see, but certainly felt. She pulled her shawl up, burrowed into her seat, and tucked her hands into her dress grabbing hold of the wrapped daguerreotype. The driver sat outside the enclosed carriage guiding the horses. *He must be freezing*. The cold wind was bone-chilling even within the carriage bed.

They grumbled along the dirt road.

When they hit a patch noticeably quieter than the other parts of the road the driver called from over his shoulder, "they're all excited to see you. Your presence has stirred up quite the commotion. I can't tell you how many people were pining for invitations. I delivered em' all, including the one to you in fact all those weeks back. Those dogs of yours gave me quite the scare!"

His voice melted into the howl of the wind and Mary strained to hear him.

"...especially after the, and pardon me if it's inappropriate to mention, but especially after the, you know...execution."

Mary bristled and squeezed the silk parcel containing the image of her mother, as if trying to prevent her from hearing. She tried her best not to think about the trial and the hanging of Alfred Brixley. It happened so fast: the arrest and trial, his brothers turning on him, the jury's decision, all done in the span of a month and a half. He evaded capture for the better part of a year, but once brought in the process moved quickly: the trial in November, the execution in December. Mary kept expecting one evening to find a summons in place of an invitation on her porch; but that day never came.

Apparently, the testimony of his brothers and the physical evidence was enough. The newspapers claimed the jailors were quick to see him hanged due to the insufferable threats and calls for vengeance he called for at all hours. Even as the sentence was read, Alfred reportedly called out threats towards the judge. And, of course, to—

"Mary Bowcroft coming to summon the dead, it caused a stir I tell you. That you aided in capturing a murderer- say, did you hear what happened at his, you know—"

The road was smoother now, though the driver kept his voice at the same volume, nearly shouting back to her.

"The papers said another spiritualist was there, right?"

Mary had followed it carefully, of course, but the papers always had their angle. If this man's employers were as connected as it appeared, perhaps he'd heard something else. And besides, *I'm going to need to get used to questions about it.*

"A few, or so I'm told. Popping up like daisies this past month, I swear everyone's hearing things now. Hold on—*Hyay*— where was I, oh yea! Did the papers mention she was there with the crowd to see him hung?"

"I believe so. It said she fainted at the sight and claimed to hear his threats even after he'd…passed. She claimed to have heard him in the afterlife, correct?"

"That's what they printed but that's not what I heard. I heard, yea she fainted, but then she started calling out the same threats he'd made on his way to the gallows, but in his own voice!"

"That can't be true."

"I swear that's what I heard. She was crying out threats to, well to everyone in attendance and the judge and to…well to everyone. And it was in *his* voice as his body was still hanging from the gallows. Then she, or he I suppose, started choking herself. I know a guy who was there who claimed it took five men to restrain her, all the while she's calling out in that Alfred boy's voice about how she'll torment the city until he has his revenge. Gruesome, gruesome stuff."

131

If the driver truly thought it gruesome, his voice did not convey it. Still shouting, there was an elated glee to his tone.

"They brought another spiritualist in to break the possession. I suppose that boy is where he belongs now. Good riddance. Especially after what they did to that poor peddler. I think the brothers should've got it too, but they turned so quick I reckon the judge just wanted it over. Doubt they'll ever do anything like it again after seeing what became of their brother."

In the distance Mary could make out the faint outline of the city against the night sky.

"How many will be there tonight?" she asked.

"I delivered eight invitations, not including yours that is. I doubt any of em' will miss it. So, eight, plus the Mr. and Mrs., so ten total. Again, not including yourself. They've seen to setting up the parlor for the crowd already. Had to put two tables together to have enough seats. Good thing they…"

The man kept talking though Mary only half listened. It was seven and a long night lay ahead, and already she was tired and wished to be at home. Another parlor, another distant voice that might reach out, another stunned audience…it was all so tiresome.

The gatherings in less than a y'ar's time had grown unbearable. She'd been hesitant to take them in the first place, but something about only using her recently acquired skill for herself seemed so selfish. If she'd been randomly selected, as it seemed to be the case, how fair was it to keep her abilities to herself. Besides, the money was good, and it was easy enough to think of them as a way to practice.

So, the seances began. The first one had gone so poorly it was a wonder it didn't all end there: a dead Aunt rambling about the wretched state of her house, which was inherited by her nephew.

After spending months trying to contact her mother, Mary was surprised she'd been able to find the right spirit, difficult though she was.

Red faced and expecting to be kicked out, Mary was surprised that once the lights were turned on, she was greeted by a table of smiling and giggling faces.

"That was definitely her," someone at the table muttered.

She was paid well that evening, and had since been invited to several similar parlors.

But what at first seemed a general interest or a sincere desire to communicate with the dead by her hosts quickly turned into a vogue display of wealth. No longer was she brought in to make contact with a dead daughter or to pass on a message to a grandfather who had passed suddenly; no, now she was asked to call to Alexander the Great or summon some ancient Pharaoh. She was a parlor trick, nothing else. And when she wasn't asked to do ridiculous summonings she was an animal in a menagerie, paraded about as a living talking-piece for all to ooh and aah over.

Why me? The question crept into her mind once more as she watched Rochester grow closer as the driver continued to talk about her hosts. Perhaps she was in the right (or wrong, Mary couldn't decide yet) place at the right (or again, wrong) time. She could also be predisposed to it, having lost both her mother and father and spending so much time alone made her a conduit to the other side. Or maybe it was a perfect maelstrom of all those things. The best insight she'd gotten was from the murdered peddler.

"You were just the only one to listen, I suppose."

Mary's skin crawled, and not from outside chill.

She would do this one, and maybe one or two more, but that was it. She was done. If her mother couldn't be found, then Mary no longer wanted to be a part of whatever she was mixed in with. She would quit.

"That's the house up there, just another minute."

Chapter 6

Everything seemed to be made of gold. Even the wallpaper was decorated with little golden emblems that sparkled against the beige and white striped backdrop.

Of all the parlors Mary had seen, this was by far the most impressive.

The house sat on the corner of a busy street that was unknown to her, towering above the other houses in the vicinity. As she'd been helped off the carriage Mary looked around to find a landmark, anything that might help her figure out where she was, but to no avail. None of the shops or taverns were familiar, and before she could ask the driver for information on their whereabouts another servant appeared in the doorway and whisked her inside. The young woman couldn't have been any older than Mary, and as she called to her in a thick Irish brogue Mary once again bristled at the pageantry of the whole ordeal.

They entered a giant hallway with multiple doors on either side. Somewhere from within the sound of conversation and laughter spilled out into the main hallway, and Mary began walking towards the direction she thought the voices were coming from.

The young woman who'd escorted her stepped into her path before Mary managed more than two steps.

"A few of the other guests are in the drawing room, but I was instructed to show you the parlor so you could…set up, Miss Mary."

"Set up, I don't need to—"

"It's in there. The pocket doors close if you'd prefer, Miss Mary. Your coat," the servant extended her arms out and waited as Mary removed her overcoat. "I can take your shawl too."

"No thanks, I'll keep it with me."

"Very well. This way then." She escorted Mary to the parlor. Once there, the servant disappeared leaving Mary alone in the golden room. The feeling of frustration passed momentarily and was replaced by awe. A towering mirror rested atop the largest fireplace and mantle Mary had ever seen. Wrapped about the mirror was gilded gold carved in intricate designs, culminating with a face at the very top that reminded her of a medieval jester peering down towards her. Besides the mirror, two pedestals with marble statues of Minerva and Venus sat in front of large rectangular windows.

Next to gold, marble was the next most frequent feature in the room: two marble-topped tables sat opposite each other on the far walls, both were decorated with the same blue and white china Mary's mother had been proud to own a single plate of, yet here multiple sets were heaped about. The French Rococo furniture surrounding the room was gold as well, with arm rests as intricate as the mirror's frame. Clearly it had been moved from the center of the room to make space for tonight's addition: two giant tables that nearly filled up the room and were covered in a wine-red cloth that matched the window drapes.

Mary worked her way around the table carefully, worried that if she accidentally bumped into something mirror, statues and furniture all included would come clattering down and shatter into a million pieces.

*Set up...*such a strange way to tell her to wait in the parlor for the other guests.

Maybe it's a saying in Ireland.

Mary didn't know if she should take a seat or stay standing. She opted to stand as, even if she'd been certain about finding a chair, she didn't know which one she'd be expected to occupy. Sometimes they'd place Mary at the head of the table, other times in one of the side seats. It was always a crapshoot: the decorum and seating arrangement for contacting the dead in high society had not been established yet, as it were.

As she gazed about the room lost in the gaudy display of wealth, Mary failed to realize she was no longer alone.

"Are you Miss Mary, the medium?" a voice said from the open pocket doors, startling her. She hadn't heard any footsteps approaching and was caught off guard. She turned and found a child, certainly no older than eleven, leaning on the door. He was dressed in pajamas and barefoot, which explained how he was able to sneak up on her.

Mary smiled.

"Yes, my name is Mary. I suppose they're calling us mediums now?"

The young boy nodded.

"You're the fourth one I've met. The other three were older than you." He stopped and added for emphasis, "*much* older."

"Oh, and did your parents have them over, too?"

"Yup," his smile glowed with pride. "They won't let me sit in, they say it's too scary for me, but I'll sneak down and watch 'em set up. They don't even know I'm here."

"Set up. Someone else said that earlier. What do you mean, set up?"

137

"Oh, you know, tying all sorts of things under the table and such. I saw one of 'em hand something behind the window too. I asked one what they were doing, and she was startled as you when you first saw me, but then she said it's part of the process. Are you going to tie anything up?"

Mary shook her head slowly. "No…no. I suppose that's not part of my process."

The sound of the conversation grew closer, and a look of fear crossed the boy's face.

"Bye Miss Mary, it was nice meeting you." He scampered off, silent as when he'd first arrived.

With how quickly everything happened, it was only natural some would try to take advantage of it. Mary tried to figure out how tying something under the table or behind a wall might be of use to fake a conjuring.

Maybe for the rapping noises?

She didn't have long to dwell on it as only a few seconds after the boy vanished   the servant who had led her in appeared, gesturing towards the table. Following her was a crowd of well-dressed men and women who strolled into the parlor without so much as a sideways glance at the surrounding splendor.

Mary still hadn't been introduced to her hosts, and as those entering the parlor chatted amongst themselves and took their seats, Mary once again felt like a performing animal at a traveling circus.

Dance when we want you to, but not a word before or after.

Three empty seats remained, one of which Mary assumed was hers. She made her way towards the nearest one and lowered her eyes as she went. The table grew quiet.

"You must be Miss Mary," a man said from the doorway.

Mary stopped in her tracks.

He looked to be in his thirties; in his hand was a brandy snifter that he rose in her direction.

"I'm Mr. Hearns, your host for this evening. I do apologize we weren't around to make introductions, Thomas here," he gestured towards one of the seated men at   his left, "was telling us a bit about his trip to Washington, weren't you, old boy?"

The man grunted and the table laughed. Mary smiled though *very* aware she wasn't a part of the joke.

"Anyways, we are *delighted* to have your company. My wife-Frances do come here-has been following your exploits with the keenest eye. She promised tonight would be one no one in attendance would ever forget. Oh, here she is."

Frances stepped into the doorway beside her husband who had to scoot to make space on account of her giant hoop skirt.

"I hope the ride over wasn't too dreadful. I know those roads can be quite bumpy, especially with the weather and all. We would have sent the sleigh if there'd been any snow this month," Frances said.

Mary felt the gaze of everyone in the room; it burned and made her want to twitch and run for the door. But she couldn't do any of those things without ruining her modest reputation, and some things are worse than being uncomfortable. So instead, she tried to make herself seem as confident as Leah or Maggie had stood in front of a hostile audience forty times as large. Still, it was of little use.

A plaything is what I am.

"The carriage was nice, thank you for sending it. I was used to wagons, so the drive over seemed quite smooth."

Her hosts made their way to the empty chairs and took their seats, motioning for Mary to join them. She sat next to Frances who turned and smiled. There was a genuine look of kindness across her face that set Mary at ease for the first time that evening. The lights were dimmed, and the servant brought in a candle she placed in the center of the two tables.

"Shall we co—"

"Samuel, darling, before we start, I was hoping Miss Mary might be willing to answer some questions that I've been just burning to know."

"Me as well," chimed one of the men sitting across the table. In the candlelight everyone's faces seemed to hover, the shadows of the room swallowing their already dark attire, leaving behind only floating heads peering in her direction.

"Frances, you asked your questions to the last one."

"Her answers lacked substance dear, wouldn't you agree?" Those around the table chuckled. Despite their chuckles—clearly at the expense of some earlier girl in her same line of work—once again Mary felt more comfortable. Frances turned to her and touched her arm. "I hope we're not bothering you. I am so genuinely curious. We've had a few other spiritualists over and were perhaps hoping for a change of pace, but if you'd prefer to do things in your own way I'll—no, *we'll* certainly understand."

"No, no, questions would be fine," Mary said looking around the candlelit faces.

"How did you know it was the man, oh what was his name…Alfred! How did you know he and his brothers murdered that poor peddler? I heard you were leaving a lecture of the Fox sisters: is that true?"

"Yes, I was at Corinthian Hall a year or so back as they were forming another committee to investigate the sisters…" Mary began to choose her next words, carefully weighing each one, but in the dimly lit room filled   by strangers, one of whom appeared genuine at least, she felt the weight of the loneliness crash down on her. Always selecting her words, worried she might be called a fraud (which, what little did that matter if frauds were apparently finding work?), the endless feeling of despair that she would never contact her mother, the eyes that followed her wherever she went, and the whispers she could never hear that she knew followed in her wake. It was time to open up, just the slightest bit.

"I can't tell you *why* I found out. I've asked myself that many times since. I remember leaving the hallway after the Fox sisters spoke and all those angry spectators were calling them frauds and being stuck in a large crowd, then darkness. It only lasted a second though. I woke, I suppose is the closest word, back in the lecture hall but it was empty. I thought I'd fainted and been left behind. I'll admit, it wasn't the first strange thing that happened to me around that time."

"You weren't alone though, were you? I heard a crowd gathered around you after you fainted, someone cried out to get water. They thought the shock of the evening had worn on you." Frances said. The surrounding faces all leaned a little closer.

"That's what I'm told. Though I was alone, it seemed at least to me. I kept searching for a way out and all the exits were locked. Then…"

The faces grew larger as they inched forward   again.

"Do go on," Frances insisted.

"It's rather gruesome."

"Go on, go on" the gathering, choir-like, said in unison.

"The murdered peddler approached me. That poor boy, William Richards, and he looked like he must've when they found him washed up. His body was decaying yet still bleeding, and he told me what happened to him and who the guilty parties were, and that they'd have the rings and handkerchiefs he'd been sent to sell."

"That's terrible," a woman at the table said. "So young to suffer such a horrible fate." The heads around her shook in agreement.

"When I came to, I was helped by that crowd you mentioned. Later I was told I'd been repeating the words the murdered boy had told me in the vision. They said I was speaking in a voice other than mine, his voice, though I don't know if I believe it; none of those there knew me, so how would they know my voice?"

"But it might have been, you were entranced, correct?" Hearns asked, leaning over the table to look directly at Mary.

Mary shrugged, trying not to demonstrate how upsetting the thought was…especially when thinking back to the story the driver told her about Alfred's execution. It was such an intrusive idea having the dead speak through you; Mary had decided not to dwell on *those* parts of the reports a very long time ago.

"Perhaps, maybe I was speaking in his voice," she mused. "After the past months everything seems believable. That part of the story always seemed…fantastic. I try not to think about it."

"What about the water? They said you had pond water coming from your mouth, it was green and filled with algae," Hearns asked again.

Mary shuddered. "I haven't thought about that since that evening either, I suppose."

"I'm sorry," Frances said, again lightly touching her forearm.

"You've been doing gatherings since, haven't you?" a gruff voice asked from opposite her. He cleared his throat, "Dr. Martin Van Chase. Pleased to meet someone with your illustrious talents, I should add."

"Yes. It started out just a month or two after the first incident. I took them for many reasons, only planning on doing one or two at first, but by the end of February this year I was receiving daily invitations for parlor divinations. They've kept me busy. I try to do only a few a week, as they are rather…draining."

Dr. Martin continued: "I've, or rather, *we've* heard yours are different. The past few have been so…dreary and uninspired. Frances' questions practically sent the last one running for the hills as she changed her answers frequently. I can't say any of us were impressed with *that* meeting. We have faith yours will be different."

"What are the others like? I must admit, save for the first demonstration at the Corinthian Hall I've yet to see one other than my own. Are they similar to the Fox sisters?" Mary asked, her curiosity still piqued after her brief encounter with the young boy.

"Oh, you know. A few thuds here, a rap or two there. The voice of some distant relative calling from beyond the grave. In the span of a year, while the Fox sisters were away touring, it seems like several of those able to communicate with the deceased have recently found their new calling."

The light of the candle reflected off the lens of his glasses, giving him the appearance of an owl. He spoke like he was delivering a university lecture, his voice bored and self-assured.

"Yet we've heard you are all together novel is this new phenomenon we are witnessing in our current day. Tell us before your demonstration, if you wouldn't mind, what your past—what did you call them now? Divinations, I quite like that—*divinations* have comprised of."

"Oh, I haven't a formula, I suppose. Each one is different, though the trend seems to be that everyone joins hands around the table lately. Sometimes when I go to the Otherside it's only darkness. I can hear a voice, or voices, and they call out to me. Sometimes they're random, while other times they know someone at the table and wish to pass along a message. At other times I stay in the room, and like the Corinthian Hall it's empty save for some spirit who approaches me. A few gatherings I've been whisked away to other locations. I never know what to expect, to be honest. It's all so...so..."

"Chaotic?" Dr. Martin looked over the rims of his glasses.

"That's right. There's no rhyme or reason to any of it, it seems. I haven't the faintest idea why I can see the Otherside, nor any idea how to control myself within it. I feel like an intruder more often than not."

"Well, well...I am certainly intrigued, Miss Mary. I'm sure there'll be time for questions afterwards but for now," Thomas set his hands on the table and looked around, "let's get started."

***

Something was different.

The darkness was still everywhere, but now it frothed and turned like a tumultuous sea bludgeoned by a storm overhead. The ripple became a wave, then waves, and the space around her vibrated with a charged energy that seemed directed at her. There was no change of color to signify the increased motion above, but still she knew. She could see it, even if not in the same way she saw the shore of Lake Ontario or the skies above. Sense it, perhaps. Something around her stirred.

Mary tensed, waiting for an attack or rush, but the vast expanse above her seemed content to simply unveil its power above and below and around her. At any moment it could crash down, it seemed to say, and there was nothing she could do about it but wait and see.

She was at the mercy of the void.

A wind brushed across her face and tugged at her hair. It was warm and smelled like edge of a stagnant pond during a particularly hot day, or a dead peddler boy screaming about his unjust murder.

Mary knew both well.

She waited and waited for the scenery to change: to be taken back to the empty parlor or some abandoned road to listen to some rambling spirit carry on about its untimely demise. But nothing happened save for the tempestuous display of power above. She cried out, but her voice was drowned out by both the wind and the crashing around.

Slowly through the gulf of darkness silhouettes emerged. The outlines of people stretched on endlessly until they looked like nothing more than little dots, and still they went on. In every direction too, no longer constrained to the laws of the earth. How many, Mary couldn't even begin to guess. Perhaps before her was the endless sea of those who had lived before and perished.

Every version of them too, that voice said, *the sides of them that loved their family, and the side of them that hated them for ruining their ambitions. The version of them that loved their spouse, and the one that wanted to love another... The whole human experience, laid out for you to see and hear if you'll only listen.*

At a loss for what to do, Mary relaxed and tried to make sense of the gathering around her. The babble of millions of voices in countless languages sounded, converging into little more than a hum.

Then something appeared amidst the never-ending gathering. It was a familiar outline. She racked her memory to place them

Statues. Minerva and Venus. The parlor.

A glimmer of gold flashed through.

***

The parlor was a scene from a nightmare.

The candlelight illuminated faces trying to cry out in horror, but in place of their screeches only black sludge dripped down from each mouth. The garbled screams sounded like water rolling and bubbling over rocks in a stream, Mary tried to stand, to call out for help. All around them voices called out from the shadows.

"Thomas, this is your father, you dishon—"

"Jennings I should have disowned you, you ungrateful—"

"Hannah, your brother should have received the inheritance you conniving—"

Behind them all an orchestra of wails sounded, howling and filling the room with cries of suffering. Despite the statues the parlor had transformed. Although gold was still the prevalent color, everything else seemed changed. Different furniture lined the walls, and the faces on the portraits were different than Mary remembered.

The spirit of the room, something within her said as the chaos raged around her.

You must go back.

***

Fog rushed around her feet, all the way up to Mary's waist. She was in the cemetery, but she wasn't alone. There, standing beside her tombstone was her mother. Her mother glanced down at her tombstone with a look of sadness, then towards Mary.

"Mary, you have to go back to wherever you were. You shouldn't be here. You have to go," her voice was urgent, yet gentle.

"Please, I have to talk to you. I never got to say good—"

"How would that have made any difference? Mary, you have to leave this place. I never told you this, but on your father's deathbed the last thing I promised him was I'd keep watch over you, and I wouldn't let anything bad happen to you. Something bad is coming, Mary. I love you now as I always have, sweet girl. I'm so proud of you. I'm so, so proud of you. Go back Mary. Shut the veil, quickly."

There was nothing she could do. As soon as she uttered her final sentence Mary's mother dissipated into the fog below. Mary sprinted towards the tombstone and began clawing at the fog. She dug and sobbed, then dug some more, but each time her hands came up empty as the fog swirled about unbothered by her actions. The tears flowed and still Mary tried to find her mother, but it was hopeless.

I didn't get to tell her.

In an act of desperation, she herself didn't understand, Mary took the beloved daguerreotype of her mother, carefully unwrapped the silk protection, and opened the leather binding. The silver-plated image of her stared back up at Mary as she slowly lowered it into the fog, letting it rest on whatever the ground below which only now could she make contact with.

Perhaps, if Mary had time to unpack the final conversation with her mother and her subsequent act, she might have seen the last gesture as the closing of a chapter: the realization that the promise of contacting her mother in the afterlife was not something she wanted to further dedicate her life to, and that the daguerreotype, cherished though it was, would always be a reminder of her strange dips into the other side. Or, she might have justified it as leaving her mother a piece of her in life: a reminder of what her time in this world (whatever that means) had looked like. Maybe she would have simply seen it as following her gut and that same voice that told her to bring it in the first place.

As it were, things started to move too quickly for Mary to have any of these thoughts. The chance to process the night, sadly, would not be afforded to poor Mary. Once the offering to her mother disappeared from view, completely swallowed by the fog, Mary was back in the

***

Parlor.

Faces horrified and streaming with tears stared at her in the candlelight. Opposite of her the Doctor was sobbing softly, only the sound of his gargled moan filling the room.

"How did he know…how did he *know*…" Hearns' voice finally broke the horror-struck silence.

Somewhere within the house a plate clattered, dropped by a servant preparing a meal of coffee and desserts. Eyes darted nervously to the door, sweat trickled down temples and a few men, looking to save face before the light was turned on, dabbed at tears of terror. The gravity of Mary's meeting with her mother quickly subsided as she was pressed to deal with the table of shell-shocked socialites. Hearn's continued to mumble though his voice regained some confidence as he went on.

"The spirits can be…ungrateful at times. Sometimes I think they say things they never would have in person," Mary tried to sound comforting, but given the fearful and shamed looks of those surrounding the table it did little good. "The Otherside can change some of them and sometimes they show a different side of themselves than was the one we knew. I'm sorry. I'm so sorry you all suffered. I didn't mean for that to happen, I'll never conduct another—"

Frances placed her fingers on Mary's arm.

"It's not your fault, Mary. The lights." She turned to her husband who quickly scurried to turn on the gaslights about the room.

A quick hiss, a spark, and light spilled across the table and its surrounding occupants. All were pale, glistening with perspiration, and the air of sophistication that had permeated the room and surrounded the gathering was long since gone, replaced instead with the stale-stench of terror sweat. Only Frances seemed unshaken.

"Well, as Mary said, the spirits can be cruel. I suppose they're not all that different from living in that regard. I think it best we adjourn to the drawing room and forget this whole evening."

The fear passed: faces turned red with embarrassment. Whether from the secrets revealed by the dead or the fearful response, Mary couldn't tell. It seemed no one knew how to proceed. All eyes fell to her, and when Mary looked away, they next moved on to Frances.

"I think it best we not only forget this evening, but expunge some of those dreadful things we heard from our memories. Nothing but cruel lies, I'm sure. Besides, I don't know about you, but *I* didn't see anything, only heard. So, who's to say it was even who they claimed—"

"You knew my father, dammit. That was his voice sure as the day is long," said a man who to that point had been silent. He slammed his hands down on the table; it shook loudly, its legs scraping on the floor.

On instinct, Mary looked about the room worried the mirror or statues might come crashing down, same as when she first entered. Everything stayed in place, and she felt a strange sense of release.

Why should she care if this parlor was sullied, or robbed, or crashed down, or burned…

Perhaps it was Frances' kindness, or maybe it was an appreciation of beauty which was hardwired in Mary, whatever the case, she was happy to see the outburst had no effect.

"He said he should have disowned me." *Jennings, that was the name used by the voice saying something about "disowning", Mary recalled.* The string of insults hurled from the spirits was fresh in her mind despite everything else. Frances cleared her voice, clearly buying time as she figured how to address the sensitive topic. Mary decided to try to help.

"Cruel. Yes, that's what I was trying to say earlier. You have to understand the Otherside, the afterlife is…what was it you said," she pointed to the man with glasses who stared in shock, his professorial demeanor reduced to one who had been corrected by a student and was struggling to respond as the class chuckled around them.

"Er…ahem…"

"Chaos, I think it was."

"Yes. Yes, Chaos," He tugged on the lapels of his jacket, which seemed to pull him to composure. "And tonight was certainly evidence of that."

"Perhaps the afterlife, or whatever it is, is all the thoughts. All the vicious and nasty and confusing bits of a human, along with the best parts of them. I've often gone to a cemetery behind my house trying to contact…someone special to me." Mary was rambling trying to rephrase what the voice had said.

Her face felt warm, but everyone seemed to relax so she continued.

"Sometimes they talk to me, sometimes they appear to be suffering, and other times they just want to tell me their story. Like Mrs. Frances said, it's not all that different from the living. I don't know what the void is…I think it's mostly bad—maybe completely wicked for that matter—but that doesn't mean that's all there is. It just means…"

She took a deep breath and looked down.

"It's just what chose me, I suppose. I'm so sorry. I ask for—"

"Oh Miss Mary, don't blame yourself. It was I who invited you. Let's all join together in the drawing room and have drinks," Frances said, stopping the tears Mary felt welling in her eyes.

The other guests stood up from their chairs, silent like scolded school children scared a misstep might set their teacher into a fit of rage. It was Hearns who finally broke the silence.

"Well, we did promise this would be like no other night. Bravo Miss Mary, let no one say the Hearns are liars."

A few polite chuckles followed and, though forced, the mood lightened immediately. Within half an hour enough brandy had poured to steel nerves and erase the worst parts of the evening. Even

Mary felt herself relax. It wasn't what she'd wanted, but that final conversation occurred. Though she didn't get to say her piece, at least she got to hear her mother one last time. After seeing what could have been she was grateful for that brief interaction. Even in the vast expanse of whatever lay beyond her mother was caring and good and sweet and all those things she remembered.

Chapter 7

Mary said her goodbyes and left that evening. She promised Frances she would stay in touch. When she stepped outside the carriage was already waiting. The driver opened the door with a slight bow.

"Sounds like they got their money's worth. Heard a few of them whispering about some of the things they experienced...I'd guess most of them saw a little more than was there, by the sounds of it. Seemed like they were frightened good though. Were Mr. and Mrs. Hearns good hosts?" he lowered his voice for the last sentence.

"They were." Mary felt a twinge of guilt for being curt, but she was tired. All she wanted was to collapse into her bed and forget about everything. It didn't help that the drawing room conversation extended well past when Mary had wanted to leave, and as the men drank their brandy and the women their tea, it was all Mary could do not to close her eyes and nod off. Everyone else seemed deathly afraid of allowing a moment of silence, so they chattered a mile a minute asking questions, which if not responded to quickly enough would become rhetorical as the asker plowed on. The gathering was still underway when Mary left, but finally she'd been able to let Frances know, amidst a rambling monologue from her husband, that she needed to get back home. She had a feeling the party would extend later than anyone planned, as she doubted anyone wanted to go home that evening after what they'd witnessed.

"They were excellent hosts," she managed to add as she stepped up into the carriage. "I'm sorry sir, I'm rather tired."

"Of course. A late evening, it was. Is, rather. By my count it's nearly ten thirty. We'll get you home as quick as we can to those guard dogs of yours. I bet they remember me!"

Mary smiled in appreciation, and soon the carriage was off. As the view outside the carriage changed from buildings and houses to farmland, the excitement of the day continued to weigh on her. Shutting her eyes, she bundled herself in the shawl. Although it was still cold out the carriage seemed warmer, more comfortable, than it had before. She grew drowsier, her thoughts going from the evening to strange, abstract memories. Thoughts from her childhood which she'd long since forgotten and places she'd visited long ago that now lazily drifted across her thoughtstream like flotsam down a creek.

It wasn't long before Mary was asleep.

***

"Hold now!"

The driver's shout startled Mary awake. She blinked her eyes to clear them and slowly the interior of the carriage took shape through the haze of sleep. She remembered she was in a carriage heading home from a dinner party.

I must have slept the whole drive.

She looked outside the window expecting to see the familiar sight of the giant trees leading to her property, but it was too dark, and the edge of the forest was too distant to see. That meant they were still some ways away.

"Is everything alright?" she asked.

"There's a tree blocking the way now. Funny, it wasn't there before. Musta' just fell. No worries, I think it's small enough for me to move on my own. Not a thing to concern yourself with, Miss Mary. I'll see to it quickly and we'll be on our way."

The carriage rattled as the driver made his way down, shaking slightly with each movement. She closed her eyes again, felt the warmth of the shawl, and began drifting back to sleep, but the sound of talking outside the carriage brought her to only seconds later.

Is he talking to himself out there?

She strained to hear better, leaning forward and focusing on the voice. Then voices. There was more than one person out there.

They sound angry.

A shout rose above the others who were talking out there. Mary couldn't tell if it was the driver or someone else whose voice she heard.

Maybe they think he knocked over the tree?

The thought was absurd. No one could possibly think a carriage, especially one this small, could take down a tree. Even if it was old and rotted at the base. Then another thought occurred.

Robbers.

It was a trap. The tree was laid out to stop a wagon or a carriage making its way along the road. The route was remote enough so that no one could call for help or alert the authorities in time for it to matter. Another shout was followed by what sounded like laughter. Mary could make out at least four distinct voices, though they weren't clear enough to understand what they were saying.

But why would they choose this road, it would make more sense to choose one near the dock. I mean, no one really takes this route late at night except...

They were waiting for her.

She ducked down in the carriage trying to avoid being seen.

They must think I have money on me from the Hearns.

She had kept her word to Ford and stopped carrying money while traveling, even when being escorted such as tonight, and the Hearns had promised to send a servant with the payment the next day.

Maybe they would just want the carriage.

The voices drew closer, and Mary considered running. Even if she didn't know where they were exactly, she knew the surrounding woods better than most. She could get back home and maybe get the dogs or the rifle her father left behind or…

There was a knock on the carriage door. They were close enough so that she could hear them talk.

"Don't knock on the damn thing, I said open it. Open it now," one of the unfamiliar voices said.

"You ain't gonna do nothing with that gun, right?" The driver asked. A loud thud followed by a moan followed.

"Open the fucking thing. He's useless."

"Don't do any more of that, okay? That's not the plan we agreed on."

"Just open the damn thing. I don't need a bloody sermon."

The carriage door swung open and three cloaked figures stood before Mary. One held a lantern in one hand and a pistol in the other, the other two had rifles. The three men all stared at her. They were complete strangers, and save for a scar running along the jawline of one of the men with the rifles, there was nothing to make them stand out of a crowd.

The lantern reflected on their pale drawn faces, which paired with the cloaks—clearly meant for camouflage—gave them a ghostlike appearance. All three looked tired. There were deep bags under their bloodshot eyes that all burrowed into Mary, forcing her to look away.

The driver was at their feet, crumpled on the ground with trickles of blood running from both nostrils. He began climbing to his hands and Mary started to step down to help him.

"Uh uh uh…you stay there. Don't move from that carriage, ya got it?" Said the man with the pistol as he pointed it at Mary. "Get down right there, got it? I want to see your hands too."

Mary listened, sitting down on the edge of the carriage and placing her hands in her lap. From her perch the three men towered over her, though they kept a few feet distance. The man who spoke looked down at the driver as if he was concerned, or as if something had gone wrong. No one said anything during the strange impasse, which lasted for minutes. Finally, it was the driver who broke the silence.

"There ain't no money in there bo—" the driver said, his voice shaking.

"We don't want no *fucking* money. We're here for her," the man said, gesturing towards Mary with the lantern, his voice louder and surer than before. The smell of whiskey filled the air following the plumes of steam from his breath. It hit Mary like a wave. When he spoke again, he teetered slightly as if about to fall.

"You have no idea just who we are, do ya?" He chuckled as did one of his companions.

Mary looked to their faces to see if she'd missed something, but didn't recognize any of them. The two men who were laughing pulled their hoods down so that it covered most of their faces. The third remained silent, squeezing his rifle so tightly his knuckles bulged and went white. While the other two seemed to be enjoying their little game and were clearly in the cups, their third companion grimaced in rage.

"No, I do—"

"Good, good. Stop looking at me. Look at the ground," he commanded. "You're going to do everything we ask *hiccup* alright?"

"Just let her go, she doesn't have no money either. Her hosts didn't pa—"

Thwack The butt of the rifle swung in a downward arc catching the driver on the side of his face. He let out a grunt as his arms, which had been supporting him as he got to his feet, collapsed from under him and he fell face down on the road. Mary let out a soft cry, and even the man's two companions seemed taken back.

"Jesus Christ Ma—"

"Don't say my FUCKING name."

"Well shit, you didn't have to—"

"Don't tell me what I didn't and did have to do. Rat!"

The other two exchanged nervous glances while the one with the pistol crouched down next to the driver. In the light of the lantern Mary could see his face had swollen, and directly on his cheekbone was a giant purple knot that forced his eye closed. He had regained some semblance of consciousness though, and was once again on all fours fighting his way up. The man leaned in close to his face.

"I'd stop doing that if I was you. I'd *really* stop moving if I was you, in fact. Sit there nice and quiet and you'll have a helluva' better night than you're gonna if you don't stop." His voice was deadpan with no hint of emotion making its way through. Though wobbly, the driver took his advice, pushing back on his hands so that he was sitting on the road in between Mary and the ambushers. Turned sideways, it was tough for her to see if his face was growing worse, but the eye she could see was glossy with confusion.

"That's better," said the man who'd been doing most of the talking to this point, having managed to find his voice after being jarred from the attack. "No more moving like he said, got it?" His tone was different though. He sounded worried. The driver barely nodded, his face scrunching in pain as he moved his head the slightest. The eye that could open still flickered around from person to person in disoriented confusion.

Mary was more scared than she'd ever been in her life. Not only did they know who she was, but it was her they'd set out to trap. Apparently, the trio had watched her movements enough to know she would be coming back on this road late and night, and…

Trio.

That was when it dawned on her.

"You're the Brixley brothers, aren't you? The ones from the trial; Alfred's younger brothers." The pitch of her voice rose as she spoke, there was a hint of pride at making the connection that slowly transformed to fear once more. They were armed: who knew what they were capable of doing?

"GodDAMN it," said the brother who to that point had remained silent. He then belched loudly, and let out a nervous giggle.

Mary looked from face to face, placing names from the sketchings of the three of them that every newspaper had run on the day they were captured: the leader, the second oldest brother, was named Samuel. The one with the scar who'd struck the driver was Matthias, and the one who'd just swore was Robert. Samuel and Robert glanced at each other with the same nervous look they had when Matthias attacked the driver. The revolver wavered and lowered in Samuel's hand as he spoke.

"If you tell anyone about this we'll be back, and a lot meaner next time. You hear me? Consider this a warning. No more mentioning anything about us, you hear. In fact, we'd really like it if you went to the papers in, say, a day or two, and mentioned you had another *vision*, and that whatever the hell you saw told you it was just Alfred. Just clear our names, alright. We'll leave you alone then."

"Can you please do that?" Robert asked, his voice pleading.

"Yea we can't go nowhere no more without people pointing and blaming us for that whole mess. I swear it was Alfred, like I said on the st—" Samuel's voice even took on a begging nature, but he was interrupted by Matthias before he could continue.

"Will both of you shut your fucking mouths this instant?"

He glared at them, spending a second staring each one down until they averted his accusing gaze. When he was done, he turned to Mary. Matthias eyes reflected the light from the lantern in his brother's hand giving them a particularly devilish appearance. The scar along his face had healed poorly, and though the wound appeared old it still puckered with ridges that looked ready to split back open with any contortion of his face. His eyes were wild and evil in the flickering light of the lantern.

"You killed my brother, you know that? You said some things that shouldn't a been said aloud, and you killed Alfred." He paused waiting for a response; an argument perhaps, or the point that his brother was guilty of the similar crime.

Mary remained quiet. He continued after the silence simmered long enough.

160

"These two," he gestured towards his brother whose eyes were still averted towards the ground, "wanted to give you a little scare, with their guns and big talk. I guess what they really wanted to do though is clear their name, same as they did up there before that bastard judge," he spit on the ground. "Blaming it all on Alfred. Poor bastard was so surprised he couldn't even respond at first. He was an idiot, you know? You killed a damn idiot. That's why they said it was all his idea, that he killed the little shit peddler when he found him on that road, they knew he'd just ramble and make threats instead of dragging us all down with em' like he could have. Too dumb to figure out how to get revenge so he decided to just threaten it instead. Just got real riled up at all the wrong people. Just an absolute fucking idiot who couldn't control himself...but he was kin."

"Now you don't got kin, do you Mary?" He took the rifle in his hand and extended his arm all the way in her direction as he asked the question. The barrel wavered only an inch from her face.

I'm going to die tonight.

She closed her eyes and waited for the blast.

"I asked you a question. ANSWER THE FUCKING QUESTION!"

"No, my mother and father are dead. I don't have any siblings either." Her voice quivered.

"That's the problem. I had *different* plans than the two of them. Plans I didn't make anyone else privy too, you see. I don't talk and yell like Alfred did, I plan. You getting it, now? The way *I* see it, and eye for an eye woulda made us even; you killed Alfred with your little act, so I ought to take a kin of yours. That fair?" Matthias leaned his head down, so it was directly level with Mary and stared into her eyes with his wide in feigned sincerity. "It seemed fair to me," he added.

"We didn't talk about this Matthias," Samuel said, lowering the lantern. His voice shook more than Mary's had staring down the rifle.

"We didn't talk about turning on Alfred either, now did we. You just started singing the first chance you got after that little prick all but walked him up to the platform." He turned his head and spit in Robert's direction. "And we didn't talk about asking her, who got us into this whole crock a shit in the first place, to clear our names round town so you can go to the taverns again, did we? I guess we all got our own plans, huh?"

"They were gonna get us all, it's the only choice we had. 'Sides, it was Alfred's idea to take all those rings. We told him to dump it with the body. None of this would'a happened if he listened. Well and if you didn't…" Samuel's voice trailed off as Matthias shot him a look that made Mary's blood run ice cold. "Ah, you know I didn't mean it. The boy didn't give us no choice."

"That's right. And I'll have you know in front of them and the lord almighty himself I ain't endin' up like Alfred, you hear?"

His brothers nodded, then Matthias turned back to Mary.

'Eye for an eye's the way I saw it, and you ain't got no kin to make it even now do you?" He let the rifle fall through his hand until the butt landed with a thump on the frozen ground below. Holding the gun by the barrel with one hand he pulled back this cloak at his waist to reveal a large hunting knife attached to his belt. Matthias grabbed the wooden handle and pulled it from the leather sheath.

"So, I guess we gotta make you pay instead."

162

Mary's heart pounded as she watched Matthias hold the knife at his side, the tip of the blade aimed in her direction. "I ain't decided if I'm gonna leave you alive yet, you ain't gonna be talkin' after I'm done that's for sure, but one thing that'll help your odds is if you tell me the truth: how the hell did you know about that peddler boy? Did you see us or somethin'?"

"I swear I didn't," Mary managed to get out. Her teeth chattered as the adrenaline surged through her body. *I have to make a break for it. He's going to kill me no matter what.* "I didn't mean for anything bad to happen to your brother or you, I swear. I don't even remember talking about it. I fainted—"

"But you did talk about it, and you knew what happened. So, I'll ask once more before I start to get angry," he held the knife up in front of him pointing it in between her eyes, "how the hell did you know what happened to that goddamned peddler boy?"

"He...he told me. When I fainted at the Corinthian Hall, I saw him and he told me you all killed him. His throat had been cut and...when I was unconscious, he spoke through me and told them all what happened."

"Who?!"

"The people who came to check on me."

"You think I believe that crock o' shit? You were walking home, and you saw through the trees. Tell me the truth!"

He dropped the rifle to the ground, ripped back the hood of the cloak, then stepped forward and pressed the knife sideways against her cheek. The blade was cold and even though the edge wasn't pressed in yet, it stung. Matthias leaned forward until he was only an inch away from her face, his rank breath smelled of whiskey and rot and it filled her nostrils. She pulled back slightly, and he followed, his long stringy hair, which had been pulled up in the

163

hood, now dangled to his shoulder as unkept and wild as his beard. The scar was particularly gruesome from this distance, zig-zagging back and forth like the flight path of a fruit fly.

"I'm gonna count to three before I start carvin'. One...two..."

"I'm telling the truth. I didn't see you kill that poor boy. He told me when I passed out and I saw him in the-

***

The three brothers and the driver were gone. Mary was alone, save for a figure that appeared on the edge of the forest walking towards her. It still appeared to be night, and yet she could see much clearer than she could before. Though the leaves and foliage of spring and summer were long gone, the forest seemed thicker, fuller than normal. Fog interwove among the forest clinging tightly to the ground as it blanketed the earth. Trees with gnarled branches that reached out menacingly bristled in the wind behind the boy who approached her.

"I'm sorry it has to be this way. I wanted to meet them before I find them in this place; to give them a slight hint at what awaits them. I wanted to hear and see their fear as they come to the realization that I'm waiting for them, that I will *never* let them find peace. When they stopped you I had to act. I'm sorry, I know you find it...intrusive." The dead peddler's body was still grey and slick with water. It glistened beneath the moon above, which was unnaturally large where Mary was. Blood pumped from his slit throat with each word.

He began rambling, talking quickly as he repeated himself. "I have to tell them I'm waiting for them, that I'll never forgive them. That I will haunt them in this hellish afterlife with everything I have. That I will make them suffer as I did when my body settled into the muck and sludge and the void swallowed me in all its meaninglessness."

"They'll kill me, won't they?"

"He would have anyways. The two brothers would watch him kill you just as they had during my death while Alfred held me and Matthias dragged the knife across my neck, then they will help him get rid of your body. Perhaps you can escape, I can't help much with that. Right now, I'm giving them a pretty good scare though, that I can promise you. I'm letting them know what I'll do when I find them. Same thing I did to Alfred" The corpse of a boy who had been sent out to sell some trinkets and had his throat slit for the trouble smiled at Mary, his teeth strangely white given the condition of his body.

"Maybe you'll get to see your mom if they do get you, the mom you remember. Sorry, I get some thoughts when I'm in there pulling the strings. Maybe you'll get to meet me too: the side of me that just wanted to move away from this god forsaken place."

"But what will it be like? Her...this place...when I—"

"It's different for everyone, I suppose. All I know is you can hurt here, it's different though. Oh, can you hurt, worse than in life even since it never ends. Now Mary," the dead boy stared at her as he spoke, "run."

***

They stared at Mary like she was the devil incarnate.

Even Matthias was taken back; his mouth hung open in horror revealing rotten teeth. The knife was dropped to his side, and the

165

lantern's light still illuminated his eyes like a deer's, though now they were wide open in shock.

"How do you know that? How could you...it was his voice. He's dead, that couldn't be..." The lantern sputtered as Samuel held it in front of him, swaying in his outstretched arm as he cast the light in Mary's direction.

"Quiet," Matthias said as he stepped backwards, careful and measured with each step and never looking away from Mary. "It's just one of them tricks you'll see at shows. She learned how to change her voice. Besides, you didn't hear that peddler boy say any more than twenty words—how would you know what his voice sounded like?" He dropped down and scooped up the rifle as he spoke, eyes unwavering as he watched Mary. "That thing you said about Alfred wasn't all that nice, I ain't gonna forget that, ya hear?" The rifle raised and the barrel pointed at Mary.

"She couldn't of known about where we sunk the b—"

"This bitch followed us to the marshes after seeing us do him in. It ain't that hard to piece together. She's trying to scare us. Quit your blubbering." The rifle lowered, however. Matthias took hold of the barrel once more and drove the butt into the ground beneath. He winced as he did, and for the first time Mary realized he'd had a strange gait to his step, likely from an old injury she figured.

Robert spoke for only the second time that evening, his voice clearer and less slurred than before. Whatever had happened while Mary was gone sobered him up a bit it appeared, at least for the moment.

"I think Samuel's on to something. We best leave them alone and make our way back. They said they'd cover for us, say we never left the tavern, but they might not be so accommodating if this night turns ugly." Robert hiccupped and burped once more.

"Besides, she couldn't've known some of that even if she followed us. No need gettin' tangled up in all that spiritual nonsense on top of all this." After speaking Robert produced a large leather bladder from beneath his cloak and took a pull. He gasped as he finished the gulp of whiskey, and after catching his breath he took another long drink. His face contorted as the liquid burned.

"Now you're fallin' for it too? Shoulda known you would. Look at you, can't even do this without needing to be stone drunk."

"I agree with him. I just don't like it is all, either. Robert's right. Besides, we set out to scare her, I think she got the drift. You gonna clear our name?" Samuel held up the lantern and looked to Mary who nodded her head vigorously. If Robert agreed, he didn't say so. Mary looked to him before responding and noticed him staring off above her head, the sobering effects of the fright having quickly worn off.

"I swear I'll go right into town and say I had another vision that he's satisfied with Alfred being punished, that—"

"No, you won't. You'll go right into town and say we held you hostage. That you had another vision n' that bastard told you all three of us took a turn with the knife. Won't you?" Matthias spit at the ground as if the words he'd just spoken had left behind a bad taste in his mouth. "You can trick em', but not me. I see through all your tricks and lies."

Mary was about to explain that she wouldn't go to the officials, that if they let her and the driver continue on their way the night would be forgotten. That for the rest of her life she'd stuff the memory down until it withered away like a plant without water, until eventually it would be forgotten completely. That was what she was going to say, but Mary never got the chance.

The next minute was a blur. As the words took root in her mind, the driver, who seemed too concussed to make a stir, suddenly roared to life. With a yell he dove towards the rifle that Matthias was using like a cane.

"You fuckin' Irish bastard!" Matthias screamed as he tumbled to the ground, his voice the guttural cry of a wounded animal. As he posted on the ground to lessen the impact of his fall a loud crunch, like the snapping of a log beneath the wheel of a carriage, filled the air. Mary saw the knife tumble from his hand as Matthias instinctively brought the wounded arm up to his face to inspect the damage. He didn't have much time though. The driver grabbed onto the butt of the weapon while Matthias retained his grip with his uninjured hand and began raining kicks from the ground. The gun connected the two men as they wriggled about looking like a giant squirming python, Matthias pulling the weapon up to prevent the driver from getting his finger on the trigger or getting grabbed hold to, while the driver tried to pull himself up to do exactly that. It was a matter of seconds, but everyone else seemed frozen in a state of shock.

"One of you idiots shoot him. Shoot him now," Matthias cried out as the driver managed to clasp onto his kicking leg with the arm not gripping the rifle. Mary thought she saw the driver grin, but realized he was just baring his teeth that were soon dug into Matthias' ankle, who shouted in pain. "FUCKING SHOOT HIM!"

At once his brothers came too. Still holding the lantern Samuel raised it above the two battling men, making sure he had enough light for a good shot. He leveled the pistol at the driver's head, who was only a few feet away, closed one eye and…

He was too focused to see her coming. Robert cried out to warn him, but it was too late. Mary lowered her shoulder as she barreled forward from the step of the carriage. When she made contact all her force drove into his gut. He let out a pained grunt that was followed by the loud retort of the pistol being fired in the air as his arm swung to regain balance. As Samuel tumbled back, the whiskey he'd drunk earlier to steal his nerves gurgled in his gut, and even before he could brace himself or regain his footing, vomit began pouring from his mouth.

Robert was not faring much better. Though he'd called out to warn his brother, the sudden flurry of activity was all too much for his booze-addled brain to unpack. Of the three Robert was by far the drunkest, and though initial bursts of clarity emerged over the past few minutes, everything was now happening so quickly he could do little but watch.

Mary charged Samuel once more. With the pistol fired and now empty she felt a surge of hope. If the driver could get the rifle, or if she could help him do so, they might walk out of the night alive. Again, Mary's shoulder found its mark, this time crushing into the tall man's groin. Another loud grunt was followed by a screech as he fell to the ground and the lantern flew from his grip.

As drunk as he was Robert finally managed to realize that, the way things were going, he was in for a rough go of it if there wasn't a sudden change. Though the candle was somehow miraculously still lit, the lantern was on the ground, which made it increasingly darker than when Samuel had been using it. Robert stumbled towards the light, but about two steps in had a change of heart and turned to aim his rifle at Mary. The barrel was as unsteady as he was, and the business end looped about missing Mary for most of its circuitous path.

Standing above Samuel—who was stiff as a board laying on his side as he squeezed his legs together and grabbed his wounded groin, spittle, vomit, and mucus all coating his face— Mary kicked him once more in the gut with the tip of her foot and stepped to the side. Robert's rifle was slow to follow.

She didn't know whether she should charge Robert as she had his brother, or help the driver who still had his hands full with Matthias as the two men continued wrestling for the rifle, letting out alternating cries of pain as the fight went back and forth. The decision was made for her when Robert began to speak.

"Now things has getten, er, gotten out of hand. Let's all calm down now." His hand went under his cloak and Mary worried he was about to pull out a pistol; instead, the bladder of liquor appeared in his hand once more. "I know it wasn't right what we did," he pulled the cap off with his teeth, still trying his best to keep the rifle fixed on Mary while holding it with only one arm. He took a long swig of alcohol, his eyes never leaving Mary. "I know it was bad n' all, but you tell that boy to leave us alone."

A loud cry from beside them forced both to turn. The hilt of the knife stuck from the driver's gut; his face squished in pain as he let out a deep exhale, then a cough that sprayed blood over Matthias face. Both men still had a hand on the rifle between them, and both were sitting up facing each other as if in a booth at a restaurant having a conversation instead of being in a life and death struggle.

It was clear that if Matthias won, she was dead.

Mary started to move in their direction hoping the knife wound wasn't fatal and she might help get the rifle. She moved as fast as her feet could carry her across the few feet that separated them, planning on landing the same blow that had incapacitated Samuel to the side of Matthias head as he sat still trying to pry the rifle free.

"Stop! Stop r—"

crack

In the hours to come as the alcohol was emptied from the bladder with long frantic gulps, and as the clarity cut through the fog of the booze, Robert would claim the gun went off in his hand. As they cleaned up their mess he would say he just wanted her to stop moving, that he was amidst telling her such as the bullet accidentally left the barrel of the gun, the same one he used for hunting deer in his free time in the same swamps her friend Ford hunted, and where Mary's body would be unceremoniously laid to rest.

He would say it was all an accident. A sad mishap.

Whether an accident or an immediate drunken reaction, the gun fired. The rifle, an old flintlock Hawken style, erupted with a poof of smoke that filled the surrounding area. The horses neighed loudly, and for a moment it appeared as if they might take off over the fallen branch, but after the initial shock they settled.

As the smoke cleared the two men stopped their struggle though neither relinquished their hold on the gun and looked about: first to self, to see if they'd been hit, then to Robert who stared at the gun in his arm like he didn't know what it was, then around.

As the gun smoke thinned until only ribbons of grey were left hovering through the air the scene became clearer, and all eyes fell on a crumpled mass laying only feet away from Matthias and the driver. The ground beneath was already pooled with blood. Mary lay still.

Matthias seized the moment. In a sudden lunge he grabbed the protruding knife handle with his good hand, letting go of the rifle as he did. As the driver tugged back, finally in control of the weapon, he believed would save his life, Matthias yanked upwards with all his might, pulling the knife toward his opponent's sternum.

Blood spilled from the driver's mouth and the rifle clattered to his side. He slumped forward and moved no more.

"You shot her, didn't you? She was gonna attack me and you shot her. You got more in ya' than I thought." Matthias winced as he spoke. He labored to his feet, clutching his wounded wrist close to his stomach as he stood. Meanwhile Robert babbled, taking drinks all the while.

"It just went off, I didn't mean to," his hand shook as he brought the bladder to his mouth. The whiskey poured from the corner of his mouth as he tilted his head back. When he was done, he continued: "I swear I didn't pull the trigger. The gun's old. It just *hiccup* went off in my hand. Oh god…" he let out a long groan.

Samuel still wreathed in pain on the ground, taking drawn out gasps like a fish out of water. Matthias looked at him and let out a disappointed grunt. "Fat lotta help you were." He returned his attention to Mary.

"Lordy Robert. You got her right in the face." Matthias stooped down next to the body and leaned his head beside Mary's. There was a small, quarter size hole beside her right eye.

"Caught her right in the temple looks like, then," he pointed to a bloody crater in the back of her skull, "went all the way out. Didn't think you had it in you," he sucked his teeth and shook his head. "Takes care of that problem. But now we got a new one. What are we gonna do with them? Gonna have to do better than last time."

He chuckled at the last bit, meanwhile his brothers both cleared the tears from their eyes, albeit each was crying for entirely different reasons.

"They'll do what they did to Albert if they find us," Robert said, his voice cracking as he spoke. He shook the bladder and its contents sloshed about, then he took another sip. "We gotta get rid of them. Matthias, you killed the driver so if I go d—"

"Hush with all that. We're all on the gallows if they find em, no questions asked. Sammy, gather up your balls and start helpin'. Robby, you do the same."

The three brothers worked for the next half hour collecting the bodies and all the weapons used into a giant heap. At one point Samuel suggested using the carriage they'd arrived in to transport both Mary and the driver, but Matthias quickly overruled that idea, pointing to the fact the carriage would be hard to sink or hide.

In the end, they lugged all the evidence of their misdeeds to the wagon that had brought them there that evening, and that they had tied up down the road. Before leaving they removed the branch that had corralled the horses, and with a smack to the lead's back leg sent the carriage riding off into the night.

"Shame, it was a fine carriage," Matthias muttered as made his way to the wagon.

***

The three brothers drove past farms and forest, following nearly parallel to the Genesee River to their east as they made their way towards the coast of Ontario and its surrounding swampland. They knew the way well. With the whiskey gone, Robert took turns telling his brothers about the gun having a mind of its own and various favorite hunting spots for fowl as they drove past. All three had removed their cloaks, bundling them with the wagon full of evidence they needed to get rid of. The ox in front of them lumbered slowly, unconcerned that the wagon behind them was stuffed with murderers, bodies, and evidence linking the two.

"I'm keeping that rifle," Robert slurred as the surrounding forest turned to marsh.

"Thought you said it went off on its own. What good's a gun that does that?" Asked Matthias, barely trying to hide the amusement in his voice.

"It's served me well in the past. Musta' been the charge or the powder. No need to throw it in the lake."

"That's what Alfred said about the rings," Samuel said.

"This is different. He didn't have no rings before. I'm keeping it."

"Suit yourself."

The wagon lurched forward as Samuel, who held the reins, spurred the oxen on. The ponds and marshes on either side of the road were only partially frozen, strange for this time of the year but all the better for them.

"How far in we wanna go?" Samuel asked.

"I know a real secluded area where I hunt duck comi—"

"Keep driving 'till you hear the Lake. Got it?"

"Yes Matthias."

There were no bugs out with it being winter, but out of habit from his hunting trips Robert pulled up the neck of his shirt as far as it could go. They passed no houses, and soon the road would end.

"You don't think there's any truth to that spiritualism stuff, do ya?"

"You finally act like a man saving us back there and right away you go to this shit. You sound like a child askin' about monsters in the woods." Matthias spit out the side of the wagon.

"But that stuff she knew, and her voice changed—you all heard it!"

"Same as I said before, same tricks those travelin' magicians do. Nothin' happened but she saw us or had a lucky guess, and wanted to make a living off scamming rich folks in the parlor."

"But the voice."

"To hell with the voice, now shut the hell up and go back to your whiskey. Sammy, I think I hear 'er."

"It's empty."

"Shut it!"

The night was silent save for the occasional hoot of an owl. The wagon halted and the road had come to an end. High grasses poked through the frozen water in front of them, and throughout the patches of dry   land large fir trees towered above. It seemed both marsh and woodland had converged before the wagon.

"Grab as much as you can. We'll take the old Haudenosaunee hunting trail into the marshes." Matthias and Samuel grabbed the body of the driver, while Robert grabbed an armful of weapons, minus the rifle. "We'll come back for her," Matthias said, nodding towards Mary, whose body was draped with the cloaks.

"What if someone…" Robert's question trailed off, and no one answered. It was too late, and they were too remote; no one would find or look into the wagon. Even if they did, well, they picked the wrong night to get noisy; the swamp by the lake was certainly big enough for one more body.

The path, which was normally muddy and difficult to trudge through, was much easier to traverse in the cold. With the water frozen along the edge and the ground in a similar state the trio made good time, even carrying the broken body of the driver. When one of them shifted their grip blood, which had pooled in the cavernous wound, would slosh to the ground with a heavy splash.

On occasion, Matthias would let out a grunt of pain as either his wounded arm gave out, or the leg that still had a bullet in from a past altercation at a tavern failed to find solid ground rolled in a painful manner. A string of curse words followed each time.

"The marsh'll get rid of it," Matthias muttered every few yards, as if convincing himself. They walked about a half mile total. If they'd gone further north they'd have been greeted by a strip of wide beach covered with flotsam and driftwood and the lake, and if they turned east or west, they would have found nothing but more swamp and eventually farmland.

Instead, they stayed on the strip that they'd been following. The path continued climbing upwards slightly, and the swamp temporarily gave way to a thin forest with trees that towered high above them; even higher above, the stars and moon danced against the cosmic backdrop. A quarter mile in either direction and trees would have been a rarity, cleared by farmers or drowned by swamps that made it difficult for them to take root, but here they grew unimpeded from human hand or nature's competition. It was a place few went anymore.

About halfway up the ridge and dripping in sweat, Matthias and Samuel dropped the body. Both leaned forward and put their hands on their knees as they sucked in air. The cold air singed their lungs as they panted. Matthias looked down at his arm, which already had begun to swell.

"Are we throwing him in the Lake?" Robert asked.

"No…no…tide might bring 'em in too soon," Matthias managed between deep breaths, gritting his teeth as he spoke. "She don't have no family that I know of, but I suppose *someone'll* be looking for her, and someone will *definitely* be lookin' for him. Might even be people sent out this morning when he doesn't return with that fancy carriage they were driving. No, we couldn't get em' out far enough on a lake too prevent em' from possibly washing back in. Let's look around this bog and see what we can't find though."

"He's a heavy bastard. Let's leave him here and find the spot before we lug him there…that alright with you Matthias?"

"Sure Sammy, that's good thinkin'. Hey how you holdin' up?" The lantern caught the smirk on his face as he asked, and Samuel chose to ignore the question as he responded.

"Not far from here there's a particularly rough part. I doubt anyone goes, I think I know where it is." He gestured with the lantern off the footpath towards a small break in the surrounding marshes. "There's a few ponds surrounded by the marshes that might be a good place for…well it'll work for us, I'm thinkin'."

"As long as it's better than the one we used 'fore. Robert, you know these trails better than us—you know what he's talkin' about?"

"Think so. We gotta be careful though. There's some drop offs that sneak up on you close to the water if we ain't careful, but I think I know where he's sayin'. Watch for the gulleys though."

"Let's get there, and quick. This cold is gettin' to me."

Matthias dropped back as Samuel and Robert took the lead. They were moving downhill now, surrounded by tall ridges that jutted from the earth in all directions, forming a natural way for them to follow. They moved quickly, only occasionally stopping when the ridges made a crossroads so Robert could look for a sign that remained hidden from the other two. The deeper they went, the worse the way became. Both Samuel and Matthias slipped multiple times—sometimes their feet would catch a hidden root that snaked up from the ground, while other times the frozen edge of the marsh would give way beneath a boot and their legs would drop into freezing water below while cusses filled the air above— Robert would look back to make sure they were still there then continue moving ahead.

By the time they found the spot they were looking for, the two of them were drenched and covered in mud and gunk up to their knees, while Robert remained unsullied. The three brothers made a final push up a slight incline, their lungs burning while the candle in the lantern was the only thing guiding them through the dark, until they were looking over a body of water somewhere between a bog and pond.

"Think that's it there, right Sammy?"

"That's the one. There's another bigger one not far from here...this'll do though."

The water was covered by ice. Near the shore where the ice was thin, the green water beneath was still visible, though towards the center as the ice grew thicker it went from grey to white. The lantern shone bright enough to reflect off the frozen top, making it sparkle and twinkle like an emerald held to the light for inspection. The edges were unfrozen, and water seeped around reeds that surrounded the pond in its entirety. If it was warm, the smell of stagnant water would have bombarded them once they were within visibility; however, since it was winter, the sweet smell of fir that stood tall beside them on the overlooking ledge greeted them instead. It was tough to make out in the dark, but as Matthias strained his eyes, he noticed steep drop offs surrounding the edge of the water and walls of trees above.

It was perfectly concealed.

A few pockets of snow were still scattered along the ridge; it was noticeably chillier than it was inland.

"There's rocks here too," Matthias noted as he pointed to one sticking halfway through the ground. "We'll fill their clothes up with em' so they don't float. Not making the same mistake as last time."

The walk back went quickly. All three found a second wind, Robert and Samuel out of fear of discovery while Matthias was just sick of being out in the cold. Lucky for Matthias, the surge of adrenaline from the night still prevented the pain in his wrist from being unbearable.

They found the driver where they'd left him along with the cache of weapons, and after loading up once more they made the trek back to the body of water. Along the way the driver was dropped no less than three times, dragged by Matthias after Sam's arms grew too heavy, and treated with the general care one might afford a sack of flour or cornmeal.

When they arrived back at the water, Matthias took the largest rock he could locate from an outcrop of stones nestled within the ridge above and tossed it with all his might atop the frozen surface. It landed with a loud *crunch*, sinking halfway through the ice amidst a growing spider web of fractures. A colder winter might have required more effort, however, this one was fairly mild, and another heaved stone did the trick, breaking apart the ice enough for a clearing that a man might wade to his chest before reaching the new edge of the ice. Beyond that, the frozen lake twinkled beneath the stars and moon above.

"We gonna put him there?" Robert asked, looking down at the body.

"Too shallow. Any hunter or fisherman might find him if we dropped em' right on the edge of it. I figured we could load him up on the ice there and push him closer to the center. Don't know if it'll work—but at least they'll be a bit deeper. Less chance of anyone findin' 'em."

"You goin in there? You're crazy." Samuel said as he gathered rocks, piling them beside the mud and bloody body of the driver.

"We're all goin' in."

"No way in hell. I'll freeze solid, probably die from it."

"I agree with Sam—"

"You'll die a lot quicker if they find em'. You know Albert shit himself up there on the gallows."

"Why'd you have to bring that up...fine. I wanna be quick though. In n' out then back for her. My cloak doesn't have any blood on it either so I'm wearin' it once we go in the water, ya hear?"

"Whatever'll get you to shut the hell up." Matthias rubbed his hands together as he spoke, wincing as he'd forgot about the wrist until the pain from the movement radiated up his arm. "I'm freezing too, and you don't hear me bitchin' and moanin'. Just get more rocks."

They gathered all the rocks and pebbles they could find, working in silence as they dug into the cold, claylike dirt to unearth the partially submerged stones. When Matthias grunted in approval after dropping off another haul, both Samuel and Robert joined him.

"Think that's enough?" Robert asked.

"We'll see."

They stuffed the barrels of the weapons, minus the rifle used to kill Mary, which was still beside her in the wagon, with the small stones, then stuffed the larger ones into the shirt and pants of the driver. His clothes were slashed to ribbons already, so when needed, they tore large strips which they used like rope to bind the weighted guns to his limbs. It was bloody work and by the time they were done each man was covered with enough of the stuff to need a quick dip in the pond, even if that wasn't where they were heading.

"Grab hold of him like you did when we brought him over, Sammy. Robert, you're gonna hold his middle so he don't fold in half."

"Ah, Matthias that's where his guts is spillin..." The scowl sent his way stopped Robert mid-sentence. "Alright, alright, I'll grab him. Just flip him over so I don't gotta touch where you gutted him, alright?"

"I'm gonna strip down, I don't want my clothes bein' all wet," Samuel said. The other two nodded in agreement. In a matter of minutes all three brothers stood nearly naked, shivering and clasping their hands to their shoulders in an attempt to stay warm. Samuel moved the lantern to the waterline.

"Let's be quick," Matthias said as he positioned himself by the body.

They lifted him from the ground with a trio of grunts. They were tired and he was much heavier than before on account of the rocks.

"It's like moving one of pa's scarecrows. A fuckin' heavy one though," Robert noted as they moved towards the waterline. If some unlucky passerby were to stumble upon the scene that night, they would have been greeted by an almost occult precession: three, wild-looking naked men carrying a body into a frozen lake by the light of a flickering lantern. Upon closer inspection they might have seen that the strange, brace-like supports tied to various limbs f the sacrifice were in fact, a disassembled rifle and pistol, or perhaps they would have taken off running before such things could be noticed—who's to say? Since no one interrupted the peculiar proceeding, the brothers were able to move fast.

Matthias, who was supporting the driver's shoulders, hit the water first. He grimaced as the marsh water climbed up his body. By the time it reached his manhood Matthias was struggling not to scream. His teeth clattered and he contracted his muscles out of instinct, trying to shrink away from the frigid water that seemed to seep into his very being.

"F-f-f-f-uck-k-k-k-k m-m-m-m-m-ove f-f-f-f-f-aster," for the first time that evening his demeanor broke, his voice pleading as the water climbed higher and higher up his naked body. Robert took a deep breath and plunged into the water. Samuel went last.

The body sunk into the water as they waded towards the recently formed edge of ice. Matthias made note, though he was in no state to tell his brothers the plan was working. The water was around his neck by the time he reached the ice, and without instruction he lifted the driver's head and shoulder onto the shattered edge. With a gentle push he guided the man's body onto the ice.

"K-k-k-k-eep p-p-p-pushin'. S-s-s-oft."

They listened.

The body was soon lying face down on the ice, carefully laid out to distribute the weight as much as possible. Matthias moved to the shore as quickly as he could; with confused looks on their faces the other two followed.

Once on the shore they each shook off as much water as they could before bundling themselves in their clothes, using them as if they were blankets. It took several minutes for teeth to stop chattering, but when they did Matthias spoke before either Robert or Samuel could ask the question he knew was coming.

"I'm gonna' find a stick and see how far I c-c-an push em' out. It might be a few feet, it might be more. I don't know. Seemed like it might work. While I do that you two go get the rest of the stuff. Bring those cloaks too. Quickly!"

Robert and Samuel scurried up the ridge and disappeared into the night, leaving Matthias alone to sink the body. He rooted about the surrounding forest floor, searching for a fallen branch that might serve to push the body further across the ice. As he scoured the forest floor, the cold grew unbearable; it nipped as his skin, and even the swaddling of dry clothes did little to warm him. He began gathering a pile of kindling and sticks much too small to push the weighted body, and after fishing about his pants pocket and finding the flint and small scrap of steel he always carried with him for such occasions, he started a fire.

It was a small thing, nothing that would draw attention or risk giving away their location, but even the slight flicker of flame was enough. He abandoned searching for a larger stick for the moment and instead curled up as close as he could to the fire. Most of the small branches and leaves he scrounged up from the base of trees were still dry, and the fire soon gave way to smoke. Small wisps rose from the miniature pyre, making Matthias eyes, which were practically above the fire, water. He didn't care—the warmth was too important. He laid his clothes as close to the flame as possible, then laid on top of the makeshift mat.

It was in this prone position, eyesight obscured by both tears and smoke, that Matthias noticed a strange thing. The smoke from the fire puffed and flared, and as he coughed and spit attempting to clear the acrid taste from his mouth and the burning from his lungs, it seemed to take an unnatural shape: an almost human form, even. A woman with a billowy dress that trailed behind her like a *Corpse being dragged.*

Matthias blinked his eyes and wiped at them with his wrist. When they were mostly cleared, the figure disappeared. A figment of imagination from being cold and tired, he figured.

Before he could give it anymore thought the shrill sound of Robert's voice cut through the night.

"What are you doing? You're gonna get us found!" He charged down the ridge set to scurry the fire, but as soon as Matthias stood up, he stopped in his tracks.

"Someone's gonna see us, we're gonna get caught," Robert pleaded, his voice shrill and whining.

"There ain't a farm that could see us all the way out here, even if there was enough smoke to make it above the trees. This small fire won't be seen by no one, ya hear?"

Robert only grumbled in response.

"He made me carry her all this way, can you believe it?" Samuel said as he walked down towards the lake with Mary slung over his shoulder.

"I can believe it, 'n fact."

"See he's still on the ice." Robert looked down at the ground when he spoke.

"I suppose you're right, little brother. Let me see to that…give me one of them cloaks first though." Robert bundled it into a ball and tossed it to Matthias who threw it across his shoulders. He was still partially undressed, his clothes still laid out beside the pathetic fire.

"Warm yourself up while I see to him. She'll be next."

Matthias disappeared into the surrounding forest and swamp, returning minutes later with a dried log as tall as he was. Without a word he walked past his brothers who were crouched over the fire close as he'd been and plunged into the lake. Holding the piece of wood above his head, Matthias headed towards the body that was still supported on the ice below, though his shoes, stuffed with as many stones as they could hold while still staying on the driver's feet, dangled in the water as if he was testing the water before taking a dip, the ice beneath having broken away.

It was delicate work, especially considering the gruesome nature of it, but Matthias poked and prodded at the body trying to get it further towards the center of the lake. It was like playing billiards, something he had only done twice before, but Matthias was patient. He also wasn't above desecrating the man he'd killed, finding the man's crotch the best place to lodge the stick to drive him forward. Inch by inch turned to foot by foot, and soon Matthias had extended his arm as far as it could go with him falling beneath. Bringing the stick with him he carefully pushed against the ice and made his way back to shore.

"Thought you n' him would go crashin' in any moment," Samuel said as Matthias approached the fire.

"You two c-could only be so lucky." He fought to conceal how cold he was, but the second Matthias stepped from the water his body felt as if it'd been frozen through. "M-move aside."

Samuel scooched over, giving his brother room beside the fire. Robert threw him a cloak, the other one having been soaked through. He removed the wet one and tossed it to the ground. It landed with a loud *slap*.

"Just let me warm up a bit and we'll deal with her."

***

Mary was treated to the same process as the murdered driver. Samuel had found some rope in the wagon that he brought back with him, so large stones were tied to drag her to the bottom of the lake. By the time all was done, Mary weighed roughly the same as the driver who she soon lay beside. The ice cracked beneath their weight, though it managed to hold. Robert guessed them about twelve feet from the edge of the lake, Samuel fifteen.

"Don't matter much—there's a steep drop off not far from where the ice starts, I felt it last time I was in there. If the stones hold they'll get stuck in the sludge down there, then they ain't going anywhere. Sammy, you grabbed all the money and things they had on 'em?"

"Sure did, at least—"

"Walk a bit and bury it. Just a few feet is fine."

"But—"

"Needs to look like a robbery in case they do find em', and remember what happened to Albert? If he didn't have them damn rings on him, he might be alive, and we might not be sinkin' two bodies."

"Yea, yea…just seems like a waste."

"Well get to it."

Samuel disappeared from view, and Matthias began hunting for another rock. Meanwhile, Robert tied all the other evidence in a large bundle using the cloaks that he then filled with the stones they'd already collected. Once it was tied, he took the knot in his hand, and spinning like a shotput thrower he began spinning and spinning and…

With a final twist Robert let go of the makeshift bag.

It sailed over where they'd waded earlier and came crashing down between Mary and the Driver with a loud *crunch*. The ice gave way and the bodies disappeared into the murky green water below.

"Don't need that other rock no more," he called to Matthias, who joined him on the edge of the water.

"Nice toss." Samuel was the last to join them after burying their victims' belongings. The three brothers stared out over the lake and all the shattered ice that trailed to the final resting place of Mary and the driver.

"Never a word. Never, ever a word. This whole mess ends tonight in this damn swamp, you two hear? If anyone asks, we were drinking at Smith's Tavern and them boys said they'll vouch for us," Matthias said. "Never a word."

"Got it."

"Got it."

They doused the pathetic fire with water from the lake and made their way back to the wagon. All three thinking they were quite clever, and though Robert and Samuel both felt a pit of concern in their gut that *perhaps* they *might* get caught, they were able to drown out those voices by the time they were on their way back home. None felt any guilt, it should be mentioned, and all three were convinced the "mess," as Matthias put it, was over.

But as the oxen pulled them away from the swamps, woods, and bogs they'd spent the night traversing along the coast of Lake Ontario, something happened. Though the bodies of Mary and the driver sank deep—deep into that adjoining lake where they would stay until they became nothing more than bones—as they first lay at the bottom of the lake, something floated from the depths to the surface of the churned ice water. It came from a fold in Mary's dress, one that had been searched by Samuel and shaken every which way from the scene of the murder to the lake. One that by all logic should have been empty.

A leather case, within which was a silver-plated daguerreotype that had been left *somewhere* else earlier that evening, but had somehow made its way back to the site of Mary's burial. The veil was ripped, the curtain drawn for more than simple, one-way interlopers to whatever lay beyond this life. There, floating on the surface of the lake, case flipped open, was the image of a woman illuminated by the moon above. One who, like the peddler, and like her daughter, was to cross that bridge in search of something.

…and so started the revenge of The Lady in White.

Part 4
Three Dead Men

Chapter 8

Robert tossed and turned in his bed. The sheets wrapped about him like a noose or a

dress…a ratty, worn train of a dress, wrapping around his neck and face and suffocating him as he kicked and screamed but no one would save him. Alone! Always alone. He was drowning in the dress, in water, in sludge and mud and long, tentacle like weeds that reached up and dragged him down, deeper and deeper and —

A sudden gasp and the sheets flew off, which was followed by a hurried glance about the room. The window was open and though it was summer, and the day had been sweltering, Robert shivered as a breeze blew through the tavern room and across his sweat-soaked body. The curtains trembled in the breeze and took on a dress-like appearance. It was a little too close for comfort given the most recent in a string of nightmares, so he looked away. He thought about closing the window, but the musty smell of the room stopped him from turning thought to action. Instead, he laid back down in the uncomfortable bed, staring up at the ceiling of rough-cut planks. Above, loud creaks, grunts, and moans rattled down.

Someone was getting lucky.

Robert was approached at the bar with a similar offer, but the cost of the tavern was already bleeding him dry. In the end it was a simple economical choice, either booze or a fuck, easy choice. His mouth still burned from the cheap whiskey.

Sleep seemed a distant possibility given the dream and his upstairs neighbors loud romp, so Robert sat up. The mattress was uncomfortable as hell, stuffed only with straw, and it crunched beneath his shifting weight. His whole body screamed with pain as he moved. A moment of silence from upstairs coincided with Robert catching his breath; the void was filled with the sound of scurrying bugs burrowing into the mattress. He took another deep breath. The air was stale and rank, the open window did little to improve that. Neither did the booze sweats which soaked the sheets that hadn't been washed in the past few months at least, Robert guessed. He lit the lantern that rested on the headboard of the bed as they resumed above, let out a grunt, and reached for the bladder of whiskey that had helped him fall asleep before the nightmare.

Those horrid, wretched nightmares…

The whiskey lit his throat on fire, stinging as if he'd taken a huff of smoke as it crawled from gullet to gut. He winced and took a deep breath as the whiskey worked its charm. Across from him was a grime-smeared mirror sitting on a wooden dresser, the only piece of furniture save for the bed occupying the cheapest room Robert could find. The reflection that looked back at him was almost as bad as the dreams. His body was gaunt, skinnier than he'd been even as a child, and his face and arms were burned red with blisters forming across his shoulders and brow. The purple bags under his eyes were so dark it appeared as if he'd been socked twice in a bar fight. Robert looked and felt like a corpse.

It had been nearly a week since his last good meal. Work was hard to come by given the rumors swirling about, but he'd managed to bag a few racoons while hunting. At the end of the day rumors meant little when it came to furs, Robert found. As long as the exchange was done in private, buyers cared little about the provenance of their purchases. Those furs paid enough to last him a few weeks if he'd managed to withhold from buying booze, but that was no longer an option.

Rumors, they're just talk is all, he reminded himself. *The bodies ain't been found, and they won't. Just talk is all, and you can't hang someone on just that.*

Somehow Matthias and Sammy had emerged unscathed; both of them said Robert was seeing things, that he was overthinking the way people stared at him or whispered behind his back.

"You seein' things that ain't there," Sammy had chided him a few weeks back, "You're makin' Matthias worried you're going to say something you shouldn't. You know how he gets...'specially after Alfred. Always worried you're going to say something. You're just seeing things."

He wasn't and he wouldn't though. They were just missing the talk surrounding them, that was it. Robert was staying closer to Rochester than either of his two brothers, he was privy to things they weren't. They were tucked away back on the family farm...*they didn't know.* Besides, *he* knew they couldn't escape forever, even if they didn't realize it yet. Something deep in his gut, call it intuition perhaps, told him there would be a day of reckoning.

Another pull of whiskey. The bladder was now a quarter full. The contents sloshed within while above the noise reached a crescendo. Several more sips of liquor followed. By the time the container was returned to the headboard the romp was over. A few gruff bursts of conversation sounded from above, though Richard couldn't make out exactly what was said. This was followed by the pounding of footsteps and the slam of the door.

His eyes cast to the rifle leaning in the corner of the room. Beside it was the leather satchel that contained the black powder, paper wraps, bullets, and primers. The sight of the weapon and the satchel was comforting. Robert laid back down in the bed, which again crunched beneath him as the hay buckled beneath his shifting weight. He was lighter than he'd ever been, probably lost about twenty or thirty pounds since that night he figured; his body looked like a skeleton, the pale skin stretched tight across bones that stuck out more prominently than ever before. Still, despite how light he was, his body pushed through the stuffing until he could feel the straps holding up the mattress through the sheet and straw. It was like sleeping on a scarecrow. He shifted, burrowing into the cheap mattress until he found the most comfortable spot he could manage.

Against all odds, Robert was soon drifting back towards sleep. The lantern still burned on the headboard above, but the light dimmed, and the room grew dark enough for the whiskey and the all-consuming tiredness to take hold. His eyelids dropped, the promise of sleep lay within reach, but then the whisper startled him awake.

"Where is she?"

His eyes snapped open as he turned in the direction of the voice. He let out a shriek as he saw he wasn't alone in the room. A woman, too pale in some spots and grey in others, towered over him, her dress ripped and torn and as devoid of color as she was. She was impossible, a scream against sanity and all things right. It wasn't that her skin and dress were just bleached, she was translucent. A faint glow emanated from her body, but there was nothing warming or comforting in it. And her eyes! Deep black wells burrowed into Robert, for a moment sucking him into a vast expanse of nothing but rippling darkness that mocked his existence and...

the wriggling damned madness of this chaotic existence.

He begged and begged for her to leave him be. He swore he was sorry for the peddler and the driver and the girl, that it wasn't his idea and he'd never wanted to hurt anyone. The woman simply stared at him from above with those eyes that led somewhere Robert didn't want to go or see ever again.

Her face was like nothing Robert had ever seen before, somewhere between a skeleton and the rotted, water-logged corpse of the peddler boy they'd brought in and paraded before the jury and witnesses during the trial. A thin wrap of some strange material wrapped around her body and face, swirling about her yet clinging close like a boa constrictor wrapping around some traveling purveyor of curiosities. The wrap was solid at some points, see through in others, and it draped across her body like the sheet of a morgue. Even as it ran across her face The Lady in White never broke her incriminating gaze. At any moment Robert knew he might be drowned in her eyes if she so chose, pulled into the same muck and sludge as the bodies he'd help dispose of.

Instead, she drew closer, bending down and leaning her face so close to Robert he felt the crypt-like chill of her breath on his cheek as he lay, paralyzed, praying for rapture or forgiveness.

"I must find her as she found me."

Then she was gone.

***

Robert wept the rest of the night, praying to a God he'd never given much care to before and drinking intermittently as he tried to

195

convince himself he was hallucinating. It was simply guilt and a night terror he babbled, knowing full well it was neither. He'd seen her before, but always out of the corner of his eye as he walked down a dark country road after a hunt or staring at him through the woods, but always disappearing before he could react. She was following him, watching him, waiting for…

This one was different. The woman, whatever she was, was getting closer. Who knew what she might do next?

Robert made up his mind to visit Sammy, to see if he'd noticed anything strange, the moment the sun appeared on the horizon.

He cursed his brothers for dragging him into another mess, double-cursed them for killing someone who could contact the dead and was mixed up in all that spiritualism, and triple-cursed them for saying he was imagining things. He knew it was bad news once Matthias started acting strange that night all those months ago. Sure, it was his gun that went off and killed her…but it wasn't his fault. Matthias was seeing red that evening and the driver attacked them; he and Sammy just wanted to scare her a bit, clear their name and all. It was Matthias' fault. And then to say he was worried Robert would talk and he was seeing things was worst of all. Why couldn't they see what waited for them? Something was coming for revenge, and there was only so long they could escape. He knew they said the whiskey was making him see things, but they were wrong.

Ain't no way I imagined that.

Tomorrow he would talk to Sammy.

***

The farm was bustling when he arrived as the spring wheat was being harvested. The tall stalks that still stood glistened gold beneath the morning sun, waving back and forth as if bracing for their impending doom. It was August, and despite the early hour the air was already hot and sticky; the day would undoubtedly grow to a swelter. Throughout the wheatfield workers with large reapers swung them about in loops, striking down stalks of wheat that were quickly bundled by other workers who followed closely behind.

Even with how busy the scene was, Robert noted half the workers on site that he would usually expect given the size of the farm and the time of year. He had an inkling as to why the farm was understaffed. Standing on the hill above the field, Robert's gaze traced from group to group below until finally locating Sammy standing beside the ox-pulled wagon. The overhead cloth cover was removed revealing the contents of the cart, which were neatly stacked bundles of wheat. From the distance, the bundles took an almost humanlike form. Robert shuddered and licked his chapped lips, instantly wishing he had a drink. He surveyed the scene for another moment, watching Sammy hollar out instructions while pointing to the paid laborers who brought the bundles of wheat to him for inspection before loading it into the wagon.

The sun beat down on his neck and soon grew unbearable. Robert hurried down the hill past the busy scene until he was close enough to hear Sammy's shouts.

"Pick it up, pick it up. We need to make up some time. Jackson, that's only the third one you brought me. Who are you workin' with out there? Nevermind, nevermind pick it up is all. Well look who it is!"

Large, dark pits of sweat already covered Sammy's shirt. He wiped his brow with one hand and took his hat off with the other, holding it above him to block out the sun as he squinted towards Robert.

"You look like hell, brother. You been eatin' and sleepin'?"

"When I can." At the mention of eating Robert's stomach rumbled. He felt a twisting, writhing knot in his gut and found himself hoping Sammy might offer him some food. Food and drinks.

"Well, I'm sure we can scrounge you up a meal 'round here somewhere. Pa…well Pa is how he has been. Ain't makin' a lick of sense and rambling on, caught him out wonderin' last night in fact, but there ought to be food somewhere in the house if you'd like. Think Matthias brought it—"

"He around?"

"No, no. He's makin' a trip to the mill to talk prices," Sammy nodded and let out a whistle. "He's already fired up at the change of price from last season. Whoever he find, there is goin' to catch hell, I'll tell you what. You know him though, pretending he's a businessman or important like Pa was. He's even started writin' in this journal of his. Won't tell me about what though. Ah yes, a regular ol' man of letters, our brother. What was that thing we called him?" He started chuckling and looked towards his brother waiting for him to join in. But Robert's appearance seemed to halt Sammy, who looked down at the ground as he spoke next.

"Now, what made you make the trip out here? I thought you'd be busy trapping this fine morning."

"I gotta talk to you is all." A man wrestling a bundle of wheat rounded the wagon. Robert eyed him with suspicion. "I was hoping we might talk alone. That alright?"

"Sure thing, let's head to the…er, probably the house. Pa's there but, well you know."

"That's fine."

They walked towards the dilapidated farmhouse sitting at the edge of the property. The once mighty building seemed ready to collapse at any moment; Robert felt a sting of anger at his brothers for letting the place get so bad, but it passed quickly. There were more important things to deal with. Still, as they got closer, he had to add: "place looks like hell, Sammy. What happened?"

"It's as old as Pa, and falling apart just the same. Hey, you wanna fix it up? We got some tools in the shed over there." After he was done speaking, he gestured to a small wooden structure beside the icehouse Robert knew too well.

"I ain't going near that thing. Swore the last beatin' was the last time I'd step foot in there. Don't plan on goin' back on it, either."

"Then ain't much we can do about the house then, is there? The harvest has gotta come in if we want to see past winter. Money ain't what it used to be with all these other farms. So, the house stays unless you got an idea."

"Guess not. Pa…?"

"We got him downstairs now. Doesn't leave the room much on account of the peach whiskey barrel we got in there with him. His mind is gone, 'sides, so what's the harm in lettin' him enjoy himself. He sits down there and talks to Alfred, just ramblin' on and on about how he's gonna leave the farm to him."

They were close to the house. At one point the eight-room brick federal style house was painted yellow, that's how Robert remembered it when he thought back to his childhood during those long, quiet escapes into the woods; now, the paint had peeled or stripped and left behind only a pastel of browns, grey, and a sickly yellow-white that looked like someone suffering from jaundice. *Rotting away and decaying like the bodies...*

Robert turned his focus to the previous mention of peach whiskey, but even with that distraction the house was difficult to ignore. Wooden planks missing or smashed to bits on the front porch. Windows were covered in as much grime and soot as the mirror at the tavern. Even bricks were falling away and crumbling as if they were fleeing the structure doomed to collapse. Large weeds jutted from underneath the porch through the numerous cracks, their sickly discolored stalks looking like tendrils reaching out from below to drag them down to the depths.

"I suppose whatever you want to talk about is why you look about ready to keel over, and it's got somethin' to do with that thing we ain't supposed to mention. Am I right?" Sammy stepped over a caved in plank as he made his way across the porch. "Watch your step," he warned his brother when he was standing in front of the door. "She's ready to give up the ghost any minute."

Funny phrasing, Robert looked over his shoulder worried he was being watched. The wheat field behind him wavered in the breeze, and the forest beyond...

Was that her peeking out from the edge?

He cleared his eyes. Just a dead tree hit by lightning. Grey and singed from the flash, but from the distance the stump looked like the lady from the night before.

Sammy was talking, but his words were little more than a monotone drone in the background. He was certain he'd seen something there in the woods. His eyes were attune with picking up the slightest movement in the foliage—the shake of a leaf, the swivel of a deer's head, the slow expanse of a set of wings on a fowl about to hightail it to the sky above—and he'd seen *something* behind the scarred stump. He strained, leaning forward and focusing like he would when trying to unpack the camouflage of an animal or bird on a hunt. Was that the tail end of a dress peeking out from the bottom or just a root? It shuttered and disappeared.

"You coming, or you just gonna stand there looking?" Sammy's voice brought him back.

"Just thought I saw something is all."

"Not much to see out there in the field I reckon'. Findin' workers was tough this year. Think all the other farms are cuttin' in. That winery by the bay, Vinton I think the fella's name is, think he probably hired em all." Sammy's voice was unsure. He knew that wasn't the reason no one wanted to work for them, but he didn't want to say it because he'd be admitting Robert was right about the rumors.

"Hey, you mentioned somethin' about some whiskey?"

"Yea, yea. We'll get you a cup, though by the smell of you I doubt you need another one."

"Can you get it?"

"Yea…yea. Don't want to see the old man?"

"Not since he started talking to Alfred. That made my skin crawl something fierce. I had it in my mind to leave before then, but once that started…"

"Alright, alright. I'll be right back with a cup."

"Can you fill this too?" Robert tossed Sammy the deflated bladder he'd slung to his belt. Sammy caught it and looked down at the capsule with a shake of his head. "Sure thing. Then we can talk. You know the place, find wherever you wanna talk. I'll be back."

Sammy disappeared downstairs to where the kitchen and dining room were. Robert followed, stepping as softly as he could. He stood at the top of the stairway and peered into the basement level below. The stairs were caked with dust and mud, and even from where he stood the rank smell of sweat, piss, and shit forced him to cover his mouth. Lord knows the last time the chamber pot down there had been emptied. The bottom of the stairs where the two rooms split was unlit, a single slit of a window provided light to either space. It was like staring into a wintering bear's cavern. Same smell, same cavernous darkness.

Even before he'd left, his father had taken occupation of the dining room as his makeshift bedroom. It was cooler down there and it wasn't like meals were being prepared and served any more. Once their mother had died three years back his father's mind seemed to go with her. Constantly rambling on and on about absolute nonsense, and then when Alfred was hung…

His father's booming voice echoed up the stairwell. "Alfred says the harvest is looking good. Good…good. Hey, where you going with that, Sammy?"

"Alfred's out there thirsty seein' over the crop."

"Good…good. Hard work out there. That'll help. Tell him to bring in the Huxley boys. Hard workers those two. Alfred spoke to em' I know. Make sure they're workin' for us." Both brothers had been dead for years: killed in a bar fight.

"Yes Pa." The stairs creaked as Sammy made his way back upstairs. He stopped about halfway up when he saw Robert standing there, and motioned with a tin of whiskey to move towards his left. Robert did so and stepped into the room that had served as a nursery, library, and office throughout its existence. The shelves were empty, all the books had been sold for money, liquor or prostitutes over the past three years, and like the rest of the house the room was dirty. Large puffs of spiderwebs hung from about every space imaginable. A lone table, which had once been downstairs in the dining room, sat in the center, undoubtedly having been moved by Sammy or Matthias to make more room for their father as he sunk deeper into his confusion. The only items left on the shelves were his father's old surveying tools: a surveyor's compass, a half chain, and a few stakes all had survived sale, and instead sat collecting dust. Sitting in the empty room that was once filled with evidence of their father's position and wealth, the tools used to make the money that allowed them to build the farmhouse seemed the last vestige of the man their father once was. In a rare moment of reflection, Robert was thankful they hadn't hawked those tools.

When Sammy was beside him Robert stepped towards the table, not before accepting one of the tins of whiskey that was filled to the brim.

"Since you didn't pick, let's talk here. No one else is in the house, and I doubt Pa's listening besides. He's down there using a damn ladle to drink. Made me drag the barrel closer to his bed so he wouldn't have to move the other day."

They both took a seat at the table; Sammy tossed the filled bladder on the top in between them. "Here ya' are. Now," he took a sip from his tin before continuing. A wince, then: "now what are you here to talk about."

The peach whiskey burned less than what he was used to. Robert took two large gulps before speaking. "Now, I know what you're going to say to all this—and I don't want you runnin' to Matthias, you hear?" Sammy nodded and Robert continued. "Well...I think that spiritualist girl, you know—"

"Of course, I know, get on!"

"Well, I don't think she's dead. Well, not exactly, I think she's come back to get revenge."

Sammy looked like he was about to say something, and Robert paused. After a moment of silence passed, he picked back up. "She could talk to the dead, Sammy. She did it to get to us the first time, you know she ain't follow us like Matthias said. She spoke to the peddler and got our names. And then that night…"

"She coulda' sounded like that or played a trick with her voice, it doesn't mean he was talkin'."

Robert drained his cup then filled it back up with the bladder.

"You know that ain't the case. That was him talking. He even said Matthias was the one who—"

"I know what he—er, she said. You ain't gotta tell me. I heard all of it."

"Then you heard what's waiting for us, and you know that the dead ain't really all that dead."

"I don't know *all* that."

"I've been seein' her too. Usually just outta the corner of my eye, maybe when I'm hunting or at the tavern. This lady in white, wearing a long dress that just stares at me—but then disappears when I look back. Then last night she was in my room. She kept askin' about someone or finding her and I saw those things that peddler boy said was waiting for us in her eyes. The slithering madness or whatever he said. Sammy, we gotta figure a way outta this. We gotta turn ourselves in or tell someone where the bodies are so she can rest. I didn't know she had a daughter, and it wasn't our idea. Matthias made us again. She's comin' for us and she's gonna—"

"Quiet now!" his brother slammed his tin on the table which rattled beneath. Sweat poured down Robert's face, his mind was still going fast as his words were. Robert scowled back as he spoke. "You need to get yourself together. You're just seein' things is all, same as I told you when you first came here with all this nonsense. That girl we mu…well, she didn't have no daughter. You know that. You're doing nothing but drinking and marchin' through the woods now—course you're going to see things. Damn it!"

He looked about the room for something to throw, but after surveying the barren space and looking back towards his brother, Sammy's face relaxed "Why don't you come back here? You can work on the farm, lord knows we need the help. I know you don't like Pa's rambling down there, but we can set you up upstairs, so you don't hear him. Matthias will lay off too I'm sure, he knows we need more hands around. He's been better, swear it."

Robert knew his brother well enough to see he was lying about Matthias, clear as day, not that it mattered.

"She'll follow me. Oh god Sammy, it's cause I shot her, isn't it? I didn't want to, that damn gun just went off. You know we can't outrun this thing. At some point we're gonna get caught." Tears ran down his face and snot ran from his nose. He abandoned filling up the tin cup and like a nursing baby he latched to the bladder and began drinking.

"Jesus Christ Robert, pull yourself together. There isn't no lady in white haunting you. And you know damn well she was all alone besides. Remember the newspaper article after she disappeared? She lived by herself, and they said the they probably fell off the carriage to their deaths er—"

"You know that's not what people think. They know who done it, they just don't have the proof. You have half the hands out there working then you did last year—what do you think changed then? No…you know we stepped into something real bad that night. You might not know it yet, but you will. After it gets me, who do you think she's coming for next?"

The whiskey was taking hold. Robert felt lighter than before. *Hell, if Matthias walks in right now, I might give it to him too,* he thought as he continued drinking the peach whiskey. A trickle ran down the corner of his mouth and splattered on the table beneath. Sammy drained his tin.

"Robert, I don't have time for your ghost stories. Clean yourself up and get yourself together. You're feeling guilty and the whiskey and moving away isn't helping one bit. I ain't gonna tell Matthias what you said, even though I should. After what you said on the stand about Alfred, that would—"

"You know damn well that was your idea! You told the investigator, you told me to say all that on the stand. Hell, you woulda' first if I wasn't called as a witness before you. It was you—"

"Hush with all that. What's done is done. You should get outta here quick though. He'll be back soon, and if he sees you like this, drunk before with the sunup it ain't going to be good for anyone."

Robert wagged the half-filled bladder at Sammy.

"I ain't going back down there. You want it filled, go get it yourself. There's an old loaf of bread in the kitchen I think you should have, too. Alright?" Sammy disappeared out of the room, the sound of the front door closing behind him soon followed.

Robert stayed sitting for a moment. He knew when he stood the ground would be unstable, his legs would lock and bow in a manner they shouldn't, and his head would spin as the world around him took a little longer to settle than it typically did. The peach whiskey was good. Strong, though it didn't taste like it. He weighed the pros and cons of stealing away downstairs for another tin full and to top off. After a moment of contemplation and a few more sips, the choice was an easy one.

He readied himself to stand, looking about the former nursery turned office turned library to get his bearings before the world went all topsy turvy on him. The sun glared through the window illuminating dust particles that seemed thick enough to wade through. Robert, no longer thinking about his brother or The Lady in White and only about whiskey, grabbed the table and hoisted himself up. He then slung the bladder over his shoulder and grabbed his tin.

He was ready to descend to the basement.

Robert left the room, turned, and stared down the staircase leading to the kitchen, and the dining room, and his unwell father, and—most importantly—a large barrel of whiskey. He stepped lightly (or at least tried to), for a brief moment entertaining the thought he might sneak down there, refill, and be up before his old man was the wiser.

The first step shattered that illusion. The wooden plank let out a loud groan beneath his weight, and calling up from the cave before him he heard, "Albert, it evening already. You finished the harvest, didn't you? That's why I'm leavin' the farm to you. Come have a drink with yer Pa."

Robert hurried down the steps though his legs seemed at risk of giving out beneath the weight of the whiskey. He held his breath as he plunged into the dining room. Despite the sun shining through the small window running along the top of the wall, the room was as dark as it had appeared from the top of the stairs. It took his eyes a moment to adjust. His father's large outline appeared in the corner resting atop a mattress that had split open, spilling hay across the ground like the guts of a flayed deer. Slowly the room took form around him. Everything cleared out save for the mattress, the whiskey and a lone chair sitting in the corner facing the mattress. *That's where he thinks Alfred sits and talks to him.* His father was sitting upright beside the barrel, and as mentioned by Sammy wielding a ladle to dip into the booze.

"You ain't Albert?" he said after a moment of silence. The disappointment was evident in his tone. "Is that…is that Robert?"

"Yea Pa, it's me."

"Well, I ain't seen you all day. Come have a drink."

Robert stepped forward, leading with the tin cup in his outstretched hand. It shook and he focused on stilling the cup. *Albert hasn't really been talking to him. Just an old man losing his mind.* He'd told himself the same thing dozens of times before leaving, but each time the thought seemed less convincing. The stories about the hanging, the possession, the woman in w-

"It's got some peaches bobbin' around. Sure is sweet. Save some for Albert though, aight?"

"Okay Pa."

The barrel top was removed, and true to his word a few dried peaches bobbed at the surface. He dipped the tin into the murky brown liquid, a feeling of relief washed over Robert: *the trip to the basement was worth it.* A film had formed on the top, and as the tin entered the whiskey the ripple disturbed it revealing a much darker brown beneath. *It looks like a witches' cauldron, or…like swamp water.* He shivered and quickly emptied the contents of the tin once it emerged.

"That's my boy, that's my boy. You always were fond of the stuff." His father dipped the ladle in the barrell, pulled it out and began drinking from the hold. Streams of whiskey coursed down either side of his mouth so that it looked like he was drooling. With his father distracted Robert filled the bladder quickly, dipping it into the barrel and removing it once the bubbles stopped. He slung it over his neck then filled his tin.

"Well Pa think it's t—"

"We'll look who it is! Yer brothers visiting Alfred. He's been gone a day…no it's, it's been more than that, hasn't it?" His father looked up at him, eyes clouded with confusion. "Robert, you been gone a bit, haven't you? You left, when was it? Oh I…I can't recall." His voice cracked; he sounded on the verge of a blubbering cry from the moment of clarity.

Robert looked at the shell of a man he'd once feared like the wrath of God, imagining what was going through his mind at the moment. Knowing Robert had left, though why or when was likely still lost in the fog of his memory. Was he realizing he was living in denial; that his wife was dead, his favorite son executed, the three left were pariahs? Is that why he locked himself away and hid from the world? Was it easier to ignore those truths stuffed away in self-imposed exile? Or was it all—his decline and bad state—just the ravages of time or the random hand some deity in the sky had dealt his father, a man who might have or might not have deserved it?

It didn't matter, here he was trying to remember why Robert left. It wasn't the years of abuse or the sudden emergence of the broken man before him. Robert wanted to scream, *I left when Alfred died, and you started your goddamn conversations with him.*

A twinge of guilt rippled through his sternum.

Another sip will help with that.

That, and it might help with the sudden crawling of his skin brought about by the mention and thought of Alfred. His father mumbled on ("a week…a month…a year was it? When did little Robert leave?") while Robert drank and refilled, drank and refilled.

Meanwhile his father's words tumbled out slower and slower until he was silent. He looked up at Robert, eyes once again clouded with confusion. A moment of realization, gone before it could take. The ladle joined Robert's tin cup in the whiskey. His father was propped up sitting beside the barrel. He was a giant man, though now soft and doughy from his life of inactivity in the cellar. So different from Robert in so many ways; maybe that's why he beat him the worst. "Alfred, what's that now? I can barely hear you. What's he sayin' Robert?"

"Oh, I didn't hear. Sorry Pa."

"Well listen up then goddamnit!" The temper that he and his brothers spent days and nights cowering from flared. For a moment Robert hated him again like he had so often growing up.

How sweet revenge would be.

It'd be so easy to give him a beating like he used to dole out to them. To swing his boot right into the old man's temple, to hear the dull thud and squish as he drove his heel into his bulging gut, to listen to him whimper and plead like they used to beneath his tyrannical rage. He could lay into him as much as he wanted. Would he kill him? Probably not, but Robert hadn't meant to kill that spiritualist girl either, so who knew. There were years of getting the shit kicked out of him simmering in Robert's drunken psyche. The old fuck couldn't stop him. *So easy…but what would Alfred do?*

He felt the cold grip of his dead brother's hands around his throat and turned and looked around the room. The old bastard always had a soft spot for his oldest; no doubt he would come to save him if Robert followed through. *He's not here, the old man's just seeing shit. You're making things up in your mind just like him, getting drunk too. Get a hold of yourself you worthless piece of-*

"What's that Alfred? Yer right, yer right. Robert, you look like you've seen a ghost. You alright there boy?"

The rage subsided. "Just need more whiskey s'all." His request seemed to come from another voice, the words blending into a single jumbled hiss. He slurred with no control over his tone, but he got it out. Robert was swaying now, only vaguely aware of the shift in his balance. He lumbered forward, catching himself on the edge of the barrel just in time. Plunging the tin back into the liquid he briefly tried to calculate how many drinks he'd had; *eight, nine…twelve?* What did it matter—he would keep drinking. If he could drown out the thoughts of dead men and women and a family, he despised who tortured him and dragged him to places where he had to watch…

"Ah yes, drink up my boy. This'll right whatever's ailing you. Now hold up a minute," his father looked back and forth between the empty chair and Robert, who was scooping whiskey into his mouth as fast as he could slug it down. "Murder? Alfred what was that yer saying?" The tin cup, now empty, paused on Robert's lip. He glared down at his father, once again sweet thoughts of revenge danced across his liquor-addled mind.

Oh, to shut him and his incessant rambling up for a moment so he might enjoy a goddamn drink in peace.

But the look on his father's face tempered his anger once more. He looked…shocked. Horrified even. His eyes were wide like a fawn lying crumpled on the forest floor taking her dying breath, watching Robert approach; that look, pleading and accusatory and full of fear.

How could you kill me? Why would you want to kill me…what are you?

The gaze of a dying confused animal—a suffering one.

211

Why the sudden change, Pa?

Robert was about to ask if they could change the conversation, a request that undoubtedly would have been garbled and nearly undecipherable given his state, but before he could he noticed the mischievous glimmer in his father's eye. He wasn't *actually* horrified...he was mocking him.

"Albert you can't say that about yer brother." He paused, turning his head back towards the chair sitting in the corner. "Well, that is a hefty accusation. Robert, Alfred says yer some sort of a murderer. Tell him that ain't true. He mustuva' gotten confused. Only thing yer killin' is them critters yer always after ain't the right, little Robert." That smug, knowing tone. He was setting him up like he used to before kicking the absolute shit out of Robert. Baiting him. He was letting Robert know *he* knew, and no matter what Robert said he was caught red handed and there was hell to pay.

To hell *with him and Alfred and Matthias and Sammy.*

"You know Alfred and Matthias killed that boy good n' well. You know they were the ones who made us go out that evening. Alfred's dead...strung up in front of a crowd who watched him shit his pants as he wriggled from the noose. Truth be told, I wish I'd went. He deserved it...so do you."

He prepared for an onslaught of curses and threats—maybe even a pathetic charge—standing as firmly as his drunken state would allow. He was determined to hurt the old man, and if he couldn't bring himself to do it physically, he'd tear him down mentally. To Robert's surprise, however, his father seemed unbothered. In fact, the corner of his lip curled up in a smirk.

"Alfred...yer brother wouldn't shoot a woman, in the face no less. I just don't think he has it in him. Look at him, I mean. Drunk and shakin' and the sun's just up. No, no…maybe yer right. That is the type of man who might do such a thing."

How could he know that? Had Sammy and Matthias blamed him. Were they going to do the same thing to him they'd done to Alfred?

"Alfred, who's your friend?" The smirk grew to a wild and sinister grin exposing his yellow, rotten teeth. His eyes shone with mischief as they darted from the empty chair to Robert again. "Oh…she looks angry. I wouldn't want to be on the wrong end of her." He pointed his ladle at Robert. "She's lookin' at you boy. Ohhhhh, she wants to have a word with you."

Robert turned. The room was empty, save for the chair. His heart pounded, the clarity of fear managed to cut through the booze.

She's here. I can't see her, but she's come to get me.

Robert sprinted up the stairs followed by the maniacal laugh of his father.

"You can't run forever boy. They're coming for you! Oh, are they coming for you!"

***

By midday Robert was back in his room, clutching his rifle and watching the door. Every thud from the tavern beneath and every shout from outside the window made him scramble as he prepared for an assault by The Lady in White. The fright sobered him right up. He was being hunted, he had to be ready for anything.

…but a sip of whiskey might calm the nerves.

By the afternoon Robert was drunk for the second time that day. The Lady in White and his insane father be damned. He left the tavern with his rifle slung over his shoulder heading to the place he loved most: the woods.

The long walk took longer than normal on account of some stumbling and meandering. Before leaving Robert had managed to convince the innkeeper to add a bottle of rum to his tab for the next week; as such, a good hunt was no longer just enjoyable, it was critical. His mood lifted noticeably, in part due to a midday nap that happened upon him quite surprisingly. One moment he was on the edge of the mattress thinking every sound was a specter coming to drag him to the depths, the next (following a few sips of whiskey it should be added) he was asleep. When he awoke from the nap the morning seemed as distant as a nightmare; sure, it was there and he might remember it, but there were more pressing concerns. Maybe he *was* being paranoid and overthinking things. If Matthias and Sammy were fine, why shouldn't he be? They were as much to blame—hell, more so even the way he figured—as he was, Robert rationalized. If there were a ghost, surely all of them would be seeing her. It was probably just the whiskey, though he sure as hell wasn't going to take a break.

Once he resumed drinking in earnest, the world became his oyster. His room in the tavern seemed a little more comfortable, the light seemed to shine through the window a little brighter, and the other tenants he walked past—usually a dour bunch—seemed a little happier. Things were looking up, for no particular reason perhaps, but Robert could *feel it*. The fact he pulled off getting a bottle of rum seemed to highlight his sudden change in both mood and luck.

And when luck seemed to improve and money was needed, Robert knew just the spot to hunt.

The dirt path cooked beneath his feet as he went. Ahead, the way shimmered like a mirage sure to disappear when he got too close. He walked past fields of wheat—some acres harvested, some not—the beige stalks like dunes in an endless desert. The heat beat down on him, and even the shade cast from the old trifold hat he'd donned before setting out mattered little. His shirt and trousers clung to his sweaty body no matter how often he pulled at them trying to create some space from their clammy grip. Even his dear friend, rum, lost some of its appeal, replaced instead with the sudden want of a ginger beer. His mouth felt like it'd been stuffed with cotton or a dry rag, and as he licked at his lips their dryness only increased. It was like being in an oven.

But Robert was used to being uncomfortable. Sitting on a branch for hours, unable to move as a doe or buck sat just out of range, or trudging through muck to find a better vantage point for fowl. Heat, even as unbearable as it was this August, was easy enough to deal with. Besides, there was enough water where he was heading to take a dip when needed, and there was a creek not far ahead.

Dust kicked up beneath his feet on the lonely road, sticking to his skin and filling his nostrils. He walked quickly, his gait becoming less loopy and uncertain as the miles passed. Soon, his head began to pound with a growing headache. He thought about the bladder, now filled with rum, when he was halfway to his destination, but the chalky feeling in his mouth dissuaded him from indulging. There was that creek ahead, besides. *Some water first, then rum!*

So, he trotted along, sobering up and looking forward to the hunt. As he passed a farmhouse, a dress hung out to dry fluttered in the wind, and for a moment all the fear and dread he felt from the night before and that morning reared in his gut...but the wind subsided, the dress went slack, and those thoughts soon evaporated. *Seeing things, that's all. No different than the shakes.*

By the time he was at the forest bordering the marshes Robert was as close to stone-cold sober as he'd been for the past year. He plunged into the woods excited to find the creek which ran a hundred feet in, and followed alongside the road. When he arrived, the creek babbled and swirled as picturesque as something from a painting.

The water was clear and cascaded over smooth rocks on its way to the marshes and the Lake down the way, only occasionally interrupted by a hitchhiking leaf carried along. Above, the sunlight shone through the canopy of green, giving the foliage a translucent glow and providing shade for the parched hunter. And although it had been a dry summer, the creek was still full and ran nearly twenty feet across. He found himself a place on the edge where the water ran deep enough to guarantee it was fresh.

Robert went to his knees then cupped his hands, bringing the cool water to his cracked lips. It was as sweet and refreshing as any wine or cider he'd ever had, and he lapped up handful after handful stopping only occasionally to splash it across his sweaty brow. He laughed with childish glee at the refreshing reprieve as he continued drinking; thirsty as he'd ever been, the water sloshing in his gut mattered little. He kept drinking, leaning forward and watching the glitter of the sun reflect off the stream, giving the water an aqua hue that made the rocks and pebbles a foot below look like rare emeralds or minerals.

But soon the water changed. It was slow, at first barely noticeable, but the taste of it became less sweet. He didn't stop, he'd drank worse things before, and the growingly acrid taste was bearable. He was so parched it didn't matter besides. Just a touch bitter was all. Then all the sudden it wasn't a simple change in taste; the water turned, becoming unbearable. After the last pull from the creek the taste of rotten meat filled his mouth. He spewed it out before swallowing, but there was nothing he could do to get rid of the awful taste. His stomach began to rumble, and he felt a smolder feeling creep from his gut to his throat. He began to cough, then gag. Vomit spilled from his mouth, burning as it exited his body in waves spilling out beside the creek. His eyes watered, and when he was done vomiting and began wiping the snot, tears, and bile from his face he noticed the forest was no longer illuminated and bright. Storm clouds had formed overhead, blocking the sunlight and making the forest dark and foreboding.

Robert realized he wasn't alone.

Four glaring eyes peered towards him from the woods, watching him through foliage so dense he couldn't make out what type of animal they belonged to. His hands went to his rifle, the spoiled taste still fresh in his mouth, he lowered the gun ready to fire.

Before he could, they were gone. A sudden flutter of the branches, subtle enough he didn't have time to compress the trigger, and whatever had been watching him was gone. Their exit was so quiet, so quick, Robert stood for a moment mystified. He knew the woods, and to get surprised like that was rare enough to earn a few seconds of contemplation. After a moment, Robert relaxed his hold on the gun then wiped his mouth again, though he couldn't shake the feeling he was still being watched. He eyed the green veil around him suspiciously, gun lowered but finger still on the trigger. The woods were silent, save for the distant chirp of some songbirds.

"Ah hell," he said, then spit on the ground. The rancid taste coated his mouth, and he took a swig of rum to clear it. Robert was still uneasy, he didn't like being snuck up on one bit, but he wanted to see why the water had soured so quickly. He knelt down and scooped his hand into the running water, planning on smelling it to try to detect whatever had changed the taste, but when it emerged his hand was caked in mud and algae. He tried again, barely dipping his hand beneath the surface so he could see it the whole time; still, when he pulled his hand out it was muddier and covered with more algae and what looked like pond scum.

"The hell…"

His hand was out of the water held in front of him, yet the mud and scum climbed higher. From his hand to his wrist, until it was eventually halfway up his forearm, it seemed to pull itself inch by inch on its own accord. A tattoo of slime and filth.

He shook his arm back and forth trying to shake it off him, but the sludge stuck to him like tar. Robert plunged his hand back in the water, hoping it would clean it off. He was on all fours with his arm extended to his elbow and his face hovering above the water when he noticed the pool seemed deeper than it had before.

Like the forest, the water turned dark in an instant. The once clear turquoise water became green, and Robert watched in disbelief as the water around his submerged arm turned black. It happened so suddenly he didn't have time to withdraw his arm during the initial change, but when the water turned inky, he yanked with all his might, but his arm stayed submerged. Again, he pulled, this time with more force, but his arm didn't budge.

He was stuck.

The creek still flowed beyond, sparkling and clear as ever, but the water surrounding him on the shore was a dark pit of ichor. It grew until it was a patch large enough to take up nearly half the width of the creek. It all radiated from him, and Robert felt like a fly trapped in a spider's web.

"Help, someone help me please," he cried out, though he knew the chances of someone being on the rarely traveled country road behind him *and* within earshot was unlikely. That didn't stop him though. "Please, someone help me. I'm stuck. Please help!"

He felt something brush against his submerged fingertips. The water was cool, but whatever touched him was freezing. It traced so lightly against his fingers in any other situation it might seem a teasing touch, but Robert knew right away it was something meant to harm him, to punish him for all the evil he'd caused and been a part of. This was the day of reckoning he'd always known was coming, the one that could only be forgotten momentarily with whiskey or rum or prostitutes.

Here it was.

The touch turned to a tug. He felt the ice-cold grip of a hand pulling on his own. *She* was beneath the surface of the dark water, dragging him towards whatever eternal fate awaited him. He screamed and cried to no avail. The only response to his pleas were the disturbed chirps of birds who soon fluttered away towards quieter regions, bothered by the commotion beneath.

The grip climbed up higher, grabbing his forearm. Though he couldn't see through the dark water, it rippled and frothed from the movement below, boiling like a cauldron.

It's like her eyes, Robert realized.

What lay beneath was all the suffering he'd seen the night before as she peered down at him, all the suffering that lay ahead for him as those he'd wronged would take their revenge on him.

"I'm sorry, I didn't mean it. THEY MADE ME THEY MADE ME."

Another yank. This one was strong enough to pull him forward so that his face hovered an inch above the water. He strained with all his might to break the unseen grip, but it held firm.

"Please, please, PLEASE!"

The dark water swirled and rippled, and suddenly a face appeared on the other side. The Lady in White peered back, indifferent to his cries. A veil of some thin and ratty material wrapped around her face like a mummy's linen, though it did little to hide what lay beneath. The material winded and moved on its own accord, clinging tight in parts and disappearing in others. Her face, the same corpse-like grey it had been the night before, still peered back at Robert from beneath the surface. Her eyes were as dark as the water surrounding her, her flesh like grey driftwood battered by primordial waves. Even in her decayed state Robert noticed she looked older than the woman he'd killed, though the resemblance was uncanny.

"Where is she?" The Lady in White whispered through the veil covering her face. Piss streamed down Robert's leg, the warm liquid filled his trousers and pooled on the ground beneath.

"I don't know who she is. I don't know, I don't know. I'm sorry I killed you. It was an accident, I swear, I swear."

The grip relaxed slightly, and Robert managed to pull his arm up slightly. The part that had been submerged was discolored, bleached the same grey as the face that stared up at him. He let out a squeal and was immediately pulled back forward into the water.

Sweat dripped from his forehead and tears ran freely as he hovered above the water, but when they fell to the water beneath there was no expected ripple. In fact, for a moment the tumultuous churning beneath him ceased. The water transformed to a placid pool, only disturbed by The Lady in White who peered back like a nightmarish portrait against the still backdrop.

"Where is she? Where is my daughter?"

"I don't know your daughter, I don't, I don't! The papers said you were alone. You said you didn't have any family! I'm sorry we killed you, please let me go. It was my brothers who made me. They're the ones who made us stop you and then sink your body by the shore. It was their id—"

plunk

***

Two emaciated dogs watched from behind a bush as the man disappeared into the water, pulled down the endless tunnel by unseen hands. There was a sudden flurry of splashes from within the dark patch, a pained, howling scream that came from within the creak and reverberated through the forest before slowly giving way to whimpers and eventual silence. The pit in the creek dissipated, the clouds above cleared, and soon the forest was as it had been before the man's arrival. There was a moment of serenity by the creek; all was as it should be.

The dog's ears perked up. A whisper from the voice that trained them sounded from the forest, telling them what was next.

Then they were on the move.

Chapter 9

"Get the hell out here you no good mutts!"

Samuel grabbed for a broom lying beside the entrance of the icehouse, but the dogs weaved past him before he could get it. Not wanting to let them leave without sending a message he tried to kick them on their way out, his foot sailed far from his intended target and went into the door frame instead.

He stumbled back grabbing hold of his throbbing foot while teetering on the other, cursing up a storm the whole time until finally finding support against the bare wooden shelves running along the wall of the icehouse. As the shelves dug into his back and he squeezed the end of his boot where it hurt most, he kept a close eye on the two dogs who stared back, muzzles gleaming with slobber, holding their find triumphantly.

"I'll kill you fuckers if I see you again," he yelled, breaking the still of the farm.

The dogs scampered away without a care in the world, each carrying a large piece of pork that had been meant to serve as dinner for the next week. They were skinny, strays he assumed, though it was rare to see them so far away from the city. Samuel kept cursing at them as they trotted along until they disappeared into the surrounding field of wheat. He made a note to have a gun loaded by the door should they return, and to let Matthias know to keep his eye out for them just in case. Last thing they needed was their food running off when money was already scarce. Despite the pain,

Samuel smirked at the thought of blasting the two dogs who had robbed him of both dignity and food.

"Wonder what Robert could get for those hides," he muttered before going back to swearing.

When the pain subsided, he stopped massaging his toes through his boot and tenderly placed his foot back to the ground. It hurt like hell with weight on it, but he could walk. He turned to the nearly empty shelves looking for what might replace the pork for dinner, and was met by dunes of sawdust that swept across the barren space like sand dunes, and was used to keep the meat cold.

"Goddamnit…goddamnit."

In the back corner he noticed a towering heap of sawdust, clearly packed to keep something cold for as long as it would last in the summer heat. Even with it dug into the ground beneath a towering oak to provide some shade, the icebox would only do so much this late in the summer. Whatever it was, it was stored on the top shelf which explained how the dogs had missed it.

Samuel chuckled, "dumb mutts," he said making his way towards the clump of sawdust.

He was hungry, and between the hard work of harvesting and the whiskey he'd had earlier that morning with Robert, his stomach growled in anticipation. The sawdust stuck to his sunburned skin as he clawed at it, until eventually a newspaper wrapped package emerged.

Matthias must have purchased whatever was within; or maybe he had, his memory always seemed to get worse around harvest season.

He opened the parcel and found several stacks of bacon. Certainly enough for dinner, and maybe enough for breakfast too.

His eyes skirted towards the entrance way of the ice room. He was worried the smell of meat might bring the hungry dogs back, but the opening remained empty. Samuel quickly rewrapped the parcel and made his way outside. The sun was just beginning to set beyond the derelict farmhouse, and as Samuel emerged from the structure the horizon burned stripes of red and orange. It would be night soon. Then morning, and back to the harvest.

Matthias was still away with the wagon, likely buying some supplies for the upcoming week after he'd sold the wheat to whichever mill had offered the best price after making a scene at each one. He'd be back soon, Samuel supposed. Not that he cared one way or another. It was nice to have some time away from him, especially with how he'd been acting the past few weeks. Between him, Robert claiming he was seeing ghosts, and the incessant ramblings of his father from the basement, Samuel felt like the only sane one left. His father and Robert were harmless; Matthias on the other hand…

Down the road a plume of dust rose in the distance. It would undoubtedly be Matthias returning home. Not many people save for the workers made a trek this far, especially as the sun was going down, and especially given their reputation now.

"Damn Robert. The boy's seeing things," he muttered to himself as he carried the parcel of bacon towards the house.

Robert had always been the odd man out between the brothers, but since leaving it had only grown worse.

Since leaving and since that night, that is.

Samuel tried not to think about that night the best he could; it was tough though, especially with Matthias who seemed to revel in bringing it up.

On the horizon the ox pulled wagon broke through the plume of dust it stirred around it. It would be several minutes before Matthias arrived, and Samuel still hadn't made up his mind whether he'd mention Robert's visit earlier. Part of him wanted to see what Matthias would do, while the more rational side knew it would only make things worse. Even if it would be funny to watch him tear into Robert and watch their little brother snivel and beg for forgiveness, there was also the chance things could go sour. Matthias could take it too far; or perhaps Robert, already unhinged, would decide to take them all down with him and go to the law. Neither would be good.

Samuel couldn't make up his mind. So, instead, he stood with the pound of bacon clasped in his grip watching his older brother approach, The fat and oils seeped through the wrapping as he squeezed, making his hands slick.

Do I tell him?

Beyond being well worth the ticket price, there might be some practicality to letting Matthias know. If Robert was going to flip, if he was going to turn on them and rat them out, having the jump on him might play to their advantage. Besides, Robert had the gun in his possession. They could pin it all on him. And besides that, Matthias would be more than willing to turn on Robert, unlike Alfred. Sure, it had been Samuel who blamed Alfred at first, but that was during a private conversation with the investigators. Robert was the one who said it on the stand; he was the one who the newspapers quoted, and the jury heard and who had made Alfred act all crazy in the court.

And sure, that might have been Samuel's suggestion, but why dwell on that? Fact is, Matthias blamed Robert for Alfred, and though Samuel was pretty sure Matthias had some suspicions towards him as well, at the moment most of his vitriol was still directed towards their younger brother, and he sure as hell wasn't going to correct him.

The oxen lumbered along, close enough now that Samuel could make out their horns and slobbery muzzles. Matthias was behind them, sitting in the driver seat and looking mad as ever. He stood up with a bump in the road, as he did his body remained uneven and staggered from the accumulation of injuries he'd taken over the years.

The scar, the leg, the wrist…

Samuel had helped set or stitch most of his injuries, given they were typically acquired through unsavory endeavors. It had left his brother a gnarled, twisted figure who moved like a marionette, save when he was angry, which was often.

Matthias lowered himself back to the driver's seat, and Samuel could imagine the slur of obscenities that went along with the action. Likely the same curses he'd used in the icehouse. He watched his brother grow closer, with each passing foot his face grew more contorted in anger.

Matthias. Why hadn't he said it was his idea to kill that boy?

It was a question he'd asked himself nearly every day since he insinuated the plot and murder was all on Alfred. Had he told the truth, his life would be immensely improved. It was both of those fuckers who dragged them out that evening. One held, one slit the peddlers throat, that was all he needed to say. Instead, he'd blamed Alfred. Perhaps it was out of frustration that he was always their father's favorite, or maybe it was simply the first name that had popped in his head, and once the investigator seemed satisfied and looked at him with less suspicion, he really hadn't wanted to add anymore to the story.

*But with Matthias gone…*the thought was almost too sweet. No one giving him hell for every little thing or disappearing while he was left running the harvest. At least Robert had the common courtesy to disappear completely, Matthias left the work for Samuel then reaped the rewards.

It's just 'cause he got all of the piss and vinegar from pa.

"Hyah! Hyah!" Matthias' voice roared above the sound of the oxen's hooves. He sounded as angry as he looked. The oxen walked right beside Samuel and stopped, grunting and moaning from the trek.

"That fucking thief at the mill—what's his name again? Stanton or something—goddamn *doubled* what they was charging us. I have half a mind of burning their mill to the ground with them in it."

Spittle flew from Matthias' mouth as he spoke. Unlike Samuel, who was happy to wear his dirt-stained pants and button up linen shirt at the farm or about, Matthias was wearing trousers and an ill-fitting jacket top that looked like he was about to burst through at any moment. He would wear it any time he made his way into town, to the bay, or to any business.

He wants to be a wealthy merchant or trader with all his rotten heart.

It had taken all of his and Robert's convincing to let them sell their father's high-end goods when they needed money. "The gentleman imposter", he and Robert would mock him behind his back when he was good and out of earshot, and standing angrily above the oxen in a pathetic attempt at looking the part of a merchant, Samuel felt the urge to let him in on that little nickname.

But he caught his tongue.

"Did you—"

"Yes of course I did. There was no other choice after talking to a few of those other thieves. GodDAMNIT!" he spit on the ground and laid into the oxen with the whip.

Both grunted, though neither seemed all that bothered by his repetitive lashes. When he was done Matthias stared down at Robert with sweat dripping from his forehead, the stringy hair on top of his head falling loosely to the same side as the jagged scare, and his eyes wide in anger.

"I suppose you didn't find any more help either?"

"Now Matthias…"

"How the hell is this harvest supposed to get done with less than a dozen hands to help?" He sounded like his father before his mind went, Samuel realized. "We ought to get that no good little shit brother of yours to come back here and pull his weight."

"He's your brother too."

Should I tell him? Oh, he'd be raw as hell. Bet I'd see fireworks from him.

"He stopped being my brother the second he told on Alfred, you know that damn well. Though…" a devilish twinkle flashed across his eyes as his lips curled into a grin. "He did good work that one day."

Tell him.

"He stopped by this morning looking like hell."

"Robert?" The grin left his face, his eyes became wild.

"Yea, by the sight and smell of him he was still drunk from the night before too. I offered him that bread downstairs, and he just wanted to—"

"Wanted to what?" His brother's jaw tensed. *Not too far with it,* Samuel reminded himself. Just enough to get a reaction.

"Oh, I think he wanted to see if we had any booze 'round here. Probably going on a hunt around here and swung by. I didn't spend much time with him…*work to do in the field.*" Matthias' glared down disapprovingly. He cleared his throat, and without breaking his gaze spit to the ground beside Samuel.

"By the looks of it not much got done while I was away. The men don't respect you, that's it. Probably slackin the whole time."

"Now you know that ain't it. We barely got enough men to clear the wheat in a year, let alone a season. *Robert* seems to think it's…well, *he* said people blame us for that girl going missin'." The diversion worked as intended. Matthias stepped down from the carriage, shaking his head slowly as he went about unhitching the oxen. Next, he took them by the lead and began walking them towards the pasture. The giant animals lumbered beside him as Samuel tailed behind.

"Sure said a lot considering he wasn't here all that long, didn't he?"

"You know him…he likes to talk." Samuel squeezed the parcel of bacon as he spoke. *Too far. Too far.* "He was just talkin' to me is all. He said he ain't sleepin' all that great in the city."

"And he was drinkin' you said?"

"Well yea, but ain't we all? He said he was headin' out to hunt and trap later, I think. I don't think you gotta worry about—"

"About what? You don't tell me what I do or don't gotta worry about, you hear." The whole time he spoke Matthias tugged at the oxen. Though he couldn't see his face, Samuel could picture the look of rage likely plastered across his brother's face. Though he knew he was treading dangerous ground, Samuel couldn't help but smirk. *Serves 'em both right.* Robert for abandoning him, and Matthias for always getting them in trouble and ditching out on the farm work. *To hell with both of em'.*

"In fact, I think you two seem to be talkin' a lot considering he up and moved away."

"You know he's always out here hunting. I just told him he should come back and help around the place, that's all. He grabbed some of pa's whiskey and left not long after. Like I said, he had trapping an—"

Before he could finish Matthias was on him. He spun and leaped, grabbing hold of Samuel's collar and pulling him in he started screaming in his face. "If you two think yer doing what you did to Alfred to me, you got another thing coming. I'll skin you both before I go to the gallows, you hear? This-this-this collusion! Yes, yer collusion against me won't stand. I'll make sure of that."

Samuel squirmed trying to break free from his brother's clutches. "Matthias we ain't colluding I swear." His voice stammered, and for a moment he feared his brother would let go of his collar and go for his throat. Dropping the bacon, Samuel grabbed a hold of his brother's forearms trying to peel them off. Matthias was too strong though. His eyes bulged as his grip tightened and he pulled the collar closer to Samuel's throat.

He'll kill me. He'll kill me and not have a second thought about it.
"HE SAID HE SAW A GHOST!"

His grip relaxed. "He…he what?"

"That's why he was stopping by. Said some lady in white was haunting him, or following or something. I swear, I swear, that's why he stopped by. He looked like he hadn't slept in weeks. Stunk of booze too."

Matthias let go of his collar and pushed him back. "What the hell? Go on with it."

"He was saying he saw her in the woods, and she was coming for revenge. That it was the ghost of that," he dropped his voice to a whisper, "that girl he shot. Said a lady in a long white dress attacked him, and he kept seeing her in the woods. You know, the spiritualist coming back from the other side for revenge he was sayin'."

There was a moment of silence. The two brothers stood a foot apart: Samuel still tense, ready to run; Matthias deep in thought.

"How much do you think he's drinking these days?" Matthias finally asked, his voice sharp as a razor.

"Enough to be seein' things that ain't there. Hell, you should've seen him. Looked like hell. No *wonder* he was seeing things. So skinny I doubt he'd had a solid meal in the past week or two."

Matthias scratched his patchy beard and looked away from Samuel towards the disappearing sun. "If he's seeing this *woman* like you say, that makes me worried he might be talkin' about things too. Who's to say he doesn't have one of those fits like that girl, or that he doesn't start blabbering to whoever pours him his next drink about all our er—trouble?"

"Matthias, I don't think we gotta—"

"It was his drunken ramblings that first got us suspected, I suppose. Even before that bitch said she saw us. What's to stop that from happening again?"

His voice softened. Matthias rested his elbows on the top plank of the wooden fence around the grazing pasture and stared out towards the oxen. Samuel knew better than to answer the question right away. That might set him off again, and at the moment Matthias seemed relaxed, which strangely worried Samuel more than when he'd been shouting in his face. This was how'd been the night with the peddler; the night with the spiritualist, too.

A *calm before the storm.*

Matthias was planning something. What exactly, well that was beyond Samuel; he knew it was likely nothing good though. As he so often did, Samuel regretted trying to drive a wedge between the brothers. It always started so much fun, that's why he'd start to do it after all, but then Matthias would take it too far or Alfred would become inconsolable. He worried he'd started the final confrontation between the two. The one that seemed always simmering beneath and ready to boil over at any moment, and Samuel had gone and thrown a piece of driftwood on the flames beneath.

Matthias was going to do me in too, whatever his and Robert's business is, best it's the two of them and I'm far from it.

Still…

"You know he's just spending too much time hunting is all."

"Yea…too much time hunting. Lots of things to see in the woods, too. Dangerous things even, especially for a known drunk."

Matthias turned and faced Samuel.

"Enough of that, let's make dinner. I'm famished."

***

The brothers ate the bacon and stale bread Robert left behind in silence while their father sang a wailing ballad from the former dining room. The fireplace they'd used to cook the bacon was burning out; still, the room retained its warmth. Being in the cellar, the kitchen was still the most bearable room in the house.

"I wish he'd be quiet sometimes," Samuel said after the bread had disappeared. He picked up a burned slice of bacon and took a bite.

Matthias only grunted.

Eventually the song gave way to conversation.

"Alfred boy, have some of this bacon your brothers fried up. Burned to hell, but it will fill ya' proper. Another big day harvesting tomorrow, eh? You look tired as a dog."

"That reminds me…" his voice trailed off as Matthias shot him a sideways glance clearly meant to tell him to shut the hell up. "I'll tell ya' later." Another grunt.

"You're breaking your back out there, I know, I know. Shoulda' become a lawyer. That's how I always saw ya'. Me and yer ma thought you'd be arguing cases 'cross the state. It's alright though, glad to have you here more. Here, have some more whiskey. The bacon will dry ya' right out." The sound of the chair sliding across the stone floor made the hair on Samuel's neck stand on edge. Even Matthias turned quickly in the direction of the dining room.

"He's just putin' the plate on the chair again," Matthias said through a mouthful of bacon. "That's all it was."

His father went on talking to his dead son without a care in the world. Samuel couldn't help but be pulled into the conversation. He imagined Alfred was in there, actually sitting in that chair they'd been forced to keep down there by their father's demand. *What would Alfred say if he was in there?*

He looked over to Matthias to see if he might be similarly contemplating their dead brother's response, but he seemed preoccupied with stuffing more bacon into his mouth and washing it down with Whiskey.

He'd be pissed at you, Sammy. He'd probably come after you like Robert thinks that lady in white is. He'd know now it wasn't Robert's fault you got caught and blamed.

"…had to clear this land myself, you were just a little one…"

To hell with 'em all. What did he care about Alfred or—

"Robert…I wasn't expecting to see you back so soon."

Both Samuel and Matthias head shot up into the air, disbelief washed across their face as they turned and stared at the wooden door that led into the dining room.

"Why the hell is he mentioning Robert?" Samuel said. Matthias waved his hand in the air before shushing him.

"I want to hear goddamnit."

"Been taking a swim boy? You're all wet. You were all sore when you left earlier, I suppose I didn't mean nothing by what I said. Hey, have some of this whiskey you were so fond of. Sure, it'll do you good. You look like hell boy, worse than earlier even."

"Did he talk to Pa?" Matthias turned to face Samuel after asking, his eyebrow pulled up in surprise.

"I didn't think so. He knew there was whiskey down there though so…" Samuel shrugged, and Matthias turned back towards the dining room.

A strange noise began from beyond the door. Samuel couldn't place it; it wasn't the sound of his father sliding about the mattress or spilled hay, and it wasn't the sound of the chair being moved closer. It sounded like…

Waves.

The sound of waves crashing whispered from the dining room. Not the roar of a storm or gull that made the sea choppy and sunk men to their graves, but the rumble of Lake Ontario on a calm evening when the water close to the shore was like glass and it merely rolled a little ways out. If it was coming from a body of water, it would be calming, serene even, but from beyond the closed door where their delirious father resided, the sound was unnerving.

"Do you hear—"

"Shut the hell up! For the last time," Matthias said, his voice hissing as he quickly glanced over his shoulder to look at Samuel before turning back.

The sound of the waves continued for another moment before their father's voice rose above. It was different then it was before: clearer, less slurred—the way Samuel remembered it from his childhood.

"I always knew you would get yourself in trouble. And look at you! Hell, you deserve it…After what you did to Alfred. I suppose the whole lot blames me for your sorry state. Well, it ain't my fault you got what's coming to you. YA HEAR ME? IT AIN'T MY FAULT!"

The seas were no longer calm. Waves crashed, though that soon gave way to a crescendo of wails that called from behind the door, screeching out in agony. For a moment both men were frozen, surprised at the drastic turn of whatever was going on in the dining room. Above the pained howls rose their father's voice.

"Robert, always a sniveling wretch of a man—that's why I was hardest on you. Wanted you to become something and look at you!" A pained screech was the only reply. "They took Alfred from me and look how he suffers. Oh, look how my boy suffers."

A storm raged beyond the closed doors.

"What the fuck is going on in there?" Matthias lunged towards the closed room. He grabbed hold of the handle, but it would budge. Samuel was stuck to his seat, still leaning against the kitchen counter unable to move as his mouth hung open.

"How I suffer…seein' what's become of you! How they took my boy and tore him apart. Why are there so many of you, Alfred? Why are they all so different? Taken and swallowed in dark engulfing chaos and suffering and—"

The spell of horror and shock finally broke. Samuel pushed himself up from the counter, the stool behind him crashed to the floor. Meanwhile, Matthias stepped back and drove his shoulder into the door, which flung open with a loud *crack* just as Samuel was beginning to make his way over. Matthias stopped just short of plunging into the room, peering in.

Though there had been a lantern lit when Samuel dropped off the plate of food just a few minutes before, the two men stared into the dark space unable to see anything beyond the opening. In that room it was midnight with the moon and stars plucked by some mischievous deity; it was the bottom of a well, dug too deep and uncovering something that should have been left to slumber; it was

"THE VOID! The eternal madness of the laughing harlequin gods and the serpent of Eden and the chaos of primordial seas and skies that ripple with the gods of old and the pointless cruelty of this world that will take me as it has taken my sons," he cried out from within, his voice indignant and full of wrath like a preacher chastising his wayward flock. He was the man Samuel remembered once more; the one shrewd enough to make him one of the richest men in the county at one point, and mean enough to beat his family the next while dragging them to church the next morning.

Neither brother moved beyond the doorway. They peered in, both knowing whatever was happening in the dining room was something neither of them wanted a part of as the wailing continued, and their father continued to shout in the dissonance of madness.

"You will suffer for what you did to that peddler and the driver and the spiritualist because you must! Alfred my boy, what are they doing to you? What will they do to Robert? And Samuel and Matthias and…me?"

The first crack in the dam started in the unseen and the darkness spilled from the doorway, pooling in at their feet. Something between ink and tar leaked out from the doorway, forcing both Samuel and Matthias to jump back so it wouldn't touch them.

Run upstairs and leave this house like Robert did. Run! Run! Run!

His body ignored the command and instead planted itself just outside the reach of the liquid trickling from the dining room. Sweat dripped down his face, though the kitchen was now freezing. His frantic breath, rapid and wheezing, filled him with the chill permeating the room. Matthias, the man who seemed unflappable to him and his other brothers growing up, now whimpered in front of him as he hunched down and brought his arms to cover his face. The sudden motion was too much for the undersized dress shirt Matthias wore when he wanted to play the role of gentleman. The sweat-stained shirt finally gave up the ghost, tearing beneath both armpits as Matthias covered himself and begged for mercy.

As terrified as he was, watching Matthias grovel for his life filled Samuel with a childish glee. The years of watching him alternate between confidence and sadism all stripped away as he became a sniveling coward, no different than him or Robert. If he was going to die, this was fine by him.

The darkness spilled from the door, its tendrils reaching towards them like some sea creature from the deep as their father cried out like some mad ship captain battling the elements on their doomed ship.

"I see you, oh agent of death. You come towards me, closer each second, to drag me to the gulf of churning chaos and that hellscape that awaits. But you won't, not yet. There are others you must see to first. Go to them now, let me resume my descent before you pluck me from this god forsaken earth."

The door, that window that peered into the orderless expanse and damnation, rippled. A figure appeared, though it was impossible to make out at first. For a second Samuel thought it might be his father escaping the clutches of whatever held him beyond, but even obscured it soon became evident the figure was much too slender to be the old man.

"It ain't my fault, it ain't my fault," Matthias said.

He slunk to the ground, curling up into a ball as he leaned against the counter and watched from over his arms. Samuel, who was still enjoying the show, jumped up on the counter as the darkness grew closer. As soon as his feet left the floor, it claimed the space beneath him. Realizing it was closing in, Matthias was soon doing the same.

The figure in the doorway continued to take shape until a woman appeared, breaking through into the kitchen in a slow dragging manner. It started with a hand: a pale, claw-like hand that pushed through towards them. The fingers were gnarled like knotted branches of a tree, and long pointed fingernails stretched out like talons. The hand was splattered with the ink-like substance that dripped towards them. Next was a sleeve, torn and tattered and white. She continued forward until she stood before them, covered in dark blots that trickled down like blood from a wound. Despite this, her veil and dress remained unblemished.

Matthias let out a scream, and for the first time since seeing it the joy at his fright subsided as it was replaced by terror. Pure, unadulterated, spine-tingling, bladder-emptying fright. Samuel tried to scream, but his mouth failed to work. Instead, a gasp was all he managed as The Lady in White peered back and forth at the two of them. The white veil coiled around her body, pressing tight as it swirled and twisted around her. When the veil would lift or shift and reveal the woman beneath, the exposed flesh was sickly and grey, festering in timeless death.

She reached towards Matthias first, pointing at him as he crouched on the counter, then whispered something drowned out by the crescendo still raging behind her. She turned to Samuel next, staring at him with eyes that seemed to extend through the back of her skull to the void behind her. Still whispering, though this time loud enough so he could here, she said:

"Next. I promised I'd keep watch over her, and I will hunt you until I find her, or I will drag you to the depths."

Her mouth, covered by the veil, opened wider than should have been possible as her head leaned back. For a moment it looked as if she was about to scream as her neck bent at an unnatural angle facing up, but with a sudden jerk her head snapped back forward to stare at Samuel once more.

"I will find her and drag you to the depths to join the others."

Then she disappeared into the doorway behind, bringing the darkness with her.

The kitchen was normal once more, the doorway too. No residue or wet spots left behind: it was as if the whole thing never happened. Through the door where she'd emerged was a flickering lantern and the silhouette of his father standing in the center of the room.

Samuel looked below, and though he couldn't see anything save for the concrete floor littered with crumbs and covered by dust, he watched for a minute before moving. He touched the tip of his toe down, and when he was confident the world wouldn't give out beneath him, he placed his whole foot down. Then the next.

"You coming?" he asked Matthias when both feet were firmly planted.

"Course I am, what do you think?" Matthias peered down at the ground beneath him with distrust, but quickly launched himself down. He puffed out his chest and stood straight as he landed.

"Let's check on Pa."

"That's what I was s—"

"C'mon Sammy."

They approached the doorway, neither knowing what to expect. "Hold it," Matthias said before they entered. "I'll be right back."

"Don't leave me." Samuel's pleas were ignored as Matthias disappeared up the stairway, leaving him by himself.

"Pa…" he called out, his voice soft as if coaxing out a scared, hiding child. No response. "It's us." Silence.

Matthias clamored down the stairs behind him, the sound of his heavy footsteps joined by the clinking of metal. Samuel turned to see what his brother had brought with him, and found him holding a mini arsenal: two swords from their grandfather's time in the Revolution, pistols, and a rifle were all carried in his arms.

"You think it'll do any good against what we just saw?"

Matthias, who still looked more flustered than Samuel was used to seeing, sucked his teeth then said, "No idea…but I ain't going in there without it, that's for damn sure. I heard you calling', did he say anything?"

"Nothing. Not a word."

"Is he dead?" There was no concern in his voice. Matthias handed a saber and pistol over to Samuel, both of their hands shook as the weapons were exchanged, and both men peered nervously at the doorway. Their father still stood in the center of the room. Only his outline, made clear by the lantern within, could be seen since his body blocked the flame from providing enough light to illuminate the room. It wasn't as dark as it had been minutes before; still, it was impossible to tell *exactly* what they were walking into.

The sword and pistol provided little comfort. What they had just heard and seen seemed like the type of things that wouldn't care all that much about being shot or stabbed. Samuel had never used a sword before, so as he held it in front of him, he focused on keeping the blade steady to conceal his shaking. With the other hand he held out the pistol, though he kept his finger off the trigger. Scared as he was, the last thing they needed was to accidentally shoot his father and have all eyes back on them once more.

Samuel waited for Matthias to take the lead and step out in front. A few seconds passed, and finally he turned to look at his brother who had the rifle up to his shoulder, and the saber and pistol looped into his belt.

"You go on ahead. I got the rifle, so I'll stay behind." *He's so scared he can't move. He's sending me ahead to lead 'cause he's so scared.* If he wasn't so frightened himself Samuel would have savored the moment more. As it was, he turned and stepped into the doorway leading with the sword. "One more thing," Matthias added, his voice uncertain as the both of them stopped. "If something gets me and not you, I need you to destroy that leather book beneath my mattress, alright? Burn it for safety."

'Sure." The last thing Samuel was concerned about was getting rid of his brother's journal, but something in his voice made Samuel realize he wouldn't have accepted another answer. "Yea…I'll get rid of it."

They stepped into the dining room. Samuel started to call out to his father, but before he could get the words out a blinding light caused him to raise both the sword and pistol to his face as he shielded his eyes from the glare. *She's back. Oh god she's back.* Samuel blinked as fast as he could trying to see clearly.

"Don't shoot Sammy, don't shoot!" Matthias yelled from behind him. Samuel lowered his arms and the weapons from his face, and the room quickly fell into place around him. His father had stepped from in front of the lantern, which was glowing much more intensely than Samuel had realized, and the sudden burst of light was blinding given how dark it seemed before. The room looked exactly as he'd have expected it to, had the past few minutes not occurred. Even his father was where he should be, now sitting beside the whiskey barrel ladling the liquid into his mouth until it poured down his jowls and onto the brown nightshirt that was once white.

"What the hell happened in here?" Matthias asked, stepping forward and reclaiming the spot in front of Samuel.

He tipped the rifle so that the barrel rested on his shoulder as he stared down at his father. It was like the past few minutes had been erased: Matthias was already back to his old self. Still, Samuel promised himself he would never let go of the memory of him cowering on the floor and whimpering for mercy.

"Ah, Alfred stopped by. Didn't you see him walkin' up the stairs? Brought some friends with him, I suppose." Samuel couldn't decide if his father's voice sounded different than normal, or if he was just imagining it. The ladle remained in constant motion between his mouth and the whiskey barrel, so at least that much remained the same.

"You were yelling out, you were..." Matthias didn't finish the sentence.

His father, with the ladle to his lips held into place by one hand, raised his other in his son's direction telling him to be quiet. With a loud *smack* of his lips, he finished his most recent ladleful of booze.

"Alfred stopped by after the harvest. He was…he was…" the old man's eyes glossed over as he hunted for his train of thought. If there had been any change in his voice, surely it was gone now. He plunked the ladle down in the barrel beside him having lost his train of thought.

"The woman…the darkness…the…chaos, you were screaming about it."

"Alfred came by. Said the harvest was looking tip-top. Oh look, there he is. Alfred, tell your brothers what you need em' at tomorrow so we can get this crop. Good year for harvest…"

***

Upstairs, the sound of their father's singing resumed from below. It was less drunken revelry or bawdy limerick than normal; this night his voice was distant, more sorrowful, and brimming with pain and loss…and perhaps understanding, even if the man's clarity seemed to vanish with the specter. Any other night the change might have been pleasant as, despite his many faults, their father could certainly sing well when the mood struck him. The strange siren song from the basement filled the decrepit, once great farmhouse while Samuel and Matthias tried to drink away the things they had just seen.

Both brothers sipped tins of whiskey. On the table was a bottle they'd filled to the brim downstairs, which rested between them. It was half empty now.

"So, Alfred weren't seeing things," Samuel said after taking an especially long sip. They'd spent the last twenty minutes discussing what *they'd* seen downstairs over the melodic backdrop.

"I s'pose not." Matthias eyed him over his cup. "So, what do you suppose she wants?"

"Revenge, most likely. Seems to me at least."

"It was Robert that killed her. What's she want with us, then?"

Samuel grabbed the bottle and refilled his tin to the brim. He felt on even footing with Matthias for the first time, the instantaneous shift in their dynamic both welcome and strange. He could say what he actually thought.

"You know it ain't that simple. We were there, we helped get rid of her too. If she's out for one of us, she's out for all of us I suppose."

"Well then how the hell do we get rid of her? How do we pre-never mind, let's just focus on one thing at a time."

How do we prevent all those things we got coming to us? That first the peddler, and now their father, had made evidently clear awaited in the afterlife.

Samuel's mind filled in the blanks. He shuddered and took a pull of whiskey then looked out the window. The moon was full, and hung above the silhouette of the forest wall some hundred feet from where he sat. It's radiance and color was a bit too similar to The Lady in White for his liking; he looked away, shuddered once more, and again took another sip of whiskey.

"She kept asking for her or something, she's gotta be looking for someone to…I don't know…communicate with. What if we wind out what she wants, er- that person she's looking for, and help them connect."

Matthias just grunted then looked out the window like Samuel had seconds before. After a moment of contemplation, he said. "I hate to say it, but one of us should get Robert back here. If he's already seen her, I suppose he might know something more than we do. We should have him here to keep an eye on him besides. Scary as this *thing* is, the last thing we need his him blabberin' to some stranger and getting the sheriffs involved too."

"I'll get the boy tomorrow," Samuel said. As he watched his brother stare out the window from across the table, an idea hit him. *Communicate...find out what she wants.*

"Matthias, I...never mind. It's nothing." Matthias' eyes glanced sideways at him for a second, then returned to the window. Samuel drained his tin of whiskey as he thought. *Best I know before the rest of em'.* He reached out and grabbed the bottle, bringing it to his tin for a refill.

As the brown liquid sloshed into the tin cup, Samuel spoke once more.

"Yea, I'll go get him tomorrow so we can hash this out. I'll head into the city nice and early, alright?"

Matthias grunted.

***

It was early, but Rochester was busy. Samuel felt the city crushing down on him, suffocating him, and for a moment he wished he'd brought Matthias with him. Instead, Matthias dropped him off on the outskirts of the city earlier after telling Samuel he had business to attend to alone. So did Samuel. Though as he watched his brother pull away in the wagon, he couldn't help but regret he'd be traversing Rochester by foot.

He hated the loud noises of people screaming and carriages clattering over cobblestone streets, all the while people pushed in around him so close, he felt like he might be swallowed up in the rush. His chest felt light, and he walked faster through the crowd though it mattered little; somehow no matter how he maneuvered there always seemed to be more men in dress clothes or women with large hoop skirts who bumped into him. They'd either ignore him or look at him with a hint of disgust, embarrassed to see the country bumpkin on the same walkway as them.

Then there were the beggars. The old men and women who sat curled at the base of buildings and shops with their missing teeth and blood-soaked bandages asking for change, waving cups about or calling to him as he passed by. Or the children who would do the same, cutting him off to explain that they were orphans and needed money for food. Samuel would tell them to go to hell, but that only made them more aggressive. Speaking of hell, there seemed to be a preacher on every corner screeching about the end of days and eternal damnation as the morning sun beat down on everything, cooking the street and buildings so that those threats of hell seemed all the more imminent, while also cooking the refuse and waste pooling along the streets in stagnant puddles

He hated it here.

Samuel tried to puff out his chest and carry himself with the same reckless confidence he'd felt for a moment the night before while Matthias whimpered before his own terror settled in, but he found it impossible to muster. Every step he took seemed to intercept someone more important and adamant about getting through who would bully past him, and when he tried to be courteous and let someone by, others would squeeze past stopping his progress for minutes at a time. The whole while beggars called to him, sensing his discomfort and noting a possible easy mark. The conversations, jeers, neighs and snorts of animals pulling wagons, chime of bells ringing as doors were opened, screeches of children as they ran about underfoot all bombarded Samuel from every direction. He tried to shrink down as small as he could, but still the city pressed down on him. All he wanted was to be back at the farm, home where...

She might be waiting for you. She said you were next.

As difficult as it was, Samuel continued forward. When he first arrived at the city he'd asked around, so he knew vaguely where he was going as he weaved through the walkways of the city. A woman had told him to follow along Genesee Street until he saw Wolcott's Distillery, past that there would be a cemetery, Mount Hope, which would let him know he was close. A small brick house within view of the cemetery was the one he was looking for, then once that was done, he could find Robert.

As Samuel continued the city soon transformed from a packed metropolis to something less cluttered: sure, he saw a number of shops and houses still, but these were on larger plots of land with trees and farm animals. The residences and shops grew in size as well. Robert felt much more comfortable here. Everything was more spaced out, and finally he felt himself relax a touch. Still, he knew his mission was urgent, so his pace never slowed.

He passed the distillery, another brick building with smoke coming from the chimney and a wagon loaded with barrels of the good stuff. The horses hitched to the wagon eyed Samuel suspiciously as he walked past the courtyard.

"Dumb animals," he muttered under his breath, not that there was anyone close enough to hear him. The sun beat down from above and he adjusted his hat, his shirt clung to his sweaty body and seemed to pull at his arms as he did. Though the walkways had thinned out nicely, all around workers scurried about the courtyard rolling barrels and loading them into the wagon. Across the street was the botanical garden and a few houses set against the backdrop of trees and private gardens. He was in Brighton now, just beyond the city limits, and Mount Hope sat to his right. The cemetery was a scattered landscape of forest and grave-markers spread out as far as the eye could see, mixed within were couples strolling throughout the walkways admiring the closest green space to the city. Rolling hills sprinkled with headstones honoring the deceased and mausoleums doing the same stretched out towards the surrounding tree line.

Samuel's heart pounded, and for the first time that morning he came to a halt. The sweat pouring from him now was only in part due to the summer heat. Standing beyond the stone fence marking the property his eyes traced the landscape, looking for anything out of place.

She could be behind every headstone or mausoleum; she could be any person walking through pretending to admire the scenery…or the forest! She could be peeking out from behind any tree waiting to drag him in and have her revenge.

All the sudden Samuel wished he'd brought a weapon of some sort. Even if a pistol couldn't hurt a phantom, at least it might provide some sense of security. He felt so vulnerable there, surveying the graveyard and knowing there was nothing he could do should The Lady in White appear. *Best to be ready.* He couldn't let her sneak up on him, that would surely be the end. So, Samuel spent the next minute scrutinizing every square inch of the cemetery in front of him.

He was so distracted he didn't hear the sound of pattering paws approaching him from behind. It took a growl to make Samuel turn around.

"You're those two dogs who was stealin' from us yesterday!"

Sure enough, standing behind him were the dogs he'd found in the icehouse the day before. The dogs were bony, their matted fur clung tight in some places and drooped in others. Still, despite the fact they were malnourished the dogs struck an imposing image standing behind him, teeth bared and letting out a guttural noise somewhere between a snarl and a bark. Their tails were wagging slowly, side to side, and though he hated dogs Samuel knew enough to realize they weren't happy to see him. Besides showed bared teeth, both dog's ears were slicked back, their posture rigid, and both stood still, save for their tails, watching him. The larger of the two snapped at the air and paced forward. Samuel took a step back in the direction of the cemetery and bumped against the stone wall. He wished he had a gun again.

The dogs closed in until they were less than five feet from him, snarling and gnashing their teeth the whole time.

This is how it ends. Not the ghost, but two mangy street dogs mauling me outside the city. How did they follow me without my knowing?

When the dogs were close enough to touch Samuel made up his mind to kick the largest one. Maybe it would scare them off or maybe it would only enrage them, but it was the only chance he had to survive. He pushed off the wall with his hands, pulled back his foot as far as he could and…

The dog's ears perked up, then their heads swiveled to a point past Samuel somewhere in the cemetery. Before his boot could sail through the air the dogs were trotting away, called on to something else. Samuel watched, his eyes following them in disbelief as the animals darted down the walkway, turned into the cemetery, then continued on their way. They even stopped to be petted by a gentleman when they were about twenty feet in, nuzzling into his legs as he scratched their backs. For their efforts they were gifted with scraps from the picnic basket in his arms before they moved on once again.

"Fucking beasts. Next time they're not getting away," Samuel said, promising to himself the next time he saw them he'd make sure it was the last.

***

The parlor was small, as was the chair Samuel had been instructed to sit in. He squirmed, trying to find a comfortable position to no avail. The whole time Mrs. Livingston stared at him from behind thick glasses, her gaze both unceasing and unnerving.

"Will you do it?" He asked when the silence became unbearable. He'd told her what happened the night before—well, as much as he could without getting he and his brothers locked up—and said that he wanted to contact his lady in white to find out what she wanted. The medium had spoken very little, only adding the occasional "mhmm" to prod him on during his explanation about why he so desperately needed her services.

She took a sip of tea from the cup in front of her, the whole time her eyes burrowed into Samuel making him shift in the uncomfortable chair even more. Finally, after what seemed an eternity, she spoke.

"And you chose me because…your brother." Her voice was flat. Robert couldn't tell if he was imagining the hint of disdain, he thought he heard. He peered down at the tea in front of him, trying to focus on the floral pattern of the china as he spoke.

"I didn't know any others. I saw your name in one of the articles, and I thought you might be able to help me out. Alfred was as mean as a rattlesnake, I ain't like him I swear. I think this lady in white is tryin' to get me since I'm kin, but I didn't have no hand in any of that stuff with the peddler."

Mrs. Livingston raised one eyebrow. "And why do you think it's a woman targeting you and not the peddler or…Alfred?" She hissed his name.

"Ah, ma'am, I don't know. I don't know about any of this stuff. I just know what I seen. I know Alfred, er, possessed you when he was strung up, but I can't think of anywhere else to go. Please, can't ya' help an innocent man?"

The woman let out a sigh and set her tea down, the small table shook beneath.

"I don't know why, but I feel inclined to help you despite what your brother put me through. Did you know they said I tried to strangle myself? That his spirit forced me to call out horrible and nasty things? Well, if you read the article, I suppose you might. Now, this lady and white of yours, you say she comes to you searching for something?"

"That's what she says, that she's trying to find *her,* or someone."

"Interesting…interesting. Now, before I begin the calling, I want you to understand the process, is that understood?"

"Yes ma'am."

Mrs. Livingstone stood up from her seat, then slid the chair back. She began pacing about the portrait strewn room as she spoke, her words coming out faster with each sentence.

"Each spirit seems to come back in a different form. In fact, I've seen multiple versions of the same deceased man throughout conversations. Some seem to be the same person they were as they passed, while others…change. They become the worst parts of themselves, or something else entirely. They seem poisoned by the afterlife, perhaps."

"You said you saw the same person, with…differences?"

"Yes, it was shortly after the debacle with your brother if I remember correctly. I was still recovering from *that* encounter, but every time I closed my eyes I would see things, hear things, that I hadn't before. It was like that incident when your brother was executed, pardon me, but that new…pathways seemed to open to me. What was a whisper or a click in the past became a vision or a conversation."

As she moved around the parlor her black dress seemed out of place in the garishly colored room, which was littered with statuary and paintings similar to the ones that had once decorated his family's parlor before they were sold for booze and prostitutes. Samuel hated them all; he wished he could tear down the paintings and rip them to shreds, then smash the statues to tiny bits. It was those things his father loved most of all, except maybe Alfred.

She turned and pointed at Samuel, instantly pulling him from those thoughts. With the dark dress, glasses, and stern stare, Mrs. Livingstone reminded Samuel of the last teacher he'd had back when he was eight. All she needed was a hickory switch and the image would have been complete.

"And I saw that man, Jenson I think it was, the same night…but it was two different men. One, who looked like the daguerreotype the family brought to show me, who only wanted to tell his wife, son, and daughter he loved them, and the other? Well, he showed up after the other had disappeared he looked..." The medium looked to the ceiling to find the right word.

"Rotted?"

"That's right, like your Lady in White I suppose. He spoke in a most uncivil manner, calling for the death of his business partner— oh I forget his name, but the man must've cheated him at some point."

"Why were there two of them?"

"Oh, I couldn't tell you exactly, and I can't say I've heard anything convincing from any of the other spiritualists on the subject. I suppose the world is complex, so surely the afterlife is as well, as are people. Perhaps some people pass on nicely, while others stick around. Maybe sometimes a part of a person passes on, while another part lingers or manifests in different ways."

"You think th—"

"And maybe sometimes spirits are yanked back into this world by force or chance to see to something...or maybe they're stuck to a certain time or memory or person. Who's to say?" She paused then added, "I'm just the line between."

Her frantic pacing ended. She returned to the table and sat down, leaning in and staring at Samuel who instinctively pulled himself back from her intense gaze.

"You're scared of this woman, aren't you? You think she can harm you...do you still want to go through with trying to contact her?"

Just leave...let Matthias figure something out. You can find Robert at the tavern he's staying in and go back home. Maybe it was just a one time thing, maybe it was ju—

A statue tucked away in the corner of the room suddenly caught his eye.

"What's that?" He pointed to the statue behind the medium with a trembling finger he quickly tucked into his lap. His voice quivered when he spoke again. "What that statue?"

Mrs. Livingston's eyebrows arched, and her head shot up in surprise at the sudden change in topic. She turned and looked at where his finger had pointed.

"Oh that? It's a statue my husband purchased while traveling to Italy. The sculpture's name was...oh what was it? Rafaelle something. I'm sorry but his full name and title escape me. It's exquisite, isn't it?"

"It...it...it looks like her. The Lady in White. It looks like her."

The marble bust was of a woman, her face peered down to the ground longingly. A veil draped across her face and shoulders, wrapping around her completely. Although the covering obscured her face, Samuel could picture it perfectly. *Dark, pitch black eyes that hold you in their gaze.* And if the veil was pulled away, or if it spun around her seemingly on its own accord, sometimes falling off or revealing what was beneath, Samuel knew there would be flesh and skin greyish in hue, moldering from the poisoned waters she swam. He wanted to scream, but he managed to hold it in.

"Oh, it's nothing of the sort. My husband told me it's a style growing in popularity in Europe, as it demonstrates the artist's ability to capture the *human* form beneath. I'm told it's quite difficult and only the *most* skilled sculptures can successfully make do."

Mrs. Livingstone turned back to Samuel. "Now, I think we can...oh dear, you've grown quite pale. Should I have one of the servants fetch you a glass of water or something other than tea?"

254

Samuel cleared his throat and pulled his eyes away from the sculpture, looking back at his host. "No, I'm alright. Just…It looked like *her*. I'm alright, please continue."

"Very well then. Now, I'm used to holding these at night when connections are easiest to make, though I suppose it should still work even in the morning. Now, regarding pay—"

Samuel reached into his pocket and pulled out a small satchel that he placed on the table.

"If it's not enough I'll get more, please. Whatever you need I'll get."

"I'm sure it's enough, Mr. Samuel." Mrs. Livingstone reached out and took the satchel. She called out to a servant, who quickly appeared and took the payment away.

"Now we can begin in earnest."

***

The room was dark. Blankets had been dragged in and hung over the windows by servants who rolled their eyes when Mrs. Livingstone looked away, and the pocket doors were closed behind them as they left Samuel and her at the table, sitting across from each other. A candle flickered between them.

"I need you to close your eyes and take my hands."

Samuel was instantly aware of how clammy his palms were, and as he reached across the table he was suddenly embarrassed by his dirt-stained hands and grime caked fingernails. Without care the medium took his hands in her smaller bony grip, lowering them until both their elbows rested on the small table. The orange glow of the candle reflected back on her glasses. Samuel's mouth was dry, it tasted like the morning after a bender. He swallowed trying to wear his mouth and felt his Adam's apple bulge.

"Close your eyes," she reminded him. Samuel reluctantly listened.

"Good, good. I want you to focus on the darkness. No thoughts...focus on nothing." Her voice was sing-song soft, and Samuel tried his best to listen. Every time his mind started to go black, a thought would appear ruining his concentration.

What if she possesses the medium...did Matthias tell the workers not to come in...what was his business he needed to attend to?

"I can't do it!" He opened his eyes and looked at the medium. "I keep thinkin' thoughts."

The medium removed her glasses, set them on the table, then let out a deep breath.

"Let me ask you some questions then. *Try,* try not to think about anything other than your response. Dwell on the words, what you're saying, and nothing else. Alright?"

Samuel shook his head.

"This lady in white, what did she say to you? When did you see her? Close your eyes!"

As he responded the memories of the night before flooded into Samuel's thoughtstream. His words were lost to him, yet his mouth moved. He was talking, that Samuel was vaguely aware of, yet his sole focus was on her billowy dress. It fluttered in his mind, carried by some unseen wind. Then there was the serpentine veil coiling around her corpse-like figure, the haunting whisper of her voice telling him he's next...

The medium's questions dissipated to the background, her voice muffled as if she was speaking from a distance. Samuel knew he was answering them, but the responses seemed a voice other than his. He felt drowsy, almost as if he was in the stages before falling asleep where conscious thought melded with the abstract, and throughout the mental replay of the night before he became a spectator watching, unattached. No gut-wrenching sense of doom; no pulse pounding, sweat pouring adrenaline surge…only the events unfolding before him as his mind dulled, sinking into the recess of memory.

"Someone's here."

The words cut through loud as a cannon blast and Samuel's eyes opened at once.

"What do you…"

The words trailed off, his jaw went slack. The table had somehow become longer, impossibly so, and the previously small circular top stretched for what appeared dozens of feet. At the end he could just make out the form of the medium who was little more than a small pinpoint in the distance.

"There is someone here with us," she called from the end of the table, her voice echoing throughout the now cavernous space. "Do you feel their presence"

"No." Samuel looked around the changed parlor. "It's just us…hold on."

A chill in the air, the sound of footsteps, a distant whisper; *someone was here.* He looked about the room trying to locate the new presence.

"Don't leave your seat!"

A fog drifted from the floor, covering the ground in a swirling carpet. As his eyes traced the ground   back to the walls, Samuel realized the room had changed too. The wallpaper was no longer a floral pattern of red and beige, instead it was an older style with framed landscapes and figures spread throughout the light blue background. Some furniture was missing, some remained, and some new pieces emerged. For some reason Samuel couldn't put his finger on, these changes unsettled him more than the fog or the table. There was something…chaotic about it. No sense or order that he could figure, and the fact the veiled lady remained made it all the worse. Its head was angled differently so that it now stared at him.

Just my imagination, like the rest of this. All part of the seance.

The marble bust twitched. It tilted its neck, still peering at Samuel. He grabbed the table ready to bolt.

"Don't leave the chair," he was reminded by the distant voice. "Stay where you are, and they can't hurt you."

The veiled lady continued to twitch, the whole time its focus remained on Samuel who tried to shrink in his seat. The walls of the parlor collapsed, dropping away and leaving only darkness.

His temples pulsed and a low hum filled his ears.

Run, run you idiot, his mind screamed, though his body refused to move.

She said don't leave the chair, Samuel reminded himself, though it took everything in his power to heed the medium's advice.

"I'm in the woods, brother. By the creek we used to fish with Albert. You remember it, don't you?" Robert's voice whispered from behind.

Samuel couldn't pull his eyes away from the veiled bust. Any moment *she* might transform or burst forward to drag him to his eternal damnation.

"What are you doing here Robert?"

"Brother she almost got me. Had to leave the tavern quickly and stake out in the woods. Come and find me, quick now!"

How's he here?

Before he could examine the thought any further his fears were realized as the marble bust was swallowed in fog, and the silhouette of her shoulders and head transformed to that of a full body beneath the wall of grey.

"What do you want? Just tell us what you want?" He cried out remembering why he'd visited the medium in the first place. The Lady in White emerged from the fog drifting towards him, her dress trailing behind on the ground. "Do you see her?" He called to the medium. No response.

"She can't see her, only we can. She's coming for us Samuel, all of us. We have to stop her. I have an idea."

The Lady in White floated across the churning sea of fog, the dress and veil fluttering behind, carried by some otherworldly wind. When the veil drifted and revealed the woman beneath, Samuel was surprised to see her flesh and skin no longer moldering from decay. Instead, the woman entombed under the covering seemed…alive. The same chestnut brown hair that he'd seen matted in blood spilled out from beneath. Her face no longer pressed against the drapery like a skeleton waiting to burst from the skin; it was now full and lively. Still, the veil swirled, eventually obscuring the approaching figure once more.

"You have to tell me what ya' want. I'll do my best to get it to you."

No response, save for the soft hum of some forgotten lullaby, the melody of which Samuel couldn't place. She stopped, hovering in one place and looking around frantically.

"Mary, where are you? You know I don't like you runnin' around the cemetery."

The fog rose about her, slowly drifting upwards as she cried out. "Mary…Mary…"

"What's happening?" Samuel turned in his chair to find Robert, but the space behind him was only darkness. Still, his brother's voice responded.

"You have to come to that creek we used to fish. You'll find me there. Hurry…not…much…time…"

He turned back around to find the woman hidden behind a wall of fog, though even with her hidden Samuel knew something changed. The wind that first had blown the veil behind her now picked up, howling and screeching as it filled the fast emptiness around them. Once more the woman disappeared beneath her shroud.

"What do you want?" He screamed against the din.

"I must find her," the looming shadow from the fog said as it resumed moving towards him, growing closer with each second.

"Who?"

"Mary, you idiot. I must find Mary and then I will make you suffer for what you've done."

"But you're Mary, you're the woman we—"

The hand that shot out and grabbed hold of Samuel's neck was gnarled and covered in grey flesh long dead. As the fingers curled about his trachea and pulled him over the table, The Lady in Whites face snarled beneath the veil that slowly drifted away, revealing her face beneath.

The empty vastness of her eyes stared back.

The eternal chaos…

Samuel saw it in that moment for all it was: chaos and primordial waters that tossed and turned and punished and ignored and celebrated and remembered and forgot and waited for everyone. There was no rhyme or reason to who suffered, who came back, or who simply withered away, forgotten. He tried to close his eyes, but it was no use. She…it stared back.

Samuel felt naked, exposed, as her eyes peeled each layer of his being. He was nothing: a coward who'd followed his sociopathic brothers, poking and prodding them to make everything worse. It was *his* idea to stop the carriage, and in his heart, he knew Matthias would take it too far.

He knew.

"I am waiting for you."

***

The flickering flame of the candle, small as it was, blinded Samuel as he snapped to. The table was back to its proper size, and the gilded frames surrounding him in the dark room twinkled as they reflected the light.

"Did you see her, what did she—"

Before she could finish Samuel was out of the chair. He clawed at the pocket doors, eventually finding the crack between them in the dark and sliding them open. All the while, Mrs. Livingston continued to bombard him with questions.

"You must tell me! What did you see? What did you…"

Samuel sprinted into the main hall and out the front door, her voice following him until he was nearly a block away.

***

The creek bulged, its waters climbing higher than Samuel had ever seen.

"Robert…I'm…I'm…I'm here!" The hot summer air seared his lungs with each pant. He'd run most of the way there, and standing on the edge of the creek his legs felt like they might give out beneath him. Leaning against the closest tree he called out: "Robert, where are you? I met ya' where you said!"

A patch of maidenhair ferns beside him shook.

He wiped the sweat from his brow then leaned down closer to the brush.

"What the hell you doin' down there? You hidin' or something." He could *just* make out a patch of brown beneath that looked like it might be Robert's trousers or shirt perhaps. Samuel started pawing at the overgrowth. "Do I need to hide. What's goin—"

Before he could finish, two giant figures exploded forward, knocking Samuel to his butt and forcing him to gasp loudly as the air was knocked from his lungs. Samuel could only watch as the two dogs circled around him.

When he finally caught his breath, he cried out, "Robert, come get me man. These dogs have been tailing me since I left the farm. Come save me. Please Robert!"

The only answer was the mashing of teeth and loud growls from the dogs.

Why are they following me? He thought as pulled himself up to his hands and knees.

Before he could stand the larger of the two collided into his legs, sitting him back down to the soft earth. They kept circling him and Samuel felt his confidence surge. They were emaciated, little more than skin and bone. If they hadn't attacked yet they were just posturing, and hell, he could posture too.

"You fuckers I—"

Before he could finish his threat, the smaller dog lunged, sinking their teeth into his trachea. The dog let go quickly and stepped back, staring eye level at the still seated Samuel. It happened so quickly he didn't have time to raise his hands to protect himself. His mouth filled with a warm, metallic liquid instantly. He tried to spit it out but his body failed to respond. *The fucking thing bit me.*

When he raised his hands he noticed they felt lighter than ever before. And as he touched the wound, he found it was worse than he thought. His fingers traced deep puncture wounds that turned his throat into a slippery mush.

When Samuel tried to call out for help again the only sound emitted was a furious gurgle and subsequent bubbling, which sounded more like the creak beside him than an actual plea. His head was swimming, and when he tried to move once more, he realized his body was no longer responding to his command.

As the world spun around him, he managed to look down. A curtain of red descended down his cotton shirt, filling his lap with a pool of blood that spilled over to the ground beneath.

So much…it can't be all mine.

The calmness in which his mind was working surprised him; he knew he should be panicking, but it didn't seem to matter. Everything was so…light.

He lifted his gaze from his lap and returned it to the dog in front of him, which now seemed so distant. It was like he was staring down a tunnel as the darkness flooded his peripherals. The second one soon joined their partner from behind him. As they stared, both lowered their heads and barred their teeth. Samuel coughed in response. Blood sprayed from his mouth covering their muzzles. Neither flinched.

"Neppy…Morta…good dogs," said a harsh whisper from behind Samuel. In an instant he knew who it was, who had truly brought him here, and what was to happen. Samuel closed his eyes in resignation.

"Now attack."

***

The dogs made quick work of Samuel.

When his punctured and torn body lay still, Neppy and Morta, having obeyed their owner's command, retreated to the creek where they lapped up the water and frolicked in the cool current. As the sun began to set both dogs set out to find a meal: Morta returned with a hare, Neppy with a squirrel. The two dogs ate quickly beside the body of Samuel, which was already attracting flies that darted around the bloody heap and filled the air with their incessant drone.

It was nearly dark when they saw their owner once again. She appeared from the trees, and though her scent was different from the one they associated with her since their time as puppies, both of the dogs knew who she was.

She started walking, and they followed, returning to her side once again.

Chapter 10

Matthias approached the house with his pistol drawn.

The windows were dark, and even with the lantern he held in front it was difficult to see if there was anyone staring back out at him. A strip of light danced across each frame as he held the light in their direction trying to get a better look of what might be inside.

No candles or lanterns were lit within, which was always a welcome sign. Still, it was late, and perhaps if there was someone inside, they were sleeping. He returned the pistol to his belt and covered it with his coat jacket in case anyone was looking out. No good giving them the jump; it was best he had the upper hand of surprise should he need it. His hand hovered above the weapon ready to draw and fire in a moment.

"My wagon lost a wheel down the way…can anyone here help me?" He called out as loudly as he could.

He stepped on the porch and walked to the front door, which he proceeded to pound his fist on with as much force as he could muster. Quickly, he placed his ear on the door to hear if there was any scurrying within, but there was only silence.

It was always empty when he visited in the past, but after the night before he figured it was no good taking chances as he was on edge more than usual. Best to be safe. He'd spent the day in the city calling in the few favors he had left, asking for forwards on future deliveries, hoping the money would allow him to buy more weapons, or hire someone, or…truth be told, he didn't really have a plan; all he knew was he wanted to have the money to fund whatever he had to do to survive. It wasn't much he got, but it was something.

When Sammy never showed, Matthias assumed he and Robert had made their way back to the farmhouse without him, probably visiting a tavern or two on the way back. He was fine with that, it allowed him to make a side trip of his own.

He knocked on the door even louder than before so that the whole house shook, but again there was no response. Emboldened, Mattias slowly opened the door, and pushed in with the lantern first. He kept his hand on his pistol as he stepped inside, ready to draw and fire should there be anyone within.

The house was vacant.

The layer of dust that spread out across the floor told the story, and the few boot prints scuttled across the floor were clearly from his last visit. He looked around the abandoned farmhouse and a smile crept across his face. A tingle of elation rippled through his body: something akin to joy, though not quite. Matthias let out a long sigh as he made his way further into the house that had once belonged to Mary.

Thrill, that's what coursed through his body with each visit. The trinkets he kept from the peddler, the same ones Alfred was dumb enough to keep where they could easily be discovered, paled in comparison to walking through the house that once belonged to their victim. He'd visited the site of the murder before, that lonely spot on the country road not far from where he now stood, but the barrenness of it all was too disconnecting. Here, in *her* house, the same rush he felt that evening all came back. Matthias reveled in it.

The lantern cast its glow across the rough wood floor and the few belongings scattered across. Like always, he made his way to the seat across the fireplace.

She would have sat here. This was her seat.

Another tingle. He placed the lantern on a small table beside the seat, and reaching into his jacket pulled out his journal. The smell of old leather and must filled his nostrils, he opened it to the last entry. A burst of fear made him shiver despite the heavy and stale air of the farmhouse; there, on the last page was a small, ink sketch of the woman he'd seen last night. The ink seeped from the edges of his drawing, trickling down before blotting like blood from a deep wound. The black pit behind her where his father had screamed out in a voice of clarity covered most of the page, and in the center The Lady in White seemed to climb out towards him, ready to drag him…

He flipped quickly to the page before. Matthias didn't know what to make of the past evening even after writing and sketching it down—a typically cathartic practice for him—but he did know they needed to sort whatever *that* was quick. Robert was likely to break and go to the authorities, and Sammy wasn't much better.

He looked down at the page detailing the night's events; he'd even included the little *plan* he'd hatched regarding Robert before the night went to hell, back when he thought his brother's loose lips was the only thing he needed to worry about.

That's not why you're here.

He flipped back a few pages to the entry from January. There, every detail of the murder was laid out with every detail carefully described. The entry ran a dozen pages, and he spent the next half an hour reading every word he'd written the day after the murder.

267

This is where she lived, where she ate, where she slept each night, he reminded himself at the end of each page, looking around the house with glee.

Oh, how he loved visiting his place!

Finding it had been difficult at first, but enough people had talked about her at the tavern and around town after Alfred's death to surmise where she'd lived, despite the fact these conversations quickly hushed when they saw him near. Once he knew the rough location of her house it was as simple as keeping an eye on the only road through the area and tailing the many deliveries dropping off those damn invitations. During that time, he'd finally understood Robert's fascination with hunting. Sure, he'd though about killing her here, but those damn dogs made it impossible to get close. A blessing, he'd recently realized, as had he done the deed here there'd be more evidence linking him to the ordeal; hell, he knew everyone suspected them even if that idiot Sammy wouldn't admit it.

They'll never be able to prove it.

He'd visited the swamp where the bodies were hidden dozens of times since that evening, and the rocks had stayed true. By now, both her and the driver were likely fish food whose corpses would be unrecognizable even if they were to be discovered.

It was a shame no one would ever know the truth, save for him and his idiot brothers Matthias realized as he read about their disposal. Sure, people *suspected*, but to have their efforts go unrecognized was almost an insult. The plan he'd made was perfect: from keeping his brothers out of the loop once Sammy made up the idea to scare her, to figuring out where to catch her that evening, to the fact it was *Robert* of all people who pulled the trigger—his sniveling, wretch of a brother who he was ready to murder less than a day ago—made it all the sweeter. All of it, everything about it, he took pride in and savored. He'd helped kill the peddler; he'd planned the death of the medium; he'd now inherit the farm…Matthias would rebuild what his father had once possessed. People already looked at him with fear in their eyes, imagine what it would be like when he could afford expensive suits and luxury goods befitting a man of his standing? Soon…soon all of it would be his.

A howl hooted from outside and Matthias scurried from his seat, quickly drawing his pistol, and pointing it at the closest window. He sprinted towards the window then dropped down so only his head could be seen by someone watching. Outside the moon shone down, bleaching everything in its pale light. It was too dark to see anything in detail beyond the glass pane, but Matthias strained his eyes still.

She could be out there.

The surrounding forest offered many nooks and crannies where someone…*something*…could hide and watch him, stalking him like he'd done to Mary, waiting to seize him when he was least suspecting. The gun wavered in his hand.

If anyone comes close, I'll hear them; besides, it's not like this lady in white seems all that interested in bein' subtle.

He stowed the pistol back in his belt and turned away from the window, then made his way back to the seat. Staring into the dark abyss of the fireplace charred black from countless fires, Matthias' tired mind wandered, trying to answer questions he'd put off as long as he could.

She was real, real as I am, hell, and if there are spirits and ghosts, that means there's something after. That means…

He'd never worried a reckoning might loom on the horizon. The world was his theatre, *he was* the star. There was only Matthias, and what others experienced or saw or did on this plane surely correlated with his existence. Their suffering, their joy, their being only mattered when it intersected with him. They were expendable props, set to be moved or torn down and destroyed based on his whim.

But if there's something after…

That meant those props might be waiting for him. That Matthias, his central role, might not be so important after all. There could be a god, or a devil, or

a lady in white coming to punish you for her murder. The void of the afterlife will claim you, same as others Matthias.

He stood up from the chair and shook his head as a dog might after stepping into the rain. *No! No! No! You take care of this the same way you took care of that bitch in the first place. You must go on to great things, ya hear?!*

"I'll kill ya again," he muttered as he hoisted the lantern from the table and spun it about the room, his eyes wild and burning in the glow of the light. He kicked the chair over, then stepped around it as he headed deeper into the little farmhouse. Matthias thought about smashing the lantern to the ground, burning everything the dead medium had left in this world to rid her of those things she cherished most in life. To watch flames lick the forgotten structure, erasing any evidence of her existence as they had tried to when sinking her body. He brought the lantern high over his head, ready to do away with it all.

But where would you go on your dark and lonely nights?

The thoughts stilled his raised arm. There would be nowhere for him to go and be alone. The rush of the murder would be lost in those flames as well; he couldn't allow that. The lantern dropped to his side, but not wanting to let his indignation go without action

Matthias gathered as much saliva as he could manage in his mouth, and with a loud grunt spit it out on the ground.

Wiping the spittle from his mouth he added, "serves ya' right, ya no good witch," before heading to his next stop in the house.

The loft above.

***

Where the hell am I?

Matthias sat up, his head spinning in confusion. The mattress beneath wasn't his, nor was the room he could barely make out through the darkness.

I'm at her *house. I must've dozed off.*

The world around him took form. Matthias remembered climbing up to the loft, opening the bottom shelf of the dresser for the first time, then…

Falling asleep. I was so tired I dropped down and fell right asleep.

It all made sense. He was so tuckered out from not sleeping the night before that after he climbed up here to find another keepsake to bring back with him, he'd seen the mattress and hopped onto it for a rest.

There were a few chunks of time missing, but it all checked out to Matthias. He rubbed his temples and wiped his eyes. The candle in the lantern was no longer lit, and Matthias couldn't recall whether he'd put it out or not. If he hadn't and it had burned out while he slept, leaving the house would be rather difficult given how dark it was. Still, that meant it was still night, which meant he hadn't slept *too* long. That was good.

Matthias felt around in the darkness around him fishing for the lantern, worried that if he left the bed the edge of the loft might sneak up on him and he'd tumble over the eight-foot drop. After a minute of pawing around without much success Matthias saw the pointed outline of the lantern, which he quickly scooped up and opened. He reached in and was relieved to feel the still warm wax of the candle within. Producing a match from his jacket pocket he quickly struck it and lit the candle.

"Oh shit!" He said loudly, then quickly he covered his mouth as he remembered he wasn't supposed to be here.

Still, it took everything in him to not begin shouting for help. Though he'd initially brought his hands to his mouth to keep him from screaming in surprise, soon he was biting on the sleeve of his jacket to stop from yelling out for help.

The walls of the loft were covered completely in writing. On the ground beside where he'd found the lantern was a fountain pen and a spilled bottle of ink, he couldn't remember bringing with him. All around the exposed wood was tattooed with his neat, blocky handwriting. Not a space was left untouched. Thousands upon thousands of words surrounded him like hieroglyphics in the valley of the kings, and as he started reading the closest paragraph, he realized it was the complete contents of his journal spilled out around him. Diving to the side of the mattress he began rubbing the nearest section with the sleeve of his undershirt trying to erase it before the still wet ink could dry. It dragged across like paint from a brush, but the words remained. He felt them etched beneath his forearm. The writing done with such force each word, the entire goddamn confession for that matter, was carved into the loft.

How...?

Matthias scrambled from the ground to his feet. He'd done everything in his power to prevent the world from knowing what they, no, *he'd* done. Now, a full detailed description of his many crimes and the immense joy it brought him were into the house of his most recent victim.

Someone would find this.

Each entry, carefully labeled with his signature and the date. His name, signed like an artist on their masterpiece. He screamed, primal and wordless, as he tried to clean the walls.

It's not fair, it's not fair.

His only indiscretion was the journal; why couldn't he have that *one* thing? What had possessed him to splay out his confession on the walls while he slept? On the ground Matthias saw his crumpled jacket, which he grabbed and began dragging across the wall in wide, circular drags. It mattered little, the ink only spread into a streaky blotch, beneath which, his confession remained.

"You fucker…you fuckers. You're out ta get me, but ya can't. I'll win…I'll win goddamnit. I always fucking do!" His fists pounded against the wall and the whole house rumbled beneath the attack. Matthias did know who he was shouting out against, but a white hot rage seared through his body as he continued to hammer the blade of his hand against the tattooed walls.

It's Robert and Sammy drawin' that damn bitch in…and her…she caused all of this. The shoulda' just been quiet.

The words mocked him, swirling about like schoolboy taunts as his rage boiled over. His stringy hair flew wildy about as his attack continued to no avail.

I'll burn it down like I shoulda in the start. I'll burn the damn journal too if that's how they're gonna play.

Looking down, Matthias saw an opened drawer at the bottom of a dresser he'd often looked through for keepsakes. Tucked within the various knick-knacks was his journal, laying across was an envelope he'd never seen before.

273

Burn it down.

He turned to grab the lantern, but as his hand reached out a cold burst of wind filled the house, and the candle flickered out.

The darkness was like quicksand, pressing down and sucking him in as Matthias stood at a loss. The anger subsided—extinguished in the same chill that claimed the candle—and it was replaced with bowel-trembling fear. The same energy that filled the air when a storm loomed near charged the space. Matthias reached for his pistol, but he discovered the gun nowhere to be found.

"Where is she?" Asked a voice from below the loft.

It unfurled upwards and filled the room like noxious smoke, somehow making the surrounding darkness more oppressive. The space around him compressed; Matthias felt himself being engulfed in the impenetrable night, and though he couldn't see it directly he knew there were things moving about around him; unseen things, things not of this world that made his skin crawl and his voice crackle when he found his voice.

"I already saw you die once you...you...sunava whore. I'm a do it this time. This time it'll be me who kills ya."

The fear of what lurked about in the depths paled in comparison to what cackled below. Matthias began swimming about the floor, looking to find his pistol. The floodgates had opened, and his rambling poured out as he crawled about the floor like a drunk who had tumbled from the bar.

"That's right. This time it'll be me who does it. I was gonna' to before, don't you doubt it. That DAMN driver though."

His hand traced over something that momentarily felt like the butt of a pistol, though he quickly realized it was the handle of a bed warmer. He scooped it up then threw it with all his voice in the direction of the laughter.

"That's for ya'!"

The warmer crashed to the floor, which was quickly followed by another whisper.

"I will find her, wherever she is…but you must pay. There are *oh so* many waiting for you."

She's playing with you, but she can't hurt you. She'll disappear like before…she can't hurt you.

"I'll see em' all. I ain't scared," his voice trembled as he called down into the abyss below.

The candle lit in an instant filling the loft with light.

"You should be."

***

She was everywhere, and where she wasn't, *they* were. Yipping and howling and weaving through the trees and closing in on him. Behind every moss-covered tree, along every rough country road, no matter how fast he ran, Matthias couldn't escape. His legs trembled with each stride, but he couldn't stop. Blood squirted from his mouth with each labored breath.

She's going to kill me, you have to get away, his mind willing his increasingly tiring muscles.

Already his ankle on his good leg was swelling from the tumble down the loft, and on occasion he would feel it roll as he made contact with a loose patch of dirt or a scramble of rocks where once a creek ran. Matthias was lost, the quick exodus from the farmhouse seemed an eternity ago, and now all he could do was try to escape his pursuers.

He peered over his shoulder: behind him he could just make out the dark outline of the dogs a few feet back. They'd close in, getting so near he could smell the musk of their breath as they panted, only to drop back a few feet to resume the chase in earnest.

They were enjoying this, steering him somewhere…

If only he had his pistol. That would end this game right quick.

Matthias jumped over a log, leading with his uninjured ankle. He landed with a thud as his leg was sucked into the muddy earth. Water seeped into his boot as he fought to pry his leg free, stepping on the log behind him with his injured ankle as he yanked with everything he had in him. Matthias' eyes darted to the two dogs behind him, who had stopped their trot and now sat watching him.

"Get…Get!" He yelled. Neither dog moved, one snarled in response.

His leg was almost free. The clay-like mud pulled back, clinging to him and sucking him back in—but he was *so* close. Above the leaves rattled in the breeze. She was close, he couldn't see her, but *he knew.*

The gusts of wind pounding against his struggling and struggling form might as well have been her cold grip pushing and tearing at him. The dogs watched; a hostile, mocking audience heckling his performance.

Matthias grabbed hold of his pant leg just above his knee and pulled. The marsh finally released its hold, and the ground sucked back in where his foot had been. Matthias stumbled back nearly tripping over the log. The dogs at once became more animated behind him. There was only one way for him to go. At once he was running again, sprinting further into the swamp.

Mosquitos and gnats buzzed about as branches and brambles slapped at him, grabbing hold of him as the mud had. He tore his body every which way, freeing himself from one only to find himself ensnared by another. Another glance behind; this time *she* was right there. She floated through overgrowth that curled away from her as if repulsed, the tips of the leaves closest to her curled up into burned cocoons as if it were the end of November. Death permeated the air. The veil weaving around her grew more tattered with each passing foot, turning the same ashen grey as the withering foliage that surrounded her path until it became little more than a spider web stretching and pulling around the skeletal body beneath.

The forest became a forgotten mausoleum. No matter how fast Matthias ran, the necropolis would grow with him, he knew. But somewhere, somehow, he would find salvation. He would find a way out. The inkling of hope, that belief that he would *always* survive (because he had to, what else was there in this god forsaken world, save him?) powered him forward as he sprinted from the phantom and her dogs.

The marshes seemed to join in the attack. He was bombarded by buzzing bugs and branches that scratched and pulled at Matthias as he plowed through, clawing back at anything that he made contact with. A bramble slapped across his face and a warm trickle of blood ran down his cheek as he yanked the vine to the ground. Without slowing he wiped at the cut without thinking, then decided it was best to leave his arm in front of him to shield against the poking and prodding forest. The ground beneath his feet changed intermittently; at times his boots slid in mud, and he'd be forced to scramble to regain his footing; other times the earth was chalky and dry, and he could speed up. The woods were as indecisive as the ground: trees for a few hundred feet, reeds and high weeds the next. He was running on an old Haudenosaunee fishing and hunting trail, that much he was certain, but it was one he was unfamiliar with.

If only Robert was here. That bastard would know where to go.

The trail was there, so it must go somewhere worth going, he hoped. His body shook from excursion, fear, and rage. Matthias swore he'd see her ended, *really finished,* if it was the last thing he'd do. If he had to personally go to a damn medium to rip her back and finish her off himself, he promised himself that's what he'd do. He'd seen her killed once before, and the second time might prove even more enjoyable.

But he had to escape first.

Each breath burned, his skin was slick and itchy with sweat and from the forest, and still he pressed on. Looking back, Matthias saw The Lady in White had once again disappeared, but the dogs still followed, though they'd dropped back some.

Yes…they're slowin' down.

A moment of elation, his chest heaved as a wave of energy coursed through his body. They were getting close to the Lake. How close? It was impossible to tell in the dark with the woods and marshes blocking the view, but the rumbling of waves crashing into the shore was audible even over his heavy breathing. Once he was there, Matthias could follow along the flat beach until he reached the bay, where he could find help. Someone with a gun to shoot the dogs, perhaps. Then he could get a ride back home, get Sammy and Robert, and go and torch the-

The ground disappeared beneath Matthias feet, his gut seemed to realize what happened before the rest of him did, as it instantly tingled with a newfound lightness Matthias only knew from dreams. Still, he tried to move himself by pushing down with his feet, only to find there was nothing there as he dropped down.

He was falling.

Matthias screamed, waiting to crash into the ground and hoping it would be soft enough for him to continue his escape. With each passing second, the likelihood of that seemed increasingly unlikely. In front of him the Lake unfurled, glowing beneath the white light of the moon overhead. As Matthias braced for impact, he looked down below hoping to see a dune of sand that might cushion his landing.

There was only timeless darkness, and in the inky gulf something without form stirred. Swimming towards him, refracted in the murky nothingness below, Matthias saw what awaited him and soon his screams ceased, only to be replaced by the soulful howling of two dogs standing atop the gully looking down at the spot where Matthias disappeared from this earth.

Part 5
Echoes

Chapter 11

"All three of the brothers were reported missing, though nothing exists in the written record beyond that. They went to their grave thinking it was the woman they killed who was haunting them, though the legend...well you know it as well as most, I assume. Pieces of that story stuck around: a lonely woman patrolling the coast with her phantom dogs looking for her daughter, pushing anyone off her castle who she finds unworthy...well, you know all that as well. You heard it in elementary school like every other kid in the area, I'm sure. The *folklore* around it stuck around, even if most of it seems to be derived from other lady of the lake stories. So, there you have it."

I think I was covering my eyes at this point; the fluorescent lights of the 21st century were blinding and seemed almost foreign now compared to the world I had just been so immersed in. I stared down at the tumbler of whiskey, which had been refilled more than I care to admit, before bringing it to my lips to take another swig.

My mind was swimming with questions, some, I suppose, were historic in nature, and I admit initially chafing slightly at his assumed interpretation of historic figures' thoughts, but most were about the legend of The Lady in White, or white lady as I was familiar with her. As my mind sought to untangle what question to ask first, Dr. Dawdson, sensing I was about to badger him I'm sure, continued quickly as he stood from his seat and walked towards the window overlooking the city.

"Yes, I'm sure you think this is all further evidence of my *decline*…is that the word they use? Never mind. What I'm trying to say, what I've *been* trying to say to anyone that will listen, is that *this* story has implications beyond even the most fantastic scientific discoveries of the 21st century."

Dr. Dawdson turned back to look at me, his eyes perched wide in a look I can only describe as sorrowful. When he spoke again, for the first time that evening his tone changed from confident storyteller to that of a pleading, forgotten old man.

"Don't you *see*? If there was a moment where the afterlife pierced through to this world, here in Rochester mind you, what that might do to our understanding of the world? No longer would historians have to hunt the blurring fog of time to understand the past. Hell, there would be no bloody past."

I watched as he started pacing back and forth, visibly distraught as he sought a way to explain himself. He approached a bookshelf sitting on the wall where the window ended, waving his arms in frustration at the wall of books that extended to the ceiling.

"The back and forth, the methodologies, the historiographies, the *reviews,* all tainted by the distance of time. To actually know…"

Get him back to the story.

"How did you find out about all this? The actual history of The White Lady. As far as I know, there's several stories passed down and no one ever—"

It was like I'd fired a starting pistol with how quickly he hurried to an adjacent room, the whole time calling back to me as I swiveled in my chair trying to follow his path.

"The journal! The journal and the letter, I found them, you see. I'd found them in an archive and well, I'm not proud of it but desperate times and all I suppose, but I brought them back with me. There was no harm in it, no one had seen them before and I…"

His voice became indistinguishable as he continued to speak after disappearing into the room. At one point I heard something that sounded like, "come see", and perhaps prodded on by the liquid courage I'd been imbibing with, or, more likely, the overwhelming curiosity that first drew me to history and folklore in the beginning, I stood up and walked over towards the doorway where Dr. Dawdson had disappeared within.

As I made my way over, I felt a notable shift in the air: the loft seemed to grow dimmer, gloomier even, and it was as if all the sudden an air conditioner had flipped on directly above me. My skin prickled against the cold air, which had a sobering effect on my curiosity (and probably my general state, as I mentioned, the whiskey flowed liberally throughout the storytelling.)

He seemed uneasy there. If he starts to act strange again get the hell out, I reminded myself, not wanting to become the next poster boy for the idiom about curiosity and the cat. Peering into the doorway, I couldn't help but feel a twinge of—not fear, though that's what I initially wrote down—*apprehension* as I stared into the darkened room, thinking about the Professor's story.

Now, I should note: at this part of the evening, I was quite certain the Dr. Dawdson had simply blurred some actual research with perhaps his personal beliefs of the hereafter, and, hoping to make some *groundbreaking* discovery, slowly went down the rabbit hole as he stayed locked away in his tower, both alone and resentful. His description of characters' thoughts, moments that *no* historical record would *ever* account for, and general description of the past was, of course, impossible to know for certain. He was a lonely old man who no doubt felt scorned, and I had been a receptive audience for the past few hours. The ghost story, which he layered some history throughout, might be an interesting look into local folklore...but that was as far as I was willing to concede.

Mary, the brothers, The White Lady, the murder...nothing but lore.

Still, staring at that dark abyss filled with only silhouettes and the sound of shuffling I could imagine the terror of the brothers as they stood outside the dining room as their lucid father cried out in neo-biblical tongue. I reminded myself The White Lady was a ghost story used to scare younger siblings or told around bonfires at Durand Eastman beach by drunk and horny highschoolers, not something a grown person should be worried about...especially one who had enough to worry about already, having accepted a stranger with a reputation's invitation into their house to drink. One who had disappeared from sight into a *very* dark room.

"Uh...Dr. Dawdson, I just remembered I told my roommate I'd be home by eight, so I'm going to leave. I'll take a look at the journal an—"

The light flicked on inside the room, though it hardly mattered; the walls were so covered in ink it looked as if they had sucked out the darkness that had previously occupied the space. Long rambling sentences spun around like pinwheels, while in other spots large splotches of ink were smeared and scratched into what looked like small portals.

"But you haven't *seen!* I know what they say and think about me, but you've heard...now you have to see. I'm so close."

Dr. Dawdson was sitting in a chair in the corner, holding a journal that looked like it had been cut from the seat beneath. He waved the ancient book in the air, staring at me with both frustration and rage.

"Or are you like them? *Unwilling* to see what lies beneath the facade of this world."

Spittle flew from his mouth with each word.

Dr. Dawdson clutched the book so tightly his knuckles bulged and turned white as decades of rage poured out. Looking back, the sudden change in his demeanor should have shocked me, but in that moment, it made sense.

I stood there, frightened certainly, but unwilling to run. Something in my gut or in some hidden part of my psyche *told* me I needed to stick around. *Listen to what he says.* Curiosity intermingled with the possibility of discovery overwhelmed the fight or flight instinct, so like a doomed Lovecraftian character I chose to stare into an abyss I probably wasn't supposed to.

He leaned forward in the leather chair and held the journal out towards me like a priest with a crucifix.

"You think history and the past belongs in books? You think lives and experiences and emotions and experiences and—" He dropped the journal in his lap and wiped at his mouth and sweaty brow quickly, then continued. "You think those things just end? Evaporate into the nothingness only to be unearthed by…by…by *fuckers* like that hack Martin. No! No!"

He exploded from the seat and the book fell to the ground. Dr. Dawdson pointed towards the wall beside where I stood in the entrance. I could only watch; a stunned audience before a one man play.

"If scientists can have their multiverse theory, why can't historians see the exact thing can exist for the past? She broke through. The letter…the letter…"

He collapsed to the ground, fishing through the opened journal until he found a yellowed envelope which he proceeded to hold in the air above his head as he remained crumpled on the floor. A vein bulged along the side of his face as his eyes, staring directly at me, were so wide it looked as if his eyeballs might pop out onto the floor.

"Oh, when I found it tucked away in the journal of Matthias, I thought nothing of it. I thought I'd struck gold just finding the journal. I was going to transcribe it...I was going to write articles...the confession of a 19th century killer; book tours, the whole works...but the letter..." his voice lowered to a whisper.

"I was alone in the office. They were all gone...I thought 'what would it hurt', the letter told *me* how she did it. I felt so childish, like I was playing Bloody Mary and she was like all the others, but it worked. The other side...I saw it all! I only remember parts, but it comes to me in dreams."

"Oh, I saw it all! I was the brothers, I was Mary, I was The Lady in White, I was her mother before, and the crowd at Corinthian Hall, and the murdered driver and peddler, and the dogs, the rotten corpses of the cemetery and those same bodies in life and, and I saw it *all!* It all flooded into my mind at once. It ripped my mind apart and tore at me like a pack of rabid wolves...but my eyes were opened. Like Mary had been selected, *so was I.*"

Tears poured down Dr. Dawdson's face. I wanted to approach him, to comfort him, but I knew the flip would switch. *I knew* what would come next. Like the initial tremor of an earthquake, his voice started low.

"They took me from the building and stuffed me away in a hospital for a week or two. I can't remember much from those weeks, when I try to there's only fragmented pieces that come through. The University cut all ties, of course. They sent a few students to drop off everything they'd salvaged from my office and…"

Slowly he opened the envelope and unfurled the letter.

"Look what they DID to it!" He screamed, pointing towards a giant brown stain that covered half the paper. "The portal to the past, to everything we've ever wondered, and someone poured *fucking* coffee on a two-hundred-year-old letter. I could kill them. I've laid awake each night, thinking about wringing their necks and watching life drift from their body to the hereafter they've shut off."

A wicked smile grew across his face.

"But I'm close," he hissed. "It's coming back to me. I'm approaching death, I know that…and each night the dreams of what I saw become a little more vivid. They now start with me in the office, readying…" he gestured to the covered walls. "They're still here, the ghosts of this city. I see them when I go out, when I walk through this roach-infested dump. Since that night, they follow me, surround me. I'm stuck in the middle ground…but the veil is thinning. I'm so close to being able to control it, then they'll pay."

He threw his head back and screamed so loud the room seemed to shake.

"All of them. Every. Last. One."

With that, he rose to his feet. I braced myself for an attack, instead he bowed slightly in my direction and his voice returned to the soothing tenor he'd used to tell the tale of The White Lady.

"I do apologize if I've become a bit agitated these past few minutes. Storytelling awakens a beast in me, apparently."

I stood in a daze, while Dr. Dawdson walked over as if nothing had happened, flipping off the light and gesturing towards the main space with a view of the city. His professorial cool returned as he led me towards the window. The lights of the city sparkled all around, while the outline of the buildings against the backdrop of the night sky looked like giant tombstones jutting from the earth. The city was coming alive as the moon rose. Below I knew college students were making their way to East Ave, while families gathered together in backyards to catch up and relax after a long day of work. It seemed so new, so vibrant yet...

"Every town, every city, every forgotten nook and cranny in every backwoods has its history, you see. Rochester is no different...The past lives here as much as the present. On every block, on the faces of all those you pass on your way to class, *there* it is. We think of the afterlife as the future—some grand place we can't even imagine or fathom—but perhaps what lies beyond is merely an echo of the past. Or echoes, rather. There are so many different versions of us as we live, I suppose: changing with each lover, each tragedy, and each joy. All those experiences have to exist *somewhere.* Why shouldn't we try to access them?"

"I see in your face you don't believe in The Lady in White or anything I've shown you today, and that's alright—you're young—perhaps you'll see, someday. Perhaps sooner, I have a feeling. The past is not a place we visit to go on tour, or something we read or write. It's everywhere."

Dr. Dawdson look down at his watch,

"I apologize, it's much too late for a lecture, isn't it? I believe you were saying something about your roommate and needing to leave."

***

After the door closed behind me, I stopped in the hallway, trying to process the past few hours. The Dr. Jekyll, Mr. Hyde transformation, the obsession with an old ghost story, the strange resonance of it all I hated to admit, the fear I'd felt for my life that was drowned out and ignored…all of it simply left me in a dreamlike state. The logical voice in my head tried to explain it away: *An old man, left alone, with an obsession and possible anger issues was all I'd seen. He was smart, no doubt, but fixation and isolation can damage anyone.*

But it wasn't all that convincing, and when I finally turned around to leave, I told myself that whatever happened that night would remain one of those stories I kept tucked away, brought out only when I'd had a few too many drinks and was talking to someone I felt close with. Very Lovecraftian again, I know. The notebook in my hand remained blank, and while I still carried Dr. Dawdson's book, I was certain it would remain the only reference to him in my research buried *deeeeeep* in the endnotes.

As I made my way down the stairwell of the Hotel Celeste, that gnawing feeling of interest in the old building somehow managed to rear its head above the maelstrom of emotions I was feeling about my evening with Dr. Dawdson. I passed dilapidated floor after well-kept floor, and I remember thinking:

You're never, ever coming back here again. Why not take a look around?

And although I knew it was probably best to schedule a ride and get the hell out of the old Hotel as fast as I could, the voice in my head won out. Though it seemed so long ago since I'd spoken to her after first arriving, I'll admit Deborah's warning briefly flashed across my mind. I ignored it however, and decided to make my way down to the floor she'd first yanked me out of, which is something I'm not proud of, admittedly.

I must have gone to the wrong floor, I thought as I stepped into the hallway that I was certain was the first one I'd explored. I'd even counted the floors to be sure, yet it was all so different. The chandeliers were still there, so was the blood red carpet, yet everything had aged an impossible amount. A thick coat of dust coated everything, and above I could see the chandeliers, once gold, were rusted brown and orange. And there were portraits lining the walls, which stretched on and on and…

"Echo of the past…" A voice whispered from somewhere in the endless hall.

I stepped forward though my mind told me I shouldn't. *Turn and run,* it screeched, yet my body was pulled forward by some unseen force. I was in a trance, it seemed, my body no longer my own.

As I marched down the hallway, the portraits beside me stirred awake. Faces stretched and came alive, while shadows danced along the wall following my progression. With each step I took the surroundings changed. Like flash cuts in a film, things would wither and age in an instant, the next, they would be like new again. The whole time whispers bombarded me from every direction, sometimes I would hear slivers of conversations, other times I'd hear voices calling out to me, begging me to notice them as I continued down the hallway.

It continued for what seemed like hours, my body carrying me forward as the hall lived on without me. The last thing I remember was a woman's voice that rose above all the others.

"Did you like my story?"

When I awoke I was sitting propped up in the hallway with Deborah above me, shaking her head.

"Didn't listen to ol' Debbie, did ya?"

I shielded my eyes from the flickering light above as my head pounded. I felt hungover, and though she spoke at a normal volume Deborah might as well have been screaming at me.

"And you talked to *him*…didn't you?"

I think I managed to grunt in response, though the headache made it difficult to be sure.

"Should've listened to ol' Debbie. Since he's come around things've been different. Then you went into the off-limits place on top of it all. Did you see em'?"

That time I'm certain I managed a grunt in response.

Deborah sucked her teeth before speaking again, shaking her head in pity the whole time.

"Things have been different for all've us since he arrived. Now you too, I suppose."

As she turned and walked up the stairs she continued to mutter.

"Should've listened to ol' Debbie. No one ever listens. Should've—"

Before she could finish the sentence, I watched as Deborah disappeared, leaving behind nothing but a small patch of fog where she'd taken her last step.

And true to her warning, things have been different since I found Professor Dawdson at the decrepit Hotel Celeste in the Fall of 2015.

Jason Green

Postscript

Dr. Dawdson passed away not long after that evening, within the year in fact. I was the only one in attendance at the funeral, which came as no surprise. Perhaps in a bitter twist of fate, or perhaps through something more nefarious that I'd prefer not to dwell on, Dr. Martin, the man who had penned that first critical essay as I discovered during later research, passed away not long after. When I contacted the department he had worked for, like Dr. Dawdson, I was told he'd been *unwell* in the months before his death. I chose to stop digging and leave it at that. If Dr. Dawdson broke through, I'd prefer to imagine him using the knowledge for historical understanding, not revenge. Some rocks are best left unturned.

I've visited the supposed white lady's castle once since that evening, shortly after defending my dissertation and walking across the stage to become Dr. Green. It's nothing more than an old wall built into a steep hill, part of an old overlook where families once picnicked and looked out over the lake where The White Lady is said to haunt. I'll admit, it does look like the wall of a castle, albeit a fairly unassuming one.

That evening there were teenagers sitting on it, daring The White Lady to push them over, and couples walking about enjoying the view. I had my dog, Bruce, with me, so I decided to explore the walkways that weave through the smaller lakes and ponds that sit adjacent to the shore that I'd studied on maps in the months prior. Truth be told, we were looking for something.

We started out on a paved road, but quickly located a small trail through the woods. It was steep, and brought us down beside one of the larger ponds that had been made well after the story told by Dr. Dawdson, sometime early in the 20th century when they made this place a park. We walked on a narrow dirt path that ran along the shore, passing the occasional fisherman during our trek. Eventually we were alone. Well…

Bruce noticed them first. His big, American bulldog head tilted up as he smelled the air, he then glanced in my direction. Somehow, he knows about the change that happened that evening. Dogs just pick up on those things, I suppose.

I followed his gaze. There, walking along the bank of the water opposite us were two women. They could have been twins with how similar they looked. I saw them glance at me briefly, smile, then continue their conversation until they disappeared from view.

Two dogs with wagging tails followed closely behind.

Acknowledgements

First, an embarrassing omission from the acknowledgements of the last one: thank you to all the animal shelter volunteers and workers who spend their time selflessly giving back and helping animals in need. The work you do is amazing.

Now, to the work at hand.

(Also, this is basically a continuation of that first acknowledgement, so those mentioned in that first one are doubled-down in being appreciated here. Thank you all!)

I grew up with the story of the Lady in White, but the idea for what would become my take on that story didn't really begin to germinate until I started walking up the winding stairs of the Seward House Museum in Auburn, New York to the "education tower", where Jeffrey Ludwig, PhD and Director of Education of said museum, sat, likely musing about historic happenings and how lucky he was to have me as an education and outreach coordinator. High up in a house stuffed with so much history that it would take lifetimes to learn it all, we would discuss programming (say, our Haunted History tours, where, while writing a spiritualist-themed stop on the walking tour I first became familiar with Capron) and our love of Rochester, a city to which we both had ties. Somewhere along the line those pieces of our conversations fell into place, and now I have a book. So, thank you, Dr. Ludwig.

Also, a special thanks to Natalie Murphy, Dave Jeffery, Brad Bovenzi and Nick Neverman, all of whom have taken the time to read various stories on my behalf and offer thoughtful feedback, for which I am forever grateful. And of course, my sincerest thanks to Jess Jordan, who is an absolute encyclopedia of horror knowledge and an outstanding editor to boot, and the whole crew at Vulpine Press for that matter.

I also need to thank Zach Burhans and all the folks at the Brojo in Homer, New York. The stress of writing becomes a lot easier to manage when you're fighting for your life at the gym day in and day out. There were countless times I walked into a training session with you monsters feeling like I was drowning in a story (this story, to be exact) I couldn't move forward, only to emerge an hour or so later tired and bruised but knowing I would figure it out.

Another Auburn shoutout: Cellarmen's Folly Whiskey Company. Seriously, you all are awesome. A writer loving whiskey might be a cliche, but I just wrote a ghost story laced with 'em so I'm *certainly* not shying away from another one. Perhaps a Lady in White cocktail in the near future? Just spit-balling here.

The acknowledgement section—and the book itself for that matter—really starts with a trip up the stairs of a historic structure; so, to maintain the symmetry I've stumbled upon, I'll end this similarly to the way the novel closes: with a visit to the Castle and surrounding Durand Eastman Park. I'm a tad biased, but I think it's the best park in the world and I recommend taking a trip there if you can.

And if you do…

While exploring the repurposed stone structure that has now become the White Lady's Castle for all intents and folkloric purposes, you'll most likely notice a recently funded historic marker courtesy of the William G. Pomeroy Foundation. It tells a similar story to the one I opted to write in some 80,000 words, but does so in about 20. Some writer of yonder past wrote something about brevity and wit, so if you skipped ahead to the acknowledgments before reading the proceeding book I'd like to inform you a version of more wit is only a pleasant stroll away— just watch out for the ghosts.

Having learned the lesson that started this section, and now really leaning into that whole symmetrical narrative I've got going here, my final acknowledgement goes to organizations big and small, local and national, who preserve, show, educate, interpret, re-interpret, re-re-re-interpret, challenge and spotlight the histories and stories that *must* be remembered, and to the volunteers and staff who do that important work.

Thank you.

Zachary Finn is a lover of all things history and horror. He currently resides in central NY with his dog, Bruce, and his fiancée, Natalie. When he's not working as a research historian or writing you can typically find him somewhere lost in the woods, wandering through an old cemetery, or trying to improve his jab.

Follow him on Instagram and Twitter at @finzach135

www.ingramcontent.com/pod-product-compliance
Lightning Source LLC
Chambersburg PA
CBHW020410260626
47156CB00007B/2309